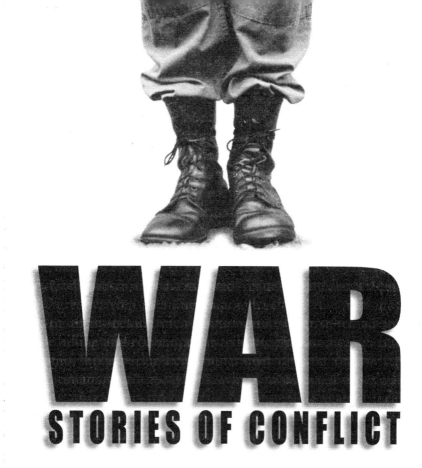

WAR
STORIES OF CONFLICT

Also by Michael Morpurgo

Arthur, High King of Britain
The Butterfly Lion
Cool!
Escape from Shangri-La
Farm Boy
Friend or Foe
From Hearabout Hill
The Ghost of Grania O'Malley
Joan of Arc
Kensuke's Kingdom
King of the Cloud Forests
Little Foxes
Long Way Home
Mr Nobody's Eyes
My Friend Walter
The Nine Lives of Montezuma
Out of the Ashes
Private Peaceful
Twist of Gold
Waiting for Anya
War Horse
The War of Jenkins' Ear
The White Horse of Zennor
Why the Whales Came
The Wreck of the Zanzibar

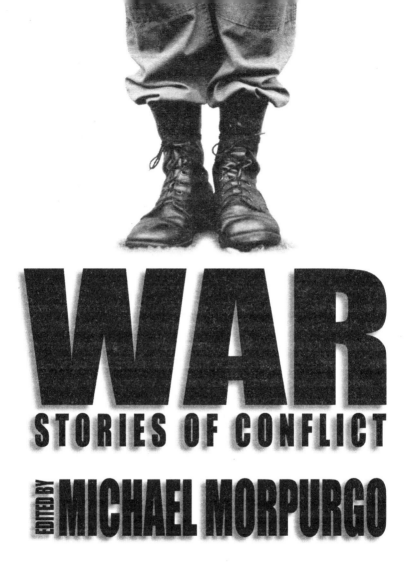

WAR
STORIES OF CONFLICT
EDITED BY MICHAEL MORPURGO

MACMILLAN CHILDREN'S BOOKS

First published 2005 by Macmillan Children's Books
a division of Macmillan Publishers Limited
20 New Wharf Road, London N1 9RR
Basingstoke and Oxford
www.panmacmillan.com

Associated companies throughout the world

ISBN 1 405 04744 5

Typeset by Intype Libra Ltd
Printed and bound in Great Britain by Mackays of Chatham plc, Kent

CONTENTS

Michael Morpurgo

I grew up in London just after the Second World War, with bomb sites all around me. For me, these were simply the best playgrounds there could be – crumbling walls to climb on, cellars to hide in, make dens in. I knew the bomb sites were there because of the war, because of the Blitz. But I never for one moment connected destruction and suffering and death to these magical playgrounds.

I first began to understand the suffering of war because of a family friend who used to visit us from time to time. He had been in the RAF and had been shot down. I knew he spent months in hospital undergoing plastic surgery. His face was terribly burnt, horribly scarred. I was told never to stare when he came, but I did. I couldn't help myself. Partly it was in awe and wonder – this was a Spitfire pilot, a war hero – and partly I was fascinated by the unnaturalness of his face. I would wonder exactly how he had been shot down, what he must have looked like before he was so dreadfully burnt. And while I wondered, I stared.

The hospital he went to was Professor McIndoe's pioneering plastic-surgery unit near East Grinstead, in Sussex. Here, this extraordinary man gave his patients, all burns victims, a new lease of life, new hope. The patients called themselves – and still do – 'the guinea pigs', because the work was so experimental.

HALF A MAN

When I was very little, more than half a century ago now, I used to have nightmares. You don't forget nightmares. The nightmare was always the same. It began with a face, a twisted tortured face that screamed silently, a face without hair or eyebrows, a skull more than a face, a skull which was covered in puckered, scarred skin stretched over the cheekbones. It was Grandpa's face and he was staring at me out of his scream. And always the face was on fire, flames licking out of his ears and mouth.

I remember I always tried to force myself to wake up, so that I wouldn't have to endure the rest of it. But I knew every time that the rest would follow however hard I tried to escape – that my nightmare would not release me, would not allow me to wake until the whole horrible tale had played itself out.

I saw a great ship ablaze on the ocean. There were men on fire jumping overboard as she went down, then swimming in a sea where the water burned and boiled around them. I saw Grandpa swimming towards a lifeboat, but it was packed with sailors and there was no room for Grandpa. He begged them to let him on, but they wouldn't. Behind him, the ship's bow lifted out of the sea, and the whole ship groaned like a wounded beast in her death throes. Then she went down, slipping slowly under the waves, gasping great gouts of steam in the last of her agony. A silence came over the burning sea. Grandpa was clinging to the lifeboat now, his elbows hooked over the side. That was when I realized that I was in the lifeboat with the other sailors. He saw me looking down at him and reached out his hand for help. It was a hand with no fingers.

I would wake up then, shaking in my terror and knowing even now that my nightmare was not over. For my nightmare would always seem to happen just a day or two before Grandpa came to stay. It was a visit I always dreaded. He didn't come to see us in London very often, every couple of years at most, and usually at Christmas. Thinking about it now, I suppose this was part of the problem. There were perfectly good reasons why we didn't and couldn't see more of him. He lived far away, on the Isles of Scilly, so it was a long way for him to come, and expensive too. Besides which, he hated big cities like London. I'm sure if I'd seen him more often, I'd have got used to him – used to his face and his hands and his silent, uncommunicative ways.

I don't blame my mother and father. I can see now why they were so tense before each visit. Being as taciturn and unsmiling as he was, Grandpa can't have been an easy guest. But, even so, they did make it a lot worse for me than they needed to. Just before Grandpa came there were always endless warnings, from Mother in particular (he was my grandpa on my mother's side), about how I mustn't upset him, how I mustn't leave my toys lying about on the sitting-room floor because he didn't see very well and might trip over them, how I mustn't have the television on too much because Grandpa didn't like noise. But most of all they drummed into me again and again that whatever I did I must not under any circumstances stare at him – that it was rude, that he hated people staring at him, particularly children.

I tried not to; I tried very hard. When he first arrived I would always try to force myself to look at something else. Once I remember it was a Christmas decoration, a red paper bell hanging just above his head in the front hall. Sometimes I would make myself look very deliberately at his waistcoat perhaps, or the gold watch chain he always wore. I'd fix my gaze on anything just as long as it was nowhere near the forbidden places, because I knew that once I started looking at his forbidden face or his forbidden hands I wouldn't be able to stop myself.

But every time, sooner or later, I'd do it; I'd sneak a crafty look. And very soon that look became a stare. I was never at all revolted by what I saw. If I had been, I could have looked away easily. I think I was more fascinated than anything else, and horrified too, because I'd been told something of what had happened to him in the war. I saw the suffering he had gone through in his deep blue eyes – eyes that hardly ever blinked, I noticed. Then I'd feel my mother's eyes boring into me, willing me to stop staring, or my father would kick me under the table. So I'd look at Grandpa's waistcoat – but I could only manage it for a while. I couldn't help myself. I had to look again at the forbidden places. He had three half-fingers on one hand and no fingers at all on the other. His top lip had almost completely disappeared and one of his ears was little more than a hole in his head.

As I grew up I'd often ask about how exactly it had happened. My mother and father never seemed to want to tell me much about it. They claimed they didn't know any more than they'd told me already – that Grandpa had been in the merchant navy in the Second World War, that his ship had been torpedoed in the Atlantic, and he'd been terribly burnt. He'd been adrift in a boat for days and days, they told me, before he'd been picked up. He'd spent the rest of the war in a special hospital.

Every time I looked at his face and hands the story seemed to want to tell itself again in my head. I so much wanted to know more. And I wanted to know more about my grandmother too, but that was a story that made everyone even more tight-lipped. I knew she was called Annie, but I had never met her and no one ever talked about her. All anyone would ever say was that she had 'gone away' a very long time ago, before I was born. I longed to ask Grandpa himself about his ship being torpedoed, about my grandmother too, but I never dared, not even when I was older and got to know him a lot better.

I must have been about twelve when I first went to see him on my own in the Scilly Isles for my summer holiday, and by then the nightmares had gone. That's not to say I wasn't still apprehensive in those first few days after I arrived. But I was always happy to be there, happy just to get out of London. I'd go and stay with him in his cottage on Bryher – a tiny island, only about eighty people live there. He had no electricity – only a generator in a shed outside, which he'd switch off before he went to bed. The cottage wasn't much more than a shed, either. It was a different world for me and I loved it. He lived by himself and lived simply. The place smelt of warm damp and paraffin oil and fish – we had fish for almost every meal. He made some kind of living out of catching lobsters and crabs. How he managed to go fishing with his hands as they were I'll never know. But he did.

It was years before I discovered why he never smiled. It was because he couldn't. It was too painful. The skin simply wouldn't stretch. When he laughed, which wasn't often, it was always with a straight face. And when he smiled it was with his eyes only. I'd never understood that when I was little. His eyes were the same blue as the sea around Scilly on a fine day. He was silent, I discovered, because he liked to keep himself to himself. I'm a bit the same, so I didn't mind. He wasn't at all unkind or morose, just quiet. He'd read a lot in the evenings, for hours, anything about boats – Arthur Ransome, C. S. Forester and Patrick O'Brian. He didn't have a television, so I'd read them too. I think I must have read every book Arthur Ransome wrote during my holidays on Scilly.

During the day he'd let me do what I liked. I could run free. I'd wander the island all day; I'd go climbing in the rocks on Samson Hill or Droppy Nose Point. I'd go swimming on Rushy Bay, shrimping off Green Bay. But as I got older he'd ask me to go out fishing with him more and more. He liked the company, I think, or maybe it was because he needed the help, even if he never said so. I'd catch wrasse and pollack for baiting his lobster pots. I'd help him haul them in and extract the catch. We would work almost silently together, our eyes meeting from time to time. Sometimes he'd catch me staring at him as he had when I was little. All these years later and I still couldn't help myself. But now it was different. Now all the fear had gone. Now I knew him well enough to smile at him when our eyes met, and, as I was later to find out, he understood perfectly well why I was staring at him, at his forbidden face, his forbidden hands.

It wasn't until the summer I just left school that Grandpa first told me himself about what had happened to him when his ship went down. He talked more these days, but never as much as the day we saw the gannets. We were out in his fishing boat. We'd picked up the pots, caught a few mackerel for supper and were coming back in a lumpy sea round the back of Bryher when a pair of gannets flew over and dived together, spearing the sea just ahead of us. 'See that, Grandpa?' I cried. 'Aren't they brilliant?'

'Better than brilliant,' he said. 'They bring you good luck, you know.'

We watched the gannets surface, swallow their catch and take off again. We caught each other's eye and smiled, enjoying the moment together.

'You know what I like about you, Michael?' he went on. 'You look at me. Most people don't. Your mother doesn't, and she's my own daughter. She looks away. Most people look away. Not that I blame them. I did

8

once. Not any more. But you don't look away.' He smiled. 'You've been having sneaky old looks at me ever since you were knee high to a grasshopper. If you looked away it was only to be polite, I always knew that. You've always wanted to ask me, haven't you? You wanted to know, didn't you? How this happened, I mean.'

He touched his face. 'I never told anyone before, not your mother, not even Annie. I just told them what they needed to know and no more, that my ship went down and after a few days in a lifeboat I got picked up. That's all I said. The rest they could see for themselves.' He was looking straight ahead of him, steering the boat as he was talking.

'I was a handsome enough devil before that – looked a bit like you do now. Annie and me got married a couple of years before war broke out. A year later, I was in the merchant navy, in a convoy coming back from America. My third trip, it was.' He looked out towards Scilly Rock and wiped his face with the back of his hand. 'It was a day like this, the day we copped it – the day I became half a man. Early evening, it happened. I'd seen ships go down before, dozens of them, and every time I thanked God it wasn't me. Now it was my turn.

'I was on watch when the first torpedo struck. Never saw it coming. The first hit us amidships. The second blew off the stern – took it right off. All hell broke loose. A great ball of fire came roaring through the ship, set me on fire and cooked me like a sausage. Jim – Jim Channing, he came from Scilly too, him and me were mates, always were, even at school, joined up together – he smothered the flames, put them out. Then he helped

9

me to the side. I'd never even have got that far without Jim. He made me jump. I didn't want to, because the sea was on fire. But he made me. He had hold of me and swam me away from the ship, so's we wouldn't get sucked down, he said. He got me to a lifeboat. There were too many in it already and they didn't want us.'

I could see it! I could see it in my head. It was straight out of my nightmare.

'Jim said that he could hang on to the side but that I'd been burned and they had to help me into the boat. In the end they did, and Jim clung on beside me, still in the water, and we talked. We had to talk, and keep talking, Jim told me, so we didn't go to sleep, because if we went to sleep, like as not we'd never wake up again. So we told each other all the stories we knew: Peter Rabbit, the *Just So Stories* – anything we could remember. When we ran out of stories, we tried singing songs instead: 'Ten Green Bottles', 'Oranges and Lemons'; anything. Time and again I dropped off to sleep, but Jim would always wake me up. Then one time I woke and Jim just wasn't there. He was gone. I've thought about Jim every day of my life since, but I've never spoken about him, until now.

'He's out there, Michael. Jim's out there, down in the deep somewhere. They all are, all the lads that went down in that ship, good lads. And there's been plenty of times since, I can tell you, when I wished to God I'd gone down with them.'

He said nothing more for a while. I'd never heard him talk like this before, never. But he hadn't finished yet.

'All we saw for days on end were gannets,' he went on. 'Except once we did see a whale, a ruddy great whale. But that was all. No ships. No aeroplanes. Nothing. Just sea and sky. Some of the lads were burnt even worse than I was. They didn't last long. We were out there on the open ocean for a week or more. No food, no water. I lost count of the days and the nights. By then I didn't know any more who was alive and who was dead, and what's more I didn't care. I only knew I was still alive. That was all that mattered to me. I lived on nothing but hope, and a dream. I had a dream and I clung on to it. I dreamed of getting back to Annie, of coming home. I thought if I dreamed it hard enough, hoped for it hard enough, it must come true.

'Then, one morning, I wake up and there's this huge destroyer right there alongside us and men looking down over the side and waving and shouting. I thought I was still in my dream, but I wasn't. Only three of us out of that whole lifeboat survived. They patched me up as best they could, and shipped me home. The next thing I knew I was in this hospital, down in Sussex it was, East Grinstead. That's where they put the pieces of me together again, like a sort of jigsaw puzzle, but the pieces were skin and bone and flesh. The trouble was, there were some pieces of my jigsaw missing, so they had bit of a job, which is why I still look a bit of a mess. But I wasn't the worst in that hospital, not by a long shot.

'Dr McIndoe, he was called. Wonderful man he was, a genius. It was him that did it, put us back together, and I'm not just talking about the operations. He was a magician in the operating theatre, all right. But it's what he did afterwards for us. He made us feel right again inside, like we mattered, like we weren't monster men. It was a hospital full of men like me, but mostly air-force boys. We were all together, every one of us patched up in one way or another, so it didn't matter what we looked like even when we went out and about. Everyone treated us right: nurses and doctors, everyone. Annie came to see me when she could. Right away I saw she didn't look at me the same, didn't speak to me like I was normal, like the nurses did. She still loved me, I think, but all she saw was a monster man.

'After a while, when the war was over, I left the hospital and came home to Annie, home to Scilly. My dream had come true, I thought. But of course it hadn't. I soon found that out. Annie tried – tried her best. I tried, too. We had a baby – your mother, Michael – but Annie still wasn't looking at me. I drank too much, said things I shouldn't have said. She did too, told me I should stop feeling sorry for myself, that I wasn't the man she'd married any more. Then we just stopped talking to one another. One day I came back home from a day's fishing and she'd left – just like that, taking my little girl, your mother, with her. She'd had enough. I don't blame her, not any more. No one wants a monster for a husband. No one wants half a man, and that's what I was, Michael, half a man. That's what I still am. But I blamed her then. I hated her. Every day it's all I could think of, how much I hated her.

'I lived with that hate inside me most of my life. Hate, anger, call it what you will. It's like a cancer. It eats away at you. She wouldn't let me see my little girl, even when she was older. I never forgave her for that. She said I drank too much, which was true – said I'd frighten her too much. Maybe she was right. Maybe she was right.'

It wasn't the moment to say anything, so I didn't. We fell into our silence again.

We unloaded the catch, moored the boat and walked together back home up the hill. We cooked the mackerel and sat eating it, still in silence. I was silent because I was reliving his story in my head. But I had one thing I needed to say.

'She wasn't right,' I told him. 'Annie should have let you see your own daughter. Everyone has a right to see their own child.'

'Maybe,' he replied, 'but the truth is, I think I do frighten your mother a little, even now. So Annie was right, in her way. Your mother came to see me for the first time after she'd left school, when she wasn't a little girl any more; practically grown up, she was. She came without ever asking her mother, to find out who her father was, she said; because she hadn't ever known me, not properly. She was kind to me. She's always been kind to me ever since. But even now she can't look me in the eye like you do. She writes letters, keeps in touch, calls me Dad, lets me visit, does her best by me, always has. And I'm grateful, don't get me wrong. But every time I came to you for Christmas when you were little, I longed for her just to look at me. She wants to, but she can't. And she's angry too, like I was. She can't forgive her mother for what she did either, for taking her away from her dad. She hasn't spoken to her mother now in over twenty years. Time's come to forgive and forget; that's what I think.'

So now I knew the whole story for the first time. We relapsed after that into our usual, quiet ways for the rest of the holidays. But by the time I left I think I was closer to him than I have ever been to anyone else in my life.

I went back a year later, this time with my mother to visit him in hospital. He was already too ill to get out of bed. He said he was a lucky man because he could see the sea from his bed. He died the second night we were there. He'd left a letter for me on the mantelpiece in his cottage.

Dear Michael,
See they bury me at sea. I want to be with Jim and the others. I want Annie there, and I want your mother there too. I want you all there together. I want things put right. Thanks for looking at me like you did.
Love, Grandpa

A few days later Annie came over to Scilly for the funeral. She held hands with my mother as Grandpa's ashes were scattered out beyond Scilly Rock. We were lucky. We had a fine day for it. The gannets were flying, and everyone was together, just as Grandpa had wanted. So he was right about gannets. Grandpa was right about a lot of things. But he wasn't half a man.

Geraldine McCaughrean

The precepts of most religions are peaceful, and yet throughout history greedy, well-meaning, bigoted, misguided, politicking or thrill-seeking men have used religion as an excuse for killing and robbing their fellow human beings. To my mind, 'holy war' is a contradiction in terms. War is the ultimate sacrilege. That's why I wrote this story.

I chose 1148 AD and the end of the failed Second Crusade as the setting, because it was a time when Christianity was being stretched out of shape in other ways. Many monasteries, founded as centres of prayer and simplicity and bound by strict rules of chastity, poverty and obedience, were changing into something quite different. Some grew both rich and corrupt, abusing their power over the ordinary people whose food and money they sapped. The abuse was so bad in parts that the locals rose up and evicted the monks.

It was the practice of knights returning from the Crusades to carve a cross in a church wall or floor – a symbol of their thanks to God at surviving. These symbols were called *ex-votos* (literally 'by reason of a vow'). You can still see them in some medieval churches today. And this is where my story begins.

EX VOTO

As his sword hit the plaster, a spark flew, then the blade's tip snapped off. Hugh's breath escaped him in a heavy sob halfway to a laugh. That it should break now – this blade that had travelled so far with him! Having weathered the blazing desert heat, the freezing desert nights, having struck limbs from bodies, heads from shoulders, having driven chain-mail links into flesh like currants into dough, it chose now to snap, inside the chapel of this peaceful English monastery. Plaster fell on to his face, like quicklime on to a corpse.

Sir Hugh shrugged – well, would have shrugged but for the wound in his shoulder. The flesh had healed but not the joint beneath, which never would. He could already foresee the nicknames they would dub him: 'Lapwing', 'Hunchback', 'the Tilt' . . . What name would his mother call him, he wondered, if she proved still to be alive? He went back to gouging away at the wall of the nave. His bad shoulder ached. The pain no longer troubled Hugh; he had endured so much that it had lost the power even to annoy him.

Morning sunbeams, shining in over the rim of the high windows, also drove long blades of light into the plastered wall. Perhaps the sun too was carving its *ex-voto*, in thanks at having survived another night. How quiet it was, this place he had chanced upon. Unusually quiet, even for a monastery chapel.

'Devil toss you on his pitchfork, you thieving dog!' said a voice behind him and a blow across his back felled him to his knees. As he fell, he assessed the degree of pain, the likelihood of death. He also began counting seconds: he had learned precisely how long an enemy took to deliver a second blow. Before his attacker could hit him again, he had rolled over and up and lunged with his sword. If the tip had not been broken, it would have pierced the abbot's belly.

The abbot was holding the candle sconce like a quarter-staff, and his lips were drawn back off his teeth in a ferocious snarl.

'An *ex-voto*! I was carving an *ex-voto*!' cried Hugh in self-defence and the abbot, recognizing a cultured voice, stood the large candlestick back on its base.

'I thought you were prising the chains out of the wall,' he said (though he did not apologize). And now that Hugh looked, he could see that the beautiful wooden font had indeed been chained to the chapel wall. 'They pilfer. All the time, they pilfer, God rot them,' said the abbot. He examined the hole Hugh had made in the plaster. 'Poor effort.'

'Not for want of gratitude to my maker,' said Hugh. 'Only for want of a fit tool.'

The abbot promptly disappeared out of a side door and returned a minute later with a mason's awl that he tossed to the knight. 'I fine you one crown for scarring church fabric . . . Here. You'll make a better job with this.' As Hugh paid, the abbot tried his hardest to see into the purse.

Hugh gladly laid aside his sword. It was much easier using the awl. He was able to scrape out the shape of a fluked cross around the dent he had already made. He worked on steadily, tongue creeping out of the corner of his mouth as he concentrated on his *ex-voto* – his note of thanks to God for bringing him safe home from the war.

He was not the first returning Crusader to carve on the chapel wall. Several 'fines' must have been paid to the abbot. Two dozen crosses were cut in the plaster – even into the marble floor around the font – some as deep as arrow slits, some as shallow as hastily dug graves. Hugh's heart filled with gratitude that these men, too, had survived the bloodbath of the Holy Wars – had dragged themselves home across desert, through hostile countries, escaped diseases, avoided capture or slavery or shipwreck or bandits or open wounds festering or rotten food . . . Each carved cross represented a miracle really.

His head also filled with the faces of those who had not survived – friends, comrades, yeomen of his own levy, his brother Luke . . .

'You use the devil's hand to work, I see,' said the abbot sourly.

'I took a hurt in my shoulder,' said Sir Hugh. 'I have to use my left hand.'

One question had rolled around inside Hugh all the way home, like a stone in his boot. Suddenly – he did

19

not know why – it found its way out of his mouth. 'Why did God not grant us the victory, Father Abbot? I know, I know – serving the Lord is a privilege . . . But you would suppose – given that He called us to go on Crusade – that God would grant us the victory. Or why—'

The question gave the abbot no difficulty at all. 'Too many sinners among you,' he said. 'The feet of the army stumbled upon their own trespasses and they were mired in sin.' It sounded like a quotation from the Bible, though Sir Hugh could not place it. He tried to picture the great army of the Second Crusade, and behind it its siege engines, forges and field kitchens, and behind them – biggest of all – a vast bundle holding all the sins of the marching men, gradually dragging them to a standstill.

'But we went on the Crusade to be forgiven, Father! The priests told us it was our duty to go and our reward to be forgiven! One thousand years less in purgatory! Our accounts wiped clean! Our souls washed in the blood of the Heathen! Why did the victory go to the heathen, Father?'

'The ways of God are not our ways,' snapped the abbot glibly. 'You brought home other rewards, I dare swear. Loot? Plunder?'

Sir Hugh thought of the contents of his saddlebag. 'Something for my sweetheart,' he admitted.

The abbot shuddered with distaste at the mention of a sweetheart but still wanted to see what loot the knight had brought. So Hugh went outside to his horse, tethered in the monastery garden. He stayed to stroke her – the winded, galled, ringwormed nag that had once been the finest in the county. Hardship had made them the best of friends. He told her about the *ex-voto* he had carved and the horse nodded her head in approval. Then Hugh got the pomegranate out of his saddle-wallet and took it back into the chapel. He had picked it in the Holy Land. The hard rind was browner now, but still as hard as eggshell.

The abbot took hold of it with a look of disgust. 'Is this all?'

'We had to travel light. It was bad. At the end. Chaos. We were lucky to get away with our skins. The ones who did.' In the back of Hugh's head familiar monsters squirmed into view – the ones he tried so hard to block out: the pomegranate hanging on its tree; the men lying under that tree as though resting in its shade; its roots soaking up their blood. Perhaps the fruit of the pomegranate tree grew red from drinking the blood of the Crusades.

A cord ran down inside the abbot's skirts. He pulled out a bunch of keys and useful implements. With a knife he ringed the pomegranate and twisted it open. Some of the seeds fell out on to his foot. The juice stained his hands. Those hands will be sticky all day now, thought Hugh absently.

He did not trouble to grieve for the loss of the pomegranate. Such things are not important in comparison with being alive. And now that it was open, the fruit reminded him too much of things he had seen after a sword stroke cut through a helmet, a limb, a horse's flank.

'How many did you kill?' asked the abbot, sniffing the fruit dubiously and giving both halves back to Hugh.

'Sorry, Father?'

'How many heathens did you kill?'

Hugh shook his head. The colourful monsters writhed in the back of his brain: black, blood-red, tripe-white, chestnut, sallow, bay . . . 'Fifty. Sixty, maybe.'

The abbot raised his hands, so that the sunlight fell on his fat white fingers. Hugh bent one knee, thinking to be blessed. But the abbot was simply doing his sums. 'Eight hundred crowns should void it,' he said.

'Father?'

'Well? Did you think to break the Sixth Commandment and not pay the price? *Thou shalt not kill*. The fine has been fixed at twelve crowns per head. Best pay me as much as you can here and now and receive forgiveness. You could wait until you reach your own estates, but the roads are rife with thieves, and if you were to die unshriven . . .'

Hunger and sickness had kept Hugh company all the way from Palestine. Now they gave him a push and he reeled with dizziness. 'I'm sorry. I fear I do not understand you, Father.'

The abbot pursed his lips impatiently. His face seemed to ask how such a stupid knight had managed to find his way home at all. 'Blood weighs heavy, young man. I counsel you earnestly to wash away your sins! Ransom your soul. Some piece of carving on a wall won't do.'

Hysteria, somewhere between laughter and tears, caught in Hugh's throat.

When the call to arms had come, his parents had dug deep to furnish him and his brother with horse, weaponry and armour, so that they might serve the holy cause – recapture Jerusalem for Christ and Christendom! Now Hugh alone was home again, penniless, his only wealth oozing from the broken rind of a pomegranate. And was his surcoat too soaked, his soul too sodden, his scabbard too brimful of blood for him to enter heaven?

'Let me be sure I understand you,' Hugh said slowly and deliberately. 'The Church sends us to war, telling us that fighting for Christ will save our souls. Then, when we come home, you tell us we are sinners for taking lives? And must buy back our innocence with twelve pieces of silver?' Rage flashed behind his eyes as red as blood.

What hatred had he ever felt for the dark-faced strangers who had confronted him over the rim of his shield, who had crossed swords with him, whose thighs had touched his as their horses collided? What wrong had he ever felt he was righting? How holy had it ever felt to wipe the sweat from his lip and taste blood on his glove?

Now this fat abbot, smug and supercilious, was telling him it had been for nothing – for less than nothing – had fitted him for nothing but damnation, had earned him nothing but the tortures of hell. And was his brother even now roasting in hell, for killing Moors at the Holy Church's command?

A red fog clouded Hugh's eyes. The same fog had helped him face a charging horde of Arab horsemen without turning tail, had let him torch a village and trample the dead under his horse's hoofs. Now it blinded him to the sacredness of his surroundings, the light-pierced beauty of the nave, the reverent respect owed to a minister of God. Hugh went for his sword. But of course he had laid it aside. His scabbard was empty.

23

All of a sudden, something flew through the sun-filled slit of the window above him and landed on the floor of the nave with a crack. It was a rock. Hugh stared at it, bewildered. More rocks hit the outside of the wall, with a noise like hoofs clipping flint. The abbot moved with remarkable speed to push shut the open door, shooting the bolt just as someone tried to enter.

Fuddled by hunger and fatigue, Hugh was slow to grasp what was going on. 'Are we under attack?'

The abbot was running full tilt from font to vestry to transept, bolting doors, shouting as he did so, 'Three thousand years in hell to you all! Devil gripe you, you godless Gadarene swine!'

As more rocks rattled down round and about him, Hugh recovered himself. The red fog cleared. He slipped back into the role of Christian knight defending the True Faith. Who but the wicked would attack a monastery chapel? He only wished he could have brought his poor mare indoors.

Cakes of dung and half a rusty ploughshare came through the lancet windows. He retreated to the centre of the nave. Fists were beating on all the doors now, filling the nave with a clamour that reverberated through the choir stalls and up the yawning emptiness of the bell-tower. Birds and bats swooped in terror through the nave. Hugh's sword still lay by the font.

'Scum! Vermin! Devil slit you, you heathen plague rats!' bawled the abbot, his voice cracking like an old stirrup leather. 'By bell, book and candle I cut you off from all hope of heaven!' He ran to the vestry and fetched out a richly embroidered surplice.

At least the man means to die in the robes of his calling! thought Hugh. And he resolved to do his Christian duty as a knight and defend the abbot with his life's blood against whatever godless fiends were outside.

The fiends outside seemed to care nothing about damnation, but redoubled their efforts to break in. A tree branch hit the window and fell back on to the person who had thrown it, who cursed.

'Who *are* they?' Hugh asked. In his weary bewilderment he had begun to imagine Moorish faces, Moorish swords, Moorish pavilions massing outside this English monastery.

'The devil's brood, that's who!' panted the abbot, kneeling beside a gigantic coffer by the door, rattling a key in its lock. It was an intricate lock, its workings a maze of rods and junctions and curlicues filling the lid of the chest. But at last the mechanism grated and clanked, and the hasp was free. The abbot threw open the lid and began pulling out various leather bags, jute sacks and church plate. 'They'd sooner buy cheese and ale than pay their tithes to me!' His spittle spattered the plates and chalices as he wrapped them in the embroidered surplice. As he worked, he shouted at the top of his voice: 'Sons of Gomorrah! Worshippers of Mammon!'

(Daughters of Gomorrah too, to judge by the shrill taunts coming through the lepers' window.) Who could they be, these witches and demons who felt no fear of God or His ministers?

'Thankless serpents and vipers!' hissed the abbot, knotting together the corners of the surplice and dragging it to the side door. 'You must hold them off, knight, while I . . . while I . . . save the treasures of St Ivo!' Suddenly remembering the saintly relic kept under the altar in a lead-lined casket, he dragged it out and shunted it down the choir, like a child trying to toboggan on thin snow. 'Want to kiss it?' he grunted.

Sir Hugh knelt and kissed the casket as it skidded past him, its hasp catching him a blow across the nose. The heart of St Ivo encased in lead made a screaming noise as the nails in its base scraped the marble floor.

'Why does no one come to our aid?' Hugh asked, realizing, for the first time, that he had seen no monks other than the abbot since riding up to the chapel door an hour before.

'Gone already – like rats from a leaky ship. Judgement fall on them! Fire and brimstone scorch their dirty hides!'

Hugh had the nightmarish impression that he must have brought war home with him, along with the lice in his hair, the fleas in his blanket, the ringworm in his horse. It was as if the ghostly spectre of war had ridden home behind him, sharing his saddle, resting its sharp chin on his shoulder. Now chaos would engulf the rolling green English countryside – and it would all be his fault!

'In the name of Christ, I charge you to defend this place!' commanded the abbot, thrusting Hugh's sword at him so that he dropped the pomegranate. 'I must save the relic of St Ivo! Defend this place, knight, and God will reward you!' And, dragging the heavy casket across the brass effigies in the aisle, the abbot disappeared into the shadowy transept.

And Hugh did wait, sword in hand.

A lifetime of obedience to the commands of Mother Church is not easily dislodged. Since childhood, the words 'Church' and 'Goodness' had been tangled tight in his breast: he was far too weary to wrench them apart now. Stones rattled down around him, and smoke began to crawl in under the doors. From time to time some kind of battering ram jarred the lock. Glancing down, Hugh saw that St Ivo's heart had crushed one half of the pomegranate and smeared it like blood and gristle across the brass faces of the dead.

The booming of the battering ram shook all logic out of his head. Once they broke in, how long could he last before they killed him? And even if he could kill every last one of them, how many more years would he have to suffer for it in purgatory before the sin was flayed from his soul?

He began to see demons clambering down the bell-ropes hand over hand, leering, jeering and cackling: *Got you! Tricked you! Fooled you! Caught you! Thou shalt not kill! Thou shalt not kill! We'll take you where we took your brother! Thou shalt not escape us now!* Hugh stood stock still, muscles so rigid, breath so pent, that he felt he was turning to stone like the effigies who lay along their tombs staring up into the vaulted roof. At last, with a splintering of wood, the door lurched open . . .

After a moment, a flock of farm boys, reddlemen, shepherds, quarrymen, housewives, weavers, hedgers and children nosed their way nervously into the church. Not Moors, then not savage, murderous heathens, thirsty for blood. Locals. The coloured light of the chapel washed over their faces and softened their scowls.

27

''Ems gone at last, then, them fat leeches?' called a tinsmith to the knight standing halfway up the aisle.

'Good riddance,' said a widow, devoutly crossing herself and curtseying to the altar. 'Helping themselves to anything they fancied. Breaking their vows. Dipping their hands in our pockets. Fleecing us these twenty years! Got no more conscience than dead ferrets, them beggars.'

They gathered glumly around the empty coffer until someone dragged it away as loot. The widow took the altar cloth, folding it four times and placing it on her head. There was little else left; the deserting monks had taken all they could carry.

Hugh watched them as he might people in a dream. He saw a miller step on the other half of the pomegranate and bend to study the mess, flummoxed by the oddness of what he had trodden in.

'Leeches, bleeding us white they were,' remarked a weaver, eyeing the knight's sword nervously as it twitched in his grasp. 'Had a bad harvest last year, but did they care 'bout our sorrows? Did they ask less? Did they tighten their belts? Not them! The religious life, they called it. We called it living off our backs. What's a monk anyway, but a man with a shaved head? Look at me.' And he showed the crown of his head where baldness had given him the look of a monk without the greedy, grasping nature of one. 'Do that give me the right to help myself to a slice of my neighbour's dinner?'

The widow came and peered at Hugh, her eyes straying over his features, and she absently licked a fingerful of apron and began to clean his face for him. 'Blessings on the Virgin Mary for bringing you safe home to your

28

mother – whoever you are. I lost my men at Damascus. If you knows where in God's earth that is, you knows more than I do. These monks – they thinks up wars to take our husbands and sons from us, but they stays home themselves, living off the widows' sweat and toil!'

'No! Surely it was God above who . . .' began Hugh but had to stop; the woman was busy folding back his lips to polish his teeth.

'Do not you believe it, lad! War's always the idea of men! God's just the excuse. Afterwards, men keeps the loot. All God gets is the blame.'

'Might be different, other places,' said the reddleman, pursuing his own train of thought. 'Monks might be saints, some of 'em, for all I know. But here . . . We've had all of them we can stomach. Been like our own private war 'twixt them and us these two months past,' he explained to the knight. 'A nest of wasps is less of a curse than a nest of godless monks.'

A ploughboy armed with a mattock took a swing at the chain securing the font to the wall. He dislodged a cloud of plaster, and cracks spread out from the hole, crazing the *ex-votos* of a dozen Crusaders.

Then a stir of excitement fetched everyone to the side door of the chapel to see a thing of interest. The boy with the mattock prised open the casket and laid bare the heart of St Ivo. It had never meant as much to the abbot as saving his hide.

And to do that, he had helped himself to Hugh's mare and made good his escape.

Michelle Magorian

When I heard that this collection of stories would be published on the sixtieth anniversary of VE day (Victory in Europe), I thought of my parents. They were unable to be there for the celebrations in 1945. My mother was nursing soldiers in a hospital in India and my father, who was in the navy, was on his way to Bombay to marry her. A few months later he was in one of many empty trucks heading for a Japanese prisoner-of-war camp to pick up survivors.

And I thought of the others who were absent, the ones who hadn't survived. Whenever I watched films about VE day, they were always about the crowds at Trafalgar Square and the street parties – but what about the ones who didn't go to Trafalgar Square and who had lost the streets they lived in?

I decided to return to the town where two of my theatre books are set and write about the theatre community there. I then discovered that on the day leading up to VE day, hundreds of people had hung around their wirelesses, longing to hear the official announcement that the next day would indeed be a public holiday. Hour after hour, tired and impatient, they waited and waited. They were waiting for peace.

And that's where my story begins.

WAITING FOR PEACE

Miss Pleasance had just finished reading a chapter of *Shadow the Sheepdog* when the school bell rang.

'Hands on laps, please,' she said and she turned to clean the blackboard.

Guy glanced at his classmates. They were fidgeting and mouthing to one another. A boy in the front row, who always came top in the mental arithmetic tests, was being nudged by two boys who sat in the desks behind him.

He raised his arm. 'Please Miss Pleasance.'

'Yes, John,' she said over her shoulder.

'It's about tomorrow, Miss Pleasance.'

'I'm sorry, John, but if there was any news . . .'

She was interrupted by a knock at the door.

The school secretary, an elderly woman with a face like a mouse, peered into the classroom. There was a murmur of excitement. Guy crossed his fingers.

'Yes, Miss Jones?

'I'm afraid there's been no announcement as yet, Miss Pleasance,' she said demurely.

'Blast!' Guy whispered.

He had been praying he would be able to stay up late to watch the opening of the week's new play at the theatre. Monday was the day of the week when he hardly saw his mother at all, because on Monday afternoons she was always busy with a dress rehearsal right up to curtain up. It meant she couldn't be there to meet him after school with his younger brother. Instead, Roger would be waiting for him on his own and they would have to go straight back to their lodgings and put up with the horrible Valerie, who would scowl and shout at him and make him feel as if she wished he would disappear forever.

Guy's eight-year-old brother was standing by a group of mothers in the playground, his gingery blond hair sticking up at all angles. One eye beamed out at Guy through the right lens of his spectacles. A wrinkled, grubby plaster on his left lens hid the other eye. His smudged face appeared to have collected even more freckles since Guy had last seen him. Roger spotted Guy, gave a gap-toothed grin and waved vigorously. As Guy approached him he said, 'Are we having a holiday tomorrow?'

'Winston Churchill hasn't made up his mind yet,' said Guy wearily.

'Did you see him?'

'Of course I didn't see him!'

'You're not to shout at me.'

Guy held his breath. Roger didn't like it when people raised their voices. If they did, he would run away and hide, which caused quite a few problems when they went to yet another new school and the teachers didn't know him.

Guy pressed his lips together and counted to ten. He edged towards the women so that he could eavesdrop.

'I was sure there'd be an announcement by three o'clock,' one woman was saying.

'Come on, Roger,' said Guy and he took hold of his hand and gripped it firmly so that he couldn't run off.

At the end of the road they turned a corner into a busy high street. They passed the lengthy queues of women waiting patiently outside grocery shops and butchers'. Guy spotted a crowd hovering round the open window of a cafe where there was a wireless.

'It'll be on the nine o'clock news,' he heard someone say.

'Nah. He won't say anythin' till tomorrer, you'll see,' said another woman behind her.

'They've already been told in France,' said another.

'They never 'ave! Where d'you hear that?' joined in an enormous woman whose battered felt hat was pulled down so firmly it looked as if it was glued on.

A pale young woman was jigging a baby in an old pram. 'I can't stand this waiting,' she complained.

'Neither can I,' muttered Guy.

They strode on past rubble and blown-away walls – the remains of a shoe shop and a hardware store – and headed for a large stone archway with a clock in it.

An excited group of women was hurrying out of the draper's, ribbons in red, white and blue dangling from their hands. Guy stepped quickly out of their way, hovered at the edge of the pavement and, when a tram had passed by, he dragged Roger briskly across the road.

He spotted a placard on the steps of the Palace Theatre.

7 MAY – OPENING NIGHT
BEDTIME STORY
BY WILLIAM ELLIS.
A SIDE-SPLITTING COMEDY BY THE AUTHOR
OF
A LITTLE BIT OF FLUFF

'Are we going to the station?' asked Roger.

Roger ate and slept steam trains. His idea of heaven was to sit on a platform and watch endless trains arriving and departing.

'Stage door,' said Guy abruptly.

'But Mummy's busy. It's Monday.'

'I know, but we can stay with Walter for a bit.'

When they stepped through the stage door they found that Walter's wife was sitting in the cubbyhole with him. They looked like twins, with their thick shocks of white hair and their blue eyes. Balanced on a tiny table, in front of a wall of pigeonholes with keys dangling below, was a wireless. A glass dome-shaped accumulator stood next to it.

'We've just had it recharged,' she said, tapping it with satisfaction.

'So the wireless won't run out of sound,' Roger said.

'That's right,' said Walter. 'We don't want it cutting out on us tonight, do we?'

'Any news?' asked Guy.

'Nothing at all. Fancy a cuppa?'

'Rather!'

Guy felt his shoulders drop. Every time his mother

worked in a new theatre he and Roger would have to go to a new school. The other children had their own friends and usually talked with a local accent. They teased them and called them 'toffs' because they came from London, but once Guy stepped into a theatre he felt welcome and at home.

'Of course the 4468 Mallard is faster,' said Roger thoughtfully.

'I take it we're talking about trains,' commented Walter, who was used to Roger's one-track conversations.

'Yes. It holds the speed record but I'd still rather go on the *Flying Scotsman* than a 4468 Mallard. All the way up to Scotland, I'd like to go. In a sleeping compartment.'

'Roger, can we stop talking about trains for one moment,' said Guy, exasperated.

'Did you know,' said Roger, turning to Walter's wife, 'that it's got a water pick-up tap.'

Guy groaned.

'It picks up water when the train is moving and scoops it up into the tank inside the tender without stopping.'

'Well, I never,' she said.

'The tender carries coal *and* water, you see.'

'Does it now?'

Guy chatted to Walter while Roger drew steam trains on a scrap of paper Walter's wife had given him. Four o'clock and five o'clock dragged by and still there was no news.

'Looks like it's school for you boys tomorrow,' said Walter.

Downcast, they left the theatre and headed for their lodgings. They were staying in a small terraced house in a street five minutes' walk from the theatre. As they reached the street Guy felt his spirits fall even lower.

'Look!' cried Roger.

Guy raised his head. There were Union Jacks draped across the windows and ribbons and coloured flags hanging outside the houses. But they failed to touch him. All he could think of was sixteen-year-old Valerie. She would be home by now.

As soon as they entered the house he quickly bustled Roger upstairs to the room they shared with their mother. His brother liked to listen to *Children's Hour* with Uncle Mac and they were already late for it. They were only allowed to listen to *Children's Hour* and *Dick Barton – Special Agent!* At seven o'clock the wireless had to be turned off so that they would have enough power left for the next day and their mother wouldn't have to traipse all the way to the other side of town to get the accumulator recharged again.

At six o'clock they went downstairs to wash their hands in the scullery. Valerie was standing at the sink washing her hands too, towering above them in her grammar-school uniform, her dark hair scraped so fiercely into plaits that her skin was taut. She looked more miserable than ever.

They washed their hands in silence, except for Roger.

'Of course, the *Flying Scotsman* is my favourite,' he said enthusiastically. 'Guy, is the *Flying Scotsman* your favourite?'

Guy sighed. 'I don't really think about it,' he said.

'I do,' said Roger. 'I *love* the *Flying Scotsman*.'

Supper was in the dining room. A wireless stood on a small cabinet on the side. Mrs Hicks, a tiny, quick-moving, elderly woman whose hands were rarely empty, bustled in and out with plates of food.

Supper was vegetable pie, after which Valerie swiftly cleared the table and carried the dishes to the scullery to wash and dry them. This was Guy and Roger's signal to go upstairs to their room. Valerie needed the dining table for doing her homework and she snapped at Guy if he disturbed her, which he did by just breathing. Sometimes she worked with the wireless on. One night when Guy came down to listen to it after Roger had fallen asleep she snapped, 'I can't concentrate while you're in the room. Go away!'

Guy made Roger clean his teeth and then read him a story in bed. While his brother drew trains in his sketch pad, Guy leaned out of the window and watched the neighbours hang out more flags. The children were playing in the street, calling out to each other, chatting easily. He guessed they had known each other for years, living in and out of each other's houses. He and his brother were still strangers. They had been in the area for less than a month. Suddenly the street was deserted and Guy realized it must be a quarter to seven. Time for *Dick Barton*.

After the episode had finished, he turned off the wireless and tried to read a book but he felt too restless to concentrate. He could hear piano music coming from the landlady's wireless. Very slowly, he crept down the stairs. The music stopped abruptly. He guessed that Valerie must have switched it off. He was about to return to his room when he heard a man reading out information. He froze.

'It is understood that, in accordance with arrangements between the three great powers,' stated the voice, 'an official announcement will be broadcast by the prime minister at three o'clock tomorrow, Tuesday afternoon, the eighth of May,'

'Not till three o'clock!' groaned Guy.

'In view of this fact, tomorrow, Tuesday, will be treated as Victory in Europe day—'

'Hurray!' he whispered and he flung his arms in the air.

'—and will be regarded as a holiday. The day following, Wednesday, the ninth of May, will also be a holiday.'

'Two days!' This was more than he had hoped for.

'His Majesty the King will broadcast to the people of the British Empire and Commonwealth tomorrow, Tuesday, at 9 p.m.'

Guy couldn't wait any longer. It was now or never. He flung himself downstairs and ran into the dining room.

Valerie was sitting motionless, gazing into the distance, unsmiling.

I expect she's annoyed the announcement has interrupted her homework, the big snooty swot, Guy thought.

Mrs Hicks was sitting at the table, a pile of stockings on her lap and a darning needle in her hand. 'Well, that was a bit of a damp squib,' she remarked, staring at the wireless.

'Mrs Hicks,' Guy blurted out, his fingers crossed behind his back, 'can I go to the theatre? Mummy said I could if there was no school tomorrow.'

40

It was only half a lie, Guy thought. He was sure she would have let him go to the theatre had she known there was to be a holiday the next day.

Walter and his wife peered at Guy from their cubbyhole. Guy rested his hands on his knees, fighting for breath. From the moment he had sprinted out of the landlady's house he had run without stopping.

'Did you hear it?' Guy gasped. He noticed that their wireless was switched off.

'Hear what?' said Walter.

'It's about VE day, ent it?' said his wife excitedly.

Guy nodded. 'Holiday tomorrow. And Wednesday,' he said, breathlessly. 'Winston Churchill's going to talk at three o'clock. King in the evening.'

'It'll be on the nine o'clock news,' said Walter. 'We'll switch the wireless on then.'

'This calls for a celebration!' cried his wife. 'I'll open the pears.' And she dived under the counter and produced an old tin with a scuffed wrapper on it.

'You stay 'ere,' said Walter to Guy as he stepped out of the cubbyhole. 'I'll wait upstairs and tell the producer in the interval.'

'Can I come with you?'

He hesitated.

'Go on, Walter,' urged his wife.

'All right, but you're not to tell anyone in the cast. They'll get so excited they might forget their lines.'

'Go on with you, Walter!' said his wife.

They walked up the stone steps and pushed open a swing door. Behind the stage was a corridor. Guy glanced at the doors which led to the dressing rooms and

41

the green room. They slipped quickly past and headed for the door which led to the stage's left wings.

Walter gave the door a gentle push and they were backstage. A wave of laughter came from the auditorium.

They crept past a table with its props neatly arranged in the order of the three acts and headed towards a young female assistant stage manager, who was sitting perched on a stool, dressed as a maid. Guy knew she would be totally absorbed in the play. It was her job to give the sound and lighting cues and prompt the actors if they forgot their lines, which they never seemed to do.

Walter pressed a finger to his lips. Guy smiled excitedly.

The ASM pressed a bell on a wooden square, which gave the sound of a telephone ringing. She was watching the downstage area intently, waiting for the phone to be picked up as her sight cue to stop it ringing.

And then Guy heard his mother speaking.

'Hello! Yes, cousin Isabel – it's *me* speaking. Eh? Uncle is – er – resting.'

There was a laugh from the audience.

'Yes, the telegram *has* come. Eh? We couldn't phone before because it's only just arrived . . . Certainly! Hold the line a minute.'

Guy could hear her walking. And then there was silence. It was frustrating not knowing what was happening on stage but, whatever his mother was doing, it was causing more laughter.

'Are you there?' he heard her ask the person on the other end of the line. 'Myra Hoffman will call in an hour's time at Sir John's flat to get the tickets for America!'

There was the sound of the telephone being replaced and the Billy Dixon Trio played the first interval music as the curtain fell to applause.

His mother appeared in the wings looking unfamiliarly plump in a shapeless gymslip and spectacles. 'Guy!' she exclaimed. 'How long have you been here?'

'About five minutes.'

'Where's Roger?'

'In bed. Mrs Hicks is keeping an eye on him and then when she goes to bed Valerie's staying up.'

'Why are you here?'

'It's a holiday for everyone tomorrow. And on Wednesday.'

'Not quite everyone, poppet,' she said, smiling. 'We'll be blocking Act One of *They Knew What They Wanted* in the morning.'

'Will you be playing someone ten years younger or ten years older?'

'Younger. An American girl who goes to the Italian part of the Napa Valley to marry a man she's never met. She thinks he's young and handsome but he's sixty, stout and Italian. But it all works out well in the end. Now, I must dash. I have to shed my padding and glasses and slip into a beautiful dress,' and she kissed him on the forehead and made for the door which led to the corridor.

The ASM now joined them. 'Is it true,' she asked, 'about VE day?'

'Yes,' said Guy.

'I wonder if I can get to London after tomorrow night's performance,' she murmured to herself and picked up a tray of props and walked briskly on to the set.

'Guy, you nip up to the gods,' said Walter and he opened the side door, which led into the auditorium. 'And keep mum!'

Guy weaved his way through the crowd of theatre-goers in the stalls and out into the foyer. He headed for the stairway and began the long climb back to the gods – the highest seats in the house. One of the usherettes recognized him and smiled, indicating an empty seat.

The lights dimmed. The audience stopped talking and the Billy Dixon Trio played the music which introduced Act Two.

The curtain rose to reveal a lounge in a very expensive-looking flat. It was dark and a telephone was ringing. A thin man wearing a hat and raincoat entered and switched on the lights, wearing an expression of such exaggerated melancholy that he looked comic. Guy guessed he was a butler.

Act Two had begun.

It was the end of Act Three. The curtain fell. As it lifted, nine performers stood in line holding hands and bowed.

The actor who played a funny red-faced gentleman called Uncle Toby stepped forward in his bow tie and spectacles.

'Ladies and gentlemen,' he began in his deep, booming voice, 'we thank you for the rapturous applause you have so generously bestowed on us this evening. Next week we are performing a play by Sidney Howard entitled *They Knew What They Wanted*. This magnificent play received a Pulitzer Prize in New York in 1925 and was an outstanding success when it ran in London. If you have enjoyed tonight's performance, which it

44

appears you have from your thunderous applause, please tell your friends and do come again next week.'

He paused.

'Before we stand for the King,' he continued, a tremor in his voice, 'I have a further announcement. It is the one we've all been waiting for. While you have been sitting here being a splendid audience, the news has come to us, via the BBC, that tomorrow is indeed VE day and that there are to be two days of national holiday.'

Through the opening chords of 'God Save the King' and the slamming of four hundred upturned seats, Guy heard a woman cry, 'It's over!'

Usually everyone filed out of the theatre after the national anthem but, before anyone could move, the cast began singing 'There'll always be an England'. The audience remained standing and joined in. The Billy Dixon Trio followed this with 'Land of Hope and Glory' and the 'Marseillaise'.

To Guy's surprise, the musicians next started to play a jaunty tune. The cast turned to one side, their hands on the waist of the person in front, and danced off into the wings, kicking their legs to each side in unison. The people in the front row of the gods were looking down into the stalls and laughing. Guy quickly ran down the aisle to join them.

'It's the conga,' shrieked two women next to him.

Down in the aisles, the audience was leaving the auditorium in the same manner as the cast, hanging on to one another and shooting their hips and legs out in strange, jerky movements.

Guy leaped up the steps back to the exit doors and ran down several flights of stairs, into a crowded and noisy

45

foyer. To his amazement, lights were spilling out of the open doors into the streets.

'Bit early for them to be flouting the blackout regulations, isn't it?' said a well-spoken elderly gentleman. 'There'll be trouble.'

'Who cares!' said his elegant companion.

There was bubbling chaos as everyone rushed to be outside, determined not to miss out on anything else, as though world events had taken a sudden shot forward while they had been cocooned in the world of the theatre.

Guy was both sorry and relieved that Roger wasn't with him: sorry because he was missing all the excitement, relieved because it was highly likely that he would be swept up in the crowd and happily wander off hand in hand with a stranger.

By the time Guy reached the stage door his mother was waiting for him. They headed briskly for the high street. Already there was a party atmosphere. They could hear singing from a nearby pub on the corner and hanging from the buildings were not only Union Jacks visible but Russian flags with the hammer and sickle, stripy blue, white and red French flags and the American Stars and Stripes. By an open window someone was playing a jazz record on a gramophone.

His mother suddenly put her arm round him as they walked. 'I was going to keep quiet till you boys were together but I might as well tell you now. I phoned the hospital this morning. They think Daddy will be well enough to be discharged in a fortnight. And when I told the producer, he said that as soon as he's demobbed there's a job waiting for him here. Isn't that good?'

46

Guy nodded. 'We'll all be together again,' he said and he leaned against her.

Their street was eerily quiet compared to the high street. It was so silent they could hear their footsteps echoing along the walls. Above them, flags and ribbons fluttered in the slight evening breeze.

They went through the usual motions of not switching on the hall light until the blacked-out front door was closed. Standing in the hallway, all they could hear was the sound of the landlady's clock ticking. Valerie was in the dining room with her schoolbooks. While Guy went off to the scullery to clean his teeth, he heard his mother thanking Valerie for staying up and keeping an ear out for Roger.

'I'll be up in a minute,' she said as he walked back through the dining room and up the stairs.

He got undressed, put on his pyjamas and waited. She was taking ages, he thought.

He listened out for the familiar creak on the stairs but he could hear nothing except Roger breathing deeply in the double bed he shared with their mother.

Tired of waiting, he slipped out of bed, slowly opened the door and crept down the stairs. Someone was crying. At first he thought it was his mother and it alarmed him, but then he heard his mother say something. He couldn't make out what it was but it sounded soothing. He realized that the cries came from Valerie. She was sobbing so hard it sounded as if her heart was breaking. He couldn't understand it. Why was she so unhappy? The war was over and there was no school for two days. Perhaps she was crying because she was upset at *not* having to go to school. He heard a chair being pushed back and the sound of a nose being blown. Hastily he crept back to his room.

Hardly had he climbed into bed when he was startled by a loud bang from outside. He threw aside the covers and ran over to the window. A huge flash of lightning lit up the sky. This was followed by another loud bang of thunder. Torrents of rain fell noisily into the empty street.

'It's almost biblical,' he heard a soft voice say from behind him. It was his mother. She wrapped her arms round him and leaned her chin gently on his head. 'It's washing it all away,' she murmured.

There was another flash of lightning.

'Sorry I took so long. I was with Valerie. Tomorrow is going to be very difficult for her.'

'Everything's difficult for her,' muttered Guy. 'She's always miserable.'

'Have you ever thought that seeing us so happy might be the cause of it?'

'No.'

'In fact, I was wondering if you could ask her to join you and Roger tomorrow morning before coming to the cafe at lunch time.'

Guy swung round, horrified. 'She hates me!' he said. 'She'll just yell at me. She'll spoil everything. Why can't she stay with here with her aunt?'

'Mrs Hicks is going to spend the day with her sister. And she isn't Valerie's aunt. Valerie doesn't have any relations at all. Mrs Hicks kindly lets her stay here in exchange for helping around the house.' She took hold of Guy's hands and looked at him squarely. 'Tomorrow, the war is going to be over for thousands of people.'

'I know. I told you,' said Guy impatiently.

'But for some people the war isn't over. There's still a war in the Far East. Valerie's father is in the navy. His ship was attacked several years ago by the Japanese and all survivors were taken prisoner. Valerie has no idea if her father is a prisoner of war or not.'

'Oh,' said Guy.

'And last year her mother and two sisters were killed by a flying bomb. Because she goes to the grammar school she arrived home later, which is why she wasn't with them. So you see, tomorrow many people will be feeling sad as well as happy, because the people they loved the most won't be there to join in the celebrations. Do you understand?'

'I think so.'

'Valerie is under a lot of strain. This year she's taking some very important examinations called School Certificate so she's working very hard, because if her father doesn't come home she's going to have to fend for herself. Maybe she works too hard at times, but it keeps her going. So will you stay with her tomorrow? For me?'

'All right,' he said dismally,

They leaned out of the window. By now all the flags and ribbons were limp and dripping.

'Let's hope we have some sun tomorrow,' said his mother.

The next day her wish came true. Guy woke to sunlight flooding into the bedroom. Roger was sitting cross-legged on the double bed, drawing more trains in his sketchbook, a *Boy's Book of Trains* lying open beside him. Draped neatly over a chair were two sets of clean clothes. A note was lying on top. Guy flung back the covers and ran to pick it up.

MRS HICKS SAID IT WAS ALL RIGHT
FOR YOU TO LIE IN AND HAVE
BREAKFAST LATE. SEE YOU AT
ONE O'CLOCK AT THE USUAL CAF
LOVE, MUMMY.

He picked up Roger's clothes and flung them at him.

Once they were both dressed they left the bedroom. As they opened the door they came face to face with Valerie. She was wearing a powder-blue dress with pink flowers on it, her Sunday-best clothes. What was different about her was that her hair was no longer in plaits. It hung round her face in waves, the hair beside her face and above her forehead in a victory roll.

Roger gasped. 'You look like the tooth fairy!' he exclaimed.

To Guy's surprise, Valerie laughed. Guy couldn't remember ever having heard her laugh. 'You don't know what the tooth fairy looks like,' Guy remarked.

'Yes, I do. I've seen her in pictures,' he said and he took her hand.

Guy followed them as they squeezed together down the narrow staircase.

'Now, what would you like me to tell you about first,' asked Roger, as if continuing the conversation from the night before, 'the valve rods, the driving rods or the coupling rods?'

Guy gazed upwards in despair.

After breakfast the three of them spent the morning at

50

the railway station watching women putting up red, white and blue decorations.

'Now the war is over,' said Roger 'do you think they'll bring back the *Flying Scotsman*?'

'I'm sure they will,' said Valerie.

'Did you know that some of the steel on the carriages is painted to look like wood?'

Guy did, thoroughly. He ignored them both and watched the crowds of uniformed men and women squeezing into the coaches, heading for London to join in the celebrations in Trafalgar Square. His father was already in back in London. He wondered how he would celebrate VE day in a hospital ward.

'Daddy said there used to be a cinema car on it,' Roger said thoughtfully.

Guy was startled to hear Roger mention his father just as he was thinking of him, but then they often had similar thoughts at the same time.

At one o'clock they left the station for the cafe. When they walked in – ducking under the multicoloured triangular flags which were hanging across the ceiling – the buxom actress who played the snobbish Lady Blundell indicated a chair for Valerie. The company seemed eager for her to feel at ease.

The owner had lined up four tables so that they could all eat together. Valerie was flanked by two of the cast. On one side was the middle-aged actor who played a London detective and a laughing foreign prince in the new play and on the other a young actor who didn't look much older than Valerie and who couldn't take his eyes off her.

'I was wondering,' he said eagerly, over a plate of

mashed potato, cabbage and a scattering of sausage, 'if you could test me on my Act One lines this afternoon? I have to be DLP for a run tomorrow morning before we block the moves for Act Two.'

'DLP?' she repeated.

'Dead letter perfect,' explained Guy's mother.

'Oh,' said Valerie shyly, 'if you think it would help.'

'It would help enormously,' said the young actor.

Guy was sitting between his mother and brother, watching. 'That means we can be on our own,' he whispered to Roger, thinking they could go to the cinema.

'Oh good,' said Roger, 'we can go back to the station. Did you know,' he said, turning to a distinguished and very elderly actor on his right, 'that the *Flying Scotsman* has a TPO? That's a travelling post office.'

'Fascinating,' said the actor, 'my life has been made all the more richer for that gem of information.'

Exasperated, Guy looked hurriedly away. He observed that the actor, who had made the announcement on stage the previous night, was pouring some brown liquid into his tea from a small silver flask. He put the flask back into his pocket and raised his cup. 'To absent friends,' he said, emotion in his voice.

Everyone picked up their cups and chinked them together. 'To absent friends!' they chorused.

Guy glanced across at Valerie and it shocked him. The sadness in her eyes was so terrible that it made his throat ache. Suddenly, he imagined being left alone, like Valerie, with no mother, no father and no Roger, and the thought of it made him feel sick.

His mother must have noticed too because he felt her fingers gently touching his arm. 'Thank you for bringing her, Guy,' she said quietly. 'I didn't want her to be alone today.'

He looked up at her. 'We're lucky, aren't we?'

She nodded. 'Very lucky. Now eat up. There's a special treat waiting for you after this course.'

'Jelly?' he cried.

'My lips are sealed.' But her voice was trembling.

'What's the matter?' he said, alarmed. 'Is there something wrong?'

'No. Everything's fine.' And she threw her arms round him and held him close.

'Don't forget *me*,' Guy heard his brother say.

His mother reached out behind him for Roger and hugged them both clumsily.

'Everything's *wonderful*!' And she laughed. 'Come on boys, it's time for us to celebrate!'

Celia Rees

Soldiers have always sought to protect non-combatants from the brutal realities of war, claiming, in the words of a song from the First World War, that 'They would never believe it.' Even at a time when we think that the camera shows us everything, there are things that we are prevented from seeing. We get only a faint echo of the screaming, a fading after-image of the horror of the immediate experience. No camera can communicate that, or the endurance and courage that soldiers have to display if they are to live with the boredom, terror, disgust and fear that they experience every day as part of the job.

The British public, by contrast, has always had an ambivalent attitude towards serving soldiers, from Rudyard Kipling's Tommy Atkins (who complains in the poem 'Tommy' that the British public has no regard for soldiers during peacetime, but is lavish with empty praise and gratitude during wartime), to the ladies who gave out white feathers to off-duty officers wearing civilian clothing. How much more would this be so for soldiers serving in a war that is unpopular in the first place?

I wanted to write a story about that. What kind of reception might a soldier receive when he comes home on leave from Iraq?

REAL TEARS

'**C**an you still do that thing?'

'What? What thing?'

I was having trouble hearing him over the music and everyone talking. He was standing next to me, hands loosely clasped, resting on the bar. His wrists were thick and sunburned. The ring he wore – third finger, left hand – was a heavy gold number, engraved with some kind of insignia. As he talked he turned it round and round.

'You know, that trick. You did it at Jake's party. You're famous for it.' He smiled. Teeth white against his tanned face. I'd forgotten how handsome he was. He was a friend of my brother's, or used to be.

'Oh.' I grinned back, catching his drift. '*That* trick. Now, let me think. A trick like that takes concentration.'

I'd perfected it when I was a small child. My brother is older than me. He won all our fights easily and used to tease me without mercy, laughing at my fury. There was only one way to get back at him. I felt the prickling pepper sting and the tears began to well and brim. It is important not to sneeze, or the effect is lost entirely. Then I blink once, twice, so that the tears spill and fall. I felt them find the channels at the side of my nose and imagined them reflecting the light, taking on a silvery glitter. I tasted salt at the corner of my mouth.

He caught a drop from my chin, held it on his fingertip.

'That's a good trick!' He grinned at me, delighted.

I smiled back. I knew it.

I took out a tissue and dabbed my face. I'm the only person I know who can cry at will. No red nose, no puffy eyes. I just look tragic, although it's good to wear waterproof mascara.

'That deserves a drink.' He turned back to the bar. 'What are you having?'

'A glass of white wine, please.'

He got served right away and I was glad he'd stood next to me. I'd been waiting ages. The bar was crowded. A level results had come out that day. Everyone was out. I was celebrating, rather than drowning my sorrows.

'What are you doing here?' I said, as we found a space to stand. Somewhere to sit was out of the question.

'I'm home for a bit. Thought I'd come out for a drink.' He looked around. 'This place has changed. We used to come here.'

He meant with my brother.

'It hasn't really. Just a different crowd.'

'I guess. I don't know anyone now.' He laughed and drained his pint. 'They make me feel like a grandad. You ready for another?'

'I'm all right, thanks.'

I watched him as he wove his way back to the bar. It

would have been easy to make an escape, drift off and join any of half a dozen different groups, but part of me thought that would be rude. He had been my brother's best friend when they were at school, and used to come to our house all the time. He never took any interest in me, of course, but I'd had quite a crush on him. At fifteen, I'd been in love. For certain and forever. I told everyone I was interested only in older men. I may even have written poems. They were at university then; he used to come to our house and hang out in the vacations. I'd drift round on hot summer days, wearing as little as possible, trying to catch his eye. I'd pretend to sunbathe and watch him and my brother doing pull-ups on the bar they'd rigged up between the house and the garage. I didn't think he'd noticed, but he must have done. I'd done the crying trick at my brother's twenty-first. At the end of that summer, there had been a falling-out. I don't remember him coming round much after that.

'Who's the fit guy?' My friend Stephanie bumped my shoulder, making me spill my drink. She'd obviously been celebrating harder than I had. 'Are you keeping him to yourself, or what?'

'I haven't decided.'

'Pass him on to me, if you can't make your mind up. He's hot!' She giggled into her vodka and Coke. 'I'm not the only one who's noticed.'

I followed her line of sight and saw that my ex was ignoring his new girlfriend and staring in our direction. He looked past, frowning hard towards the bar. I had to turn away to hide the smile on my face. That made deciding even easier.

*

'I bought you one anyway.' He gave the glass to me. 'Getting served is murder. Who's this?'

He smiled at Stephanie, who did her special eyelash-fluttering flirty laugh, the one she thinks is really seductive.

'This is Ben.' I introduced them, knowing Stephanie wasn't going anywhere until she knew his name, at the very least.

'It's such a row in here,' she said. 'Why don't we go out to the courtyard? It's just that, oh—' She waved her glass. 'I appear to be empty.'

'What would you like?'

'A Duke Doubler,' she said quickly.

'A Duke what?'

'They'll know behind the bar. Just ask for it.'

It was double shots of white rum, vodka and something else, with that blue stuff to top it off. It came in a fancy glass with parasols.

'OK. Look after my pint.'

'I've always wanted one of those. Might as well make the most of it.' Stephanie took a swig of his beer. 'I bet he's loaded. Officers earn tons of money.'

'How do you know he's a soldier?' I asked.

'Look how short his hair is, and he's built! Besides, he's got that ring. Don't you notice anything? A regimental thing. My uncle's got one like it. You'd make a rubbish detective.'

I knew anyway. That was why he'd fallen out with my brother. Jake is left wing. A trainee journalist on the *Guardian*. He couldn't believe a friend of his could want to join the forces. Ben had said, no problem – and they were no longer friends. And I never said I wanted to be a detective.

Ben came back with Steph's drink and we fought our way out to the courtyard. It was only slightly less packed but most of our friends were there, and at least it was open to the air, not choked with cigarette smoke.

As for the argument, I have to blame Steph. She was the one who told them that he was a soldier. Up to that point, all I'd been concerned about was the fact that he was older. He bought a pitcher of cocktails and beers for the boys and seemed happy enough to hang out with us, but he'd been there, done that and I was worried he could get bored with all the talk of A levels, school and university.

Ginny picked up on his job as soon as the words left Steph's big mouth. She was the one with the most definite views – on everything. Not just the war. She'd gained her clutch of A grades, but did not intend to take her place up yet. She was going on a gap year.

'I'm going to travel,' she said, 'see the world. It's important to see how other people live. Poor people who are less fortunate than we are in the West. After all, it's us who've made them like that. I intend to do what I can to make a difference.'

'Oh yeah?' Steph sneered. She'd heard the speech before and there's not a lot of love lost between her and Ginny. 'And just how is you lying on a beach with Stu going to make the slightest bit of difference to anyone? Please tell me.'

'Because I'm not going to be doing that.' Ginny's voice

was as cold as the ice in her glass. 'I'm going to the Middle East. To teach English on the West Bank.'

We all stared at her. That was news. The last plan involved Ginny and her boyfriend, Stu, spending time in Thailand and Cambodia before going to stay with his auntie who owned retail outlets in Brisbane, Australia.

'It's important to put something back.' She glared at Ben. 'Help to repair the damage *some* people are doing in that part of the world.'

'It's dangerous there.' His tone was mild, even affable. 'You be careful.'

'Oh,' she flashed back, 'and who's made it like that? You. You and those like you. Look at Iraq.' I groaned and shut my eyes. Ginny was about to make one of her great leaps of logic. 'What conceivable excuse did you have for invading that country? None at all. Now look what's going on. Children murdered. Innocent people slaughtered.'

'Hey!' He tried a smile. 'I don't do that. I'm in the Engineers, putting back the infrastructure that's been destroyed—'

The smile didn't work.

'By *who*?' Ginny was fairly squeaking with indignation. 'By YOU! Don't you feel the slightest bit *guilty*?'

'Why should I? My job is to help people.'

'Oh, please!' Ginny rolled her eyes. 'Don't even *think* about trying to patronize me. We all know what's happening out there: thousands tortured and killed every day . . .'

She was shouting across everybody, right into his

face. At first, he tried to parry what she said, set out counter-arguments. When that didn't work, he just listened. The more she battered him with words, the more silent he became. He didn't look at her – he didn't look at any of us – he just stared at the whitewashed wall, a distant, abstracted stare, as if there were scenes playing there that only he could see. The bright bloom of flame within roiling oily black smoke; people running in panic and confusion; the moment when the camera pulls back from the scene in the bomb-torn street, swinging up and away from the scrap of burned fabric, the gob of meat, the bloodstained smear that had started the day as a human being. We didn't have to see, but he did. He could smell the charred flesh, hear the screams. Best you don't know, his stare seemed to say. I'm not going to tell you, anyway, because you wouldn't believe me if I did. Hasn't that always been the way of soldiers?

'Yeah.'

'She's right.'

'What are you going to do about it, mate?'

One by one, the others joined in, taking turns to have a go at him.

'Let's leave.' Ginny stood up. 'No point in talking to someone who just won't listen.'

'Yeah. Let's go to Lyle's.'

Lyle's was the local cheesy club. A consensus formed. It was clear Ben and I were not invited.

'I'm not about to win any popularity contests with your friends.' His grin was ironic, but there was a bruised, hurt look about his eyes. The attack had been savage. 'Do you mind? I mean, you can go with them, if you want. Don't feel you have to stay with me . . .'

'Why should I mind? With a bit of luck I'll never see any of them ever again.'

Steph had been in the toilet for quite a while, probably throwing up. She came back not looking so good.

'Where *is* everybody?'

'They've gone to Lyle's.'

''K. 'S go.'

'D'you think that's a good idea?'

'Prob'ly not.' Stephanie sat down heavily, just avoiding my lap.

'Maybe we better call it a night. I think so, don't you?'

'S'pose.' Steph'll go on till the end, but the Duke Doublers had taken their toll. She knows her limits.

'Here.' Ben stood up, pulling her to a standing position. 'I'd give you a lift, but I've had a bit to drink.'

'She'll be all right. We'll go down to the rank for a cab.'

'I'll come with you.'

Exactly what I was hoping he'd say. A sudden ''Scuse me' from Steph gave me time to make further arrangements. I could say I was staying with her. She'd never remember if I'd been there or not. That's if he asked.

'My folks are away,' he said, right on cue. 'I was wondering, after we drop Stephanie off . . . I was wondering if you'd like to come back with me.'

'Yes,' I said.

Just like that. He was a really nice guy and he hadn't deserved that kind of going-over. Some part of me wanted to make it up to him. And I still fancied him, I had to admit. All that dreaming on my bed and now it was coming true. It was the kind of chance that doesn't come twice. Unrequited love about to be requited.

'Hadn't you better see about your friend?'

Lost in romantic reverie, I'd forgotten about Stephanie. I found her by the basins looking like Alice Cooper. I wiped the worst of the mascara streaks from her cheeks and made her drink some water.

'How do you feel now?'

'Fine. Jus' fine. He seems like a nice guy. Don' mind Ginny. She's a silly bitch.'

Given the state she was in, that was a long speech.

'Think you can make it?'

'Course.'

I helped her out, and then Ben took over. He held her up, walking her all the way down to the taxi stand. There was one cab there, which was lucky.

'OK. In you get.'

Ben opened the door, helping Steph into the back. I was just about to follow her when this guy began to shout.

'That's our effing cab. Get out!'

'You are joking!' Ben shook his head and grinned. 'We were here first!'

The guy grabbed Ben's arm and spun him around. He was smaller than Ben, but he made up for his lack of build with plenty of aggression.

'What did you say?' He was dancing on the pavement, jittering with rage.

'I said, "No way. You're joking."'

'I ain't, mate.'

A bunch of others stepped out from the side of the kebab van.

'I don't want to fight.' Ben put up his hands, palms out. 'I have to warn you, I'm trained in unarmed combat . . .'

'Oh yeah?'

The guy had been stepping backwards, now he lunged forward fast and hit Ben hard. Then he was gone, his mates running after him.

'You all right?' the taxi driver finally came round from his side of the cab.

'I don't know . . .'

Ben tried to straighten up but sank to the ground, bent over like a puppet. He pulled his hand from inside his coat and stared. His face creased, somewhere between grin and grimace, as if he couldn't believe what he was seeing, couldn't believe this was happening.

Steph was out of the cab. Sober in an instant.

'Don't just stand there!' She screamed at me, the taxi driver, the small group gathering. 'Call for an ambulance. Call the police!'

Phones came out. Calls were made. We knelt by Ben, cradling his head, trying to make him comfortable.

'Don't move him too much.' Steph made a pad with her wrap, pressed it against his chest. 'Hold on,' she kept saying to him. 'Hold on.'

But it was too late. She knew it, even as she said it. We looked at each other over his head. I cried then. Real tears.

Author's note: *Violence is everywhere and war is full of savage ironies. The direct inspiration for this story was a news report I read about a young British soldier on leave from Iraq. He was going home to see his mother but never reached his destination. He was murdered while waiting for a bus.*

Nina Bawden

I was evacuated from London with my school in the Second World War. My brother Peter and I were billeted with a family in Aberdare, a coal-mining valley in South Wales. My mother and my little brother, Robin, had escaped from the bombing to the farmhouse I describe in my story. I loved going there in the holidays. The farmer and his wife had a son of about my age, which was thirteen, and two daughters – one a baby and the other grown up and married to a farmer. I loved to help on the farm, but there was a lot of work to do, which was why the farmer engaged our Italian prisoner of war. He was young and very handsome and I felt very romantic about him. He once kissed me when we were cleaning out the cow shed together! But when we came home the next holidays he had gone, and the farmer's wife told me his sad story, and why he no longer wanted to work for the farmer. The farmer was now – after all – his 'enemy'. So our Italian went back to the prison camp.

A great many Italian prisoners did come back to

Wales after the war, and some of them married the daughters of the farm families they had lived with – which is why there is a surprising number of families in Wales who now have Italian names!

OUR ITALIAN PRISONER

This story started a long time ago, in the Second World War. My father was an engineer-commander in the Royal Navy on a ship that was guarding the convoys crossing the Atlantic against attacks from German submarines. Bombs were falling on London and my family had been evacuated – my brother Peter and I to South Wales and our mother and baby brother to a farm in Montgomeryshire where, up in the hills, most farmers spoke Welsh, or at least a lovely, lilting English with a Welsh curl to the words.

Peter and I went to the farm in the school holidays. It was a beautiful farmhouse that had once been an old monastery and our mother had rented an enormous room on the first floor, with windows that looked over the wide valley and the smooth blue mountains beyond. She slept with the baby in a corner of the big room and Peter and I had camp beds in the apple room, where the apples were stored in the winter, spread out on the wide, polished floorboards. That room always had a sweet apple smell even before the apples had been harvested and there were no apples there.

There was a bathroom attached to our mother's big room, but since there was no running water in the house it wasn't much use. All the water we used in the farmhouse was fetched either from the brook down the lane or, if it was for drinking, from the well in the farmyard. The lavatory was an outside privy at the end of the vegetable garden at the back of the farmhouse. It was an airy and comfortable privy with a wooden board to sit on that had three holes in it: small, medium and large, for different-sized bottoms. 'Very sociable toilet arrangements,' my mother said, which we thought very witty. But we discovered the disadvantage of having three holes in windy weather; when you threw the cut-up copies of the *Farmers Weekly* we used instead of toilet paper into one hole, it blew up through another. I wrote to my father and told him about this to make him laugh; and when his ship came into port one day and I went to meet it he gave me three wooden lids with brass knobs to lift them that the ship's carpenter had made for us to solve the problem!

Besides the farmer and his wife, the other people living in the farmhouse were their daughter, Blodwen, a cowman called Bill and a couple who lived in one of the rooms downstairs and were supposed to do a little work round the farm instead of paying rent, but they were, in fact, too old to be much use for anything beyond collecting a few chicken eggs. As the farmer said to me one day when I was helping him drive the sheep through the sheep-dip to get the maggots out of their wool, 'They'm getting a bit long in the tooth to be much use to I. Reckon I better get hold of one of them Eye-ties.'

I didn't know what he meant but my mother explained. 'An Italian prisoner,' she said. 'They're stuck in the camps and they might as well work for their keep as stay idle.'

This was quite late on in the war and there were several camps for prisoners of war in Wales – German prisoners as well as Italian – but although the farmers said the Germans were good workers, they had to be returned to their camps at the end of each day. The Italians were allowed to stay with the farm families. They were very popular with the farmers' wives, and when we came home for the summer holidays to find Angelo Benati part of the household, we understood why.

Angelo Benati was nineteen, only a year older than Blodwen. He had big, shy brown eyes and a brown gleam to his skin and was eager to help the farmer's wife as well as the farmer. He carried water to the house for her, dug the vegetable garden, and mended the punctures in Blodwen's bicycle tyres. These were things the farmer had never done for his wife or his daughter. The farmer's wife said to my mother, 'These Eye-ties, they're proper gentlemen.'

Angelo would even run to carry water for me if he saw me crossing the yard to the pump. That wasn't why I fell in love with him, of course, but it helped. He had a lovely smile and he sometimes sang me a song that ended *mia cara nina* – which means 'my dear Nina' – and looked at me so sweetly with his beautiful soft eyes that my legs trembled.

I was jealous of Blodwen, who saw more of him than I did because he ate with the farmer's family in the farm kitchen by the range fire while we had our meals upstairs in our rented room. I was surprised how carelessly she behaved towards him, ordering him about as if he were a young brother, never looking straight at him or smiling.

Or not when other people were there. Peter and I were in the hayloft above the cow shed one day. There was a trapdoor we used for spying on Bill the cowman when he was milking, because, although Bill loved the cows, he often swore at them with marvellously rude words we had never heard before. (We didn't dare repeat these words to our mother but we taught them to our baby brother, who did. She was very shocked, of course. She said to us, 'Wherever could he have heard that dreadful language?' And, of course, we said we had no idea.)

Bill and the cows were not yet in the milking shed on this particular day. We always tried to get there before Bill did and were sitting quietly in the hayloft, waiting for him, when Blodwen came running into the cow shed beneath us, swishing her flowery cotton skirt and laughing. She ran into one of the stalls and turned round to face Angelo, who had come in behind her. He followed her into the stall and put his arms round her. She stopped laughing. We couldn't see her face, only the back of Angelo's dark head as he bent to kiss her.

Up in the hayloft above them, we sat very still. Peter's cheeks were puffed out and red as he tried to stop himself giggling. I was afraid that when they stopped kissing they would look up and see us through the crack in the boards. But they didn't move. I thought, Glued together

– and wanted to giggle like Peter. I didn't dare look at him.

Then we heard Bill outside, shouting at the cows as he drove them across the farmyard. (I can't write what Bill said because the publisher would refuse to print it.) Angelo let go of Blodwen and looked up. Peter and I froze, still. We both knew what he was going to do. The only escape from the cow shed was through a hatch in the ceiling that could be pushed open; if Angelo was quick, he could get up from the stall into the hayloft without Bill seeing him.

Luckily, the hay meadow had been cut and the loft was full. By the time Angelo had jumped on to the side of the stall and thumped the hatch open, Peter and I were buried in hay. It tickled our noses but we pressed our fingers on our upper lip to stop ourselves sneezing and waited for Angelo to escape through the door at the other end of the loft.

He took his time and I thought I would burst. But as the first cow came into the shed I heard Blodwen's pretty Welsh voice calling out, 'Will I give you a hand, Bill?'

And he answered, without swearing, for once, 'There's a nice girl you are now.'

I heard Angelo let out a long sigh of relief and clatter out of the hayloft.

After that, we kept sharp eyes open. They met whenever they could: slipping out after dark to close up the hen house – Angelo first, Blodwen following a few minutes later; the privy down the bottom of the vegetable garden often provided a useful excuse, as did fetching water. Peter and I watched from the window of our mother's room and often saw Angelo filling the water can from the pump in the yard and then, when Blodwen came out to shut up the chickens, he would put the can down and follow her into the field.

We were soon not the only people who knew. Our mother said once, speaking half to herself, half to me, 'I hope her parents are keeping an eye on her. Although he seems a nice young man, he's a foreigner, after all.'

But our mother was just as 'soppy' about Angelo as Peter said I was. One day when he had carried a big can of water up to her room he showed her a photograph of his mother and father and little sister, that I knew – because he had shown it to me several times – he always carried with him. His parents looked nice, but his sister was the prettiest little girl I had ever seen: big dark eyes like Angelo's, dark hair curling round her face and dimples either side of her plump mouth. 'She's the one should be called Angel,' my mother said, seeming to put Angelo down, which was her way when she was feeling a bit sentimental, but I saw there was a gleam in her eyes. After Angelo had gone she blew her nose and said, 'Can't be helped, of course – there's a war on – but it's hard for any boy to be so far from his family.'

We knew he had letters from them, because sometimes he would tell us about something his mother or father had told him that his little sister had said or done and his eyes would have a special sparkly look about them: a happy look that was also sad, close to tears. But when the last letter came – the dreadful letter – Peter and I were not there.

We were in South Wales at school; it was the last week of term and we were counting the days to the holidays. It was a long journey to the farm – two trains with a long wait in between – and then a local bus from the last station to the end of our valley. Our mother had written to tell us that Angelo would meet us at the bus stop with the pony and trap. But when we got off the bus no one was there.

Our suitcases were heavy and got heavier as we trudged down the lane. It wasn't until we reached the white wooden footbridge over the brook that we saw our mother hurrying towards us, our baby brother trotting beside her. She waved, but she didn't look happy to see us. Peter said, 'You said Angelo would meet us; my case weighs a *ton*.'

'Sorry, darlings,' she said, a bit breathlessly. 'I thought he was going, but then . . .' She stopped, and sighed – the kind of impatient sigh she often gave when things were too hard to explain. She took Peter's case and said to him, quite sharply, 'Help your sister with her case now. You're a big, strong boy.'

She set off, up the slope from the brook to the turn in the lane where we got the first view of the farm. We usually stopped there, to enjoy the first coming-home feeling, but for once she didn't wait for us but strode on. I shouted after her, 'Mum, what's the matter? What's *happened*?'

She stopped then. She said, 'Bad news; I don't want to tell you.'

'Dad's ship?' Peter said, and I felt my heart jump. Ships were sunk in the Atlantic every day . . .

She shook her head. 'No, not your father. Sorry, I should have told you at once.'

She put Peter's suitcase down and faced us. 'It's Angelo. He's had a letter; they brought it from the camp.' She drew a deep breath. She said, 'His mother and father, his little sister. All dead. Bombed. They dropped bombs on the town. An air raid. Our bombers.'

She was crying now, tears running down her cheeks; she flicked at them with the back of her hand. 'How d'you suppose he feels? We've murdered his family . . .'

Our little brother was crying too, not because he understood but because his mother was crying. She put Peter's case down and picked up the baby. She cuddled him and said, 'Hush now, it's all right.' And then, to Peter and me, 'Come on now, get going; no point in hanging about.'

The farmer was in the yard. He raised his hand when he saw us, but he didn't smile. Nor did the farmer's wife when she came to the door. She said, 'Best come through the kitchen; not so far to carry those cases.' And she took mine from me and carried it through the kitchen and up the stairs and dumped it outside my mother's room. I said thank you, of course, but she didn't look at me.

Nor did Angelo. I went looking for him; I didn't know what I was going to say but I thought it would come to me when I saw him. It didn't. I found him when I went to the privy. He was doing something in the vegetable garden – digging up potatoes or earthing them; my eyes were too suddenly too misty to see. I said, 'Angelo . . .' and he turned his face towards me. Only for a second but that was long enough. He looked so dark and sad. Angry, too. Then he turned his back on me.

'He's going back to the camp,' our mother said. 'Nothing else for it. Well, you can see how he feels now. We're his *enemies*. But it's hard on us too . . .'

Our mother took us out for a walk. Although she said she wanted to pick wimberries up on the hill because they were nice and ripe at this time of the year, perfect for a pie, I knew it was only to get us out of the way when they came to take Angelo to the camp. But the army truck must have been late arriving. It was only just leaving, turning out of the yard when we came back.

And Blodwen was running after it, her arms stretched out in front of her, weeping. Our mother put down her basket of berries. She went to Blodwen and put her arms round her while the truck gathered speed up the lane. Blodwen put her head on our mother's shoulder. She looked at the three of us over Blodwen's bent head and whispered, 'Go along indoors now.'

Nothing was the same after that. We did all the things we usually did; we helped with the wheat harvest, we collected the eggs, I helped the farmer with the sheep and cleaned out the pigsty and Peter fetched the cows for Bill at milking time and learned how to harness the old pony into the trap. But, although the weather was beautiful and the sun shone every day, everything seemed dull and grey and droopy. It felt like the saddest thing that had ever happened in the whole of my life, but Blodwen was sadder than anyone. She looked pale and somehow withered – like a tree when a sudden frost catches the young leaves in the spring – and she never smiled at us now. Sometimes she came to see our mother, knocking on the door and then shaking her head if Peter or I answered it and starting back down the stairs. And our mother would say, 'Nina and Peter, run out now and do something useful – at least get a bit of fresh air in your lungs. Blodwen and I have things to say to each other.'

79

And once, as she closed the door on us, I heard her say to Blodwen, 'Try not to fret so, my poor girl, this wretched old war will be over quite soon.'

And it was. We said goodbye to the farmer and his wife and to Bill. We went back to London. We missed the farm and our mother kept saying we would go back for a visit some day, but our father came home from the sea and time passed. Peter and I and even our baby brother grew up, grew older, got married and had children of our own. And when my daughter was thirteen – the same age I had been at the beginning of the war – I went back to the farm.

It was twenty-five years after we had packed up and gone, but the countryside looked as I had remembered it. There were more tractors in the fields, more cars on the road, but the hills were as blue and the pastures as green. I had driven from London to a town called Ludlow to fetch my daughter, who had been staying with friends there. I had not meant to go to the farm, but the car turned towards our valley and into the familiar lane as if it had a mind of its own. The white footbridge was still there across the brook. The car splashed through the ford.

And there was the farm. And, on a tall chestnut horse, clipping down towards the brook, was Angelo Benati!

Of course, it couldn't be Angelo. This was a young man – no older, I guessed – than Angelo had been all those years ago. He drew his horse to the side of the lane to let us pass and smiled. Angelo's full, sweet smile. He said, 'You folks wanting the Benati farm? My dad's out at the moment but my mother is there.'

And I understood. This wasn't Angelo. He was – or

could be – his son. Angelo had come back after the war to find Blodwen and there had been a happy ending to the sad story, at last . . .

I smiled at the young man on the horse. I said, 'I would love to say hello to your mother.'

But as I drove into the yard my heart was in my mouth. Would she know who I was? I recognized her as she came out of the kitchen door with a bucket. She sluiced dirty water over the wall into the chicken field and looked at me as I got out of the car. She was older, of course, but still beautiful: her blonde hair in gleaming loops, blue eyes bright and shining. She smiled and, as I walked towards her, the smile broadened and became a happy laugh.

Blodwen said, 'Hello, Nina. Come to lunch.'

Margaret Mahy

In about 1940 (when I was four), my father was building a wharf in the north of New Zealand and we did live in a tin hut and a caravan. At nine o'clock each night Big Ben would chime out through our hut. This was always dramatic, but it became dramatic in quite a different way when the Japanese came into the Second World War and began edging down towards Australia and New Zealand.

But I will never forget the occasion when I remarked to my mother that Santa Claus would not bring any Christmas presents to the German girls and boys, and she pointed out to me that they were not villains or 'baddies' but ordinary people as we were, trying to live ordinary lives, and thinking that Germany was a heroic country just as we thought well of Britain (and ourselves, of course). I remember taking this new information on board and somehow feeling myself altering as I thought about it – well, I think back then I felt the *world* alter, but it amounts to the same thing. So you see, there is quite a lot in this story that is autobiographical.

THE QUESTION MARK

Toby Beckett, arms spread out on either side of him, veered from the boys' playground and bore down on the girls, making the sound of an aeroplane ('Yeeeeerooowwm!') and then that sort of sniggering sound ('E! heh! heh! heh! heh! heh!') that was supposed to be the sound of a machine-gun. And then he shouted, 'Germans! You're Germans! And I'm going to *explode* you.'

Elizabeth dropped her French knitting, leaped to her feet and held out her arms too.

'*You're* the German,' she shouted. 'I'm a Spitfire and I'm going to shoot you down.'

She and Toby circled around one another, making machine-gun snickers and wild explosion noises. It was an exciting game but, as they fired at one another, Elizabeth swung over into the boys' part of the playground. Miss Dalley, the stern teacher who taught the little ones, came marching down on them – a whole army in herself.

'Here comes the Dalley dolly!' muttered Elizabeth to Toby.

'Elizabeth! That's the boys' playground,' Miss Dalley was shouting. 'You know you're not supposed to be over there. Get back again.'

'Why are boys allowed to have all the adventures?' Elizabeth mumbled. 'I want to have adventures too.'

Elizabeth had enjoyed being a Spitfire. She felt bored at the thought of sitting down with the nearest group of girls – Sally, Christine and Joan and that lot – who were all excited about French knitting. Long coloured tails of knitted wool squirmed down through the hollow centres of the cotton reels they were using. Elizabeth picked up her own cotton reel once more, but, as usual, she was clumsy when it came to looping the stitches over the little nails in the top of the cotton reel. She would rather be holding out her arms, fighting the enemy, driving the Germans away from Britain, out of France and back towards their own country where they belonged. She would play adventure games.

'Hey, Doddy!' shouted Toby, hovering on the boys' side of that invisible line that separated them from the girls. 'Hey, Doddy! Why isn't your dad overseas like *my* dad? Is he scared of the Spitfires?'

Elizabeth leaped to her feet again. 'He's flat-out busy,' she shouted back, whipping the scarlet tail of French knitting at him. 'Someone has to do the building and stuff down here while everyone else is having fun flying around up there.'

'Your dad's *scared*!' Toby yelled. He made a squeaky, clucking sound that was supposed to remind anyone listening of a chicken. '*Scared!*'

86

'Don't take any notice of him,' said Sally Allister. 'He just wants us to take notice of him.'

Elizabeth sat down again, suddenly glad to be among the girls. But when she looked sideways at them, she saw that Joan and Christine had strange smirking expressions on their faces. Sally seemed to have noticed this too.

'Some dads are still here,' she said. 'Mine is.'

'Your dad's only got one arm,' said Christine. 'He's like Captain Hook in that book Miss House reads us.'

'*Peter Pan*,' Elizabeth said with a sigh. She had seen Sally's dad collecting milk cans out in the country, lifting one with his left hand, and hoisting another up with the hook on the end of his metal right arm. She was glad her father was at home, able to sit down in the evening and read her adventure stories, and yet she hated to be told that he was frightened of the great war game on the other side of the world. She rather envied Toby, who had a hero for a father.

That night (just as she always did), her mother turned on the radio to listen to the news.

'This is the BBC *World News*,' said a voice, sounding like the voice of a magician casting a spell.

'It looks as if the Germans might take Moscow,' said Elizabeth's father, sighing and shaking his head

'They've backed off from Britain,' said her mother. 'Russia's a lot easier.' But Elizabeth's mother always spoke as if Britain was the hero of the war game and was bound to win out in the end because the heroes of stories always won.

There were three maps on the dark wall of the hut they lived in – one of New Zealand itself – the South

Island looking rather like a drawer with a knobbly handle sticking out of its east coast, the North Island leaping up like an eager, flying, scarlet giraffe, stretching its neck towards the middle of the world. The second map showed the whole world, with New Zealand still leaping and stretching, still scarlet, but looking unexpectedly small, down in the far south. There was nothing much after New Zealand except the white borders of the Antarctic. The third map was the map Elizabeth called the War Map. There was Italy, pale purple like a bruised leg, dancing in the Mediterranean Sea. There was Spain, yellow and somehow off to one side. But then there was France (blue) and Germany (green like a sinister, rotting moss). There was Holland. And there, separated from all the other countries, by a blue sleeve of sea was Britain – gallant old Britain, as her mother always called it, sometimes touching it tenderly as she said its name – scarlet again, and still free. Other countries had been beaten back and taken over. Britain alone was confronting that savage mossy-green dragon that had devoured country after country.

'England is just wonderful,' said Elizabeth's mother. 'It's the greatest country in the world. And the English speak so beautifully.'

Elizabeth's father looked up, smiling. He had a slow, crooked smile and a dimple in his right cheek, so his smile often reminded Elizabeth of a question mark lying on its side.

Elizabeth and her parents were living, almost camping for a while, in the far north of the North Island of New Zealand – high on the neck of the giraffe – sleeping in a caravan, but eating and reading and talking by lamplight in an old tin hut. Every morning, as they crossed from bed to breakfast, they looked down a long grassy slope, across a road, past headlands rough and dark against a clear sky, and out to sea.

'Dad, why aren't you off at the war?' Elizabeth asked her father that night as he passed her her dinner on a white enamel dish.

'You keep asking me that,' he said, smiling his question-mark smile. 'Do other people ask you?'

Elizabeth's mother broke in. 'He'd go if he could,' she said, 'but he's older than most fathers. He was in the *Great* War. A lot of people don't know that.'

'They only want young, quick guys for the front line,' Elizabeth's father told her, still smiling. 'I'm too old to be worth shooting.'

'You could fly a Spitfire,' suggested Elizabeth, half holding her arms out on either side as if she might take off across the rickety table.

'Look! This is important work we're doing here,' Elizabeth's mother cried. 'This is war work just as much as flying any Spitfire. You tell the kids at school how important it is that things get from place to place. And things are hard to shift from place to place unless there are wharves for the ships to pull up to.'

Elizabeth's father was working on the edge of the sea, building a new wharf because, a year ago, the old wharf had caught fire and burned. The black bones of that first wharf were still there, sticking out of the clear green water. The tide swirled around them as it came in to lap at the beach, dancing a little mockingly before racing back out again. Elizabeth's father and his men (older men but still strong and hard-working) were driving the piles of the new wharf. An iron weight – the one-ton monkey – was hoisted by the winch up high on the derrick and then dropped down (then down again, and down again), driving the long wooden piles that would support the new wharf through sea and sand and deep into the hard land below. Pile-driving made a sound like a dull, slow drumbeat, and sometimes Elizabeth could feel that beat coming up through the soles of her shoes and into her bones.

Elizabeth's school was miles away, but each morning the milk truck came along and Elizabeth and her mother went out to the truck, her mother with a billy and Elizabeth with her school case.

'Any news?' her mother would ask as the milk-truck man filled the billy from one of the big cans of milk that crowded the back of the truck. Though Elizabeth's family had a radio, it ran on batteries and they could not always get the stations playing the *newest* news. The war was far far away on the other side of the world, and things happened overnight. Battles were won and lost while Elizabeth and her parents slept, and the war was like any good story. People were always longing to know what was happening next.

As Mr Grey, the milk-truck man, talked to her mother, Elizabeth climbed into the truck, joining Toby Beckett who was a milk-truck traveller too. Off they would go (stopping every so often to deliver milk), until they reached the school, when Elizabeth and Toby would scramble out of the truck which would drive on to collect milk from farms further up the road. In the afternoon, the local doctor, driving back from an afternoon clinic, would bring them home. She and Toby Beckett shared the back seat of the doctor's car and often talked about the war.

'I hope it goes on until I can enlist,' Toby said. 'My dad's having adventures. He's been fighting in Crete. I could go over and then we'd fight together. Side by side! Him and me!'

'My dad and I fight in Crete too,' said Elizabeth. '*Con*crete, that is.'

'Why isn't your dad away at the war?' asked Tony yet again – not making fun of her this time, simply curious. 'Is he a . . . a conscience objector or something?'

'He's a bit too old,' Elizabeth replied. 'He was in the Great War, though.' She always emphasized the word 'great', hoping to remind Toby that that other earlier war was a bigger, better war than the one his father was fighting.

'They didn't have Spitfires back then,' said Toby. He spoke as if that first world war was an old-fashioned, childish game which did not count any more.

Elizabeth was supposed to be in bed by the time the latest episode of the war story played over their radio in the evening but, if she sat quietly, her parents did not always remember she was there listening in. A serious voice would say, 'And now – the evening news.' Then, suddenly, the hut would echo to the sound of a great clock chiming, then solemnly striking nine times.

'Big Ben!' her mother often said, sounding satisfied in a curious way. New Zealand might be at the very bottom of the world map, and they might be living in a tin hut and a caravan, but the very sound of London could fly across the world to ring out there in the hut with them. They were still part of the true world.

'Holland and Belgium are small places. Of course *they* couldn't stand out against Germany,' Elizabeth's mother told her as she swept out the ashes in the fireplace. 'But France is a big country and the Germans just swept through it.' Her mother made a sweeping gesture. Ash flew off the little hand broom and into the dim air of the hut. 'And then there was Greece. And Crete. Britain's the only country that's stood out against the *Germans* so far.' She said 'Germans' screwing up her face as if the mere word tasted horrible.

'Your mother's a Christchurch woman,' said Dad, grinning across at Elizabeth. 'Christchurch still thinks it's a little bit of Britain.'

'Well, it's the most English city this side of the equator,' Mum said proudly. 'One day you'll see our Christchurch, Elizabeth. It's down in the South Island and it has a cathedral and beautiful stone buildings – parks full of oak trees with bluebells growing under them And daffodils growing along the Avon – that's the river that runs through Christchurch. When spring comes the whole city just blossoms. It's beautiful. And you can laugh at me,' she said, looking over at Elizabeth's father, half laughing herself, 'but the British are wonderful. They write such beautiful books and they speak so nicely.'

'It's beautiful here, too,' said Dad, smiling his smile that also asked a question. 'We look out at the rocks and the sea – bush grows down almost to the water.'

'It *is* beautiful,' Mum agreed, 'but it's just not the same. You know that. You came from England.'

'Years ago!' said Dad. 'And this has probably been a better place for a man like me to grow up in. I've had work – earned a good living.'

'But you *are* on Britain's side,' said Elizabeth, just to make sure.

'Of course I am,' said Dad. 'It's just that having been in that first war has mixed life up for me in some ways. But of course I want us to win – you bet I do. After all, your uncles are over there doing their bit. Their turn, this time round!'

On the shelf above the fireplace beside the radio were photographs of two of Dad's younger brothers: Uncle Stan and Uncle Cliff, one in the army and one in the air force, both overseas and doing their bit, playing the war game. Uncle Cliff might even fly Spitfires. In her mind Elizabeth saw him with his arms held out on either side of him, whisking though the air, making aeroplane noises as he went.

'I wish I could be adventurous!' Elizabeth told Toby, longingly. 'You could fight beside your dad, and I could fight beside my uncles'

'You'd have to be a nurse,' Toby said. 'Girls don't fly Spitfires.'

'I could cut my hair and dress up as a boy,' Elizabeth said, dreamily. As she said it she half believed she could. She could see herself smiling gallantly, saluting as she took the brake off – if Spitfires had brakes, that is. The plane would move forward . . . it would lift into the air . . . she would be flying . . . flying; half girl and half bird.

*

Butter was rationed because New Zealand was sending as much butter as it could to Britain. Sugar was rationed too. 'Well, we just have to back up the British,' said Mum. 'And we don't need a lot of sweets. They're bad for our teeth.'

'It would be nice to have some Christmas chocolate,' said Elizabeth. A sudden doubt overcame her. Were Christmases going to be rationed too? 'Are we going to have any Christmas this year?'

'Of course we are,' said her father. 'Maybe no sweets, but we'll have a Christmas tree.'

'And Christmas stockings,' said Elizabeth. It was good to feel that there were some things that could be relied on.

December came in. School was about to break up for the summer holidays, and just after midsummer's day it would be Christmas. But then, suddenly, everything changed.

The voices on the radio crackled differently, sounding sharp with new alarm and a different sort of fear. The summer air no longer felt open and carefree. The Germans were closing in on Moscow – the capital of far-away Russia – but suddenly Moscow did not seem to matter quite as much. A new place was being talked about. Something terrible had happened at a place called Pearl Harbour.

'The Japanese!' cried Mum.

'What?' asked Elizabeth. 'The people in Japan?'

'They've attacked the Americans at Pearl Harbour,' her father said. 'It sounds as if they've wiped out the American fleet. Listen!'

The radio talked on and on and, as it talked, the war

stopped being quite the distant adventure game it had been yesterday. Suddenly the adventure seemed much closer and more dangerous, turning its head in New Zealand's direction, baring its blood-stained teeth at them. Dangerous. But, of course, adventures were meant to be dangerous. That's what made them adventurous.

'The Japanese have bombed Hong Kong – they've bombed the British,' said Mum. 'What's going on? What's happening to the world. Well, they won't get far with the British.'

'The Germans did,' said Elizabeth.

'But the Japanese – they won't have had the practice – they won't have the planes that the British have,' her mother replied.

'They've been fighting China for a while,' said her father in a quiet voice, almost as if he was speaking to himself. 'They've probably worked out a few tactics by now.'

'The Japs won't get far,' said Toby next day at school. 'We'll fight them off.' He danced and punched the air.

'But most of our soldiers are off fighting Germans,' Elizabeth said doubtfully. 'We can't send a whole lot of people to help the Americans.' She did not know if there were any Spitfires hidden away in this part of the world.

'Oh dear! How can we possibly have a happy Christmas?' cried Elizabeth's mother. But Dad brought in the branch of a pine tree, and Elizabeth decorated it with decorations that she made herself. Sitting by the Christmas tree, looking at one another by candlelight, they sang Christmas carols full of joy and happiness even though, by Christmas Day, the Japanese had taken the whole island of Hong Kong.

The sound of Big Ben still came ringing across the world, to echo bravely in the hut, but somehow everything had changed. The distant war was no longer like a monster someone was making up. And the Japanese army kept doing things that people thought it just could not do, and it was doing them on Elizabeth's side of the world, edging down, down, down through the Pacific Ocean.

'There!' said Mum, pointing at the map of the world. 'That's Singapore. The Japanese are taking it over. And they've sunk the *Prince of Wales* and the *Repulse*. They're just sweeping down on us.'

Now, when she talked of the war, she no longer sounded as if she were telling an exciting story with villains and heroes you could rely on. She sounded quieter . . . she sounded troubled . . . she even sounded frightened.

'It seems they are good jungle fighters,' said Dad. 'We're not so good in the jungles. We need a few roads. Maybe a few signposts.'

'Well, of course we're not as good in the jungles,' Mum exclaimed crossly. 'There are no jungles in Britain. Or here! Well, there's the bush, of course, but the bush doesn't count as a jungle. Our boys just won't have had the practice.'

'I don't think there is a lot of jungle in Japan, either,' said Dad. 'Face it! They're good soldiers.'

'But not better than us!' cried Mum. 'They can't be better than us.'

Dad did not say anything aloud, but Elizabeth, watching him, thought his crooked smile was asking, 'Why not?'

*

At school there was suddenly a different feeling about the games in the playground, almost as if the boys were now practising for something real. They swept around the playground, shooting and then arguing about who had blown up whom, just as they had done before. They still made the same sniggering machine-gun sounds. Yet somehow the playground felt as if it had become a more dangerous place than it had been. Nothing had changed in the playground; it was just that everything was changing in the world around it.

'I might have to go away and be a soldier,' said Toby, sounding excited but troubled too. 'The British won't let our guys come home. If the Japs get here we'll need to have someone defending us – kids like me and even old fogey-men like your father will be called up.'

'They won't call up kids like you – not for ages,' said Elizabeth derisively.

'They might,' said Toby. 'They'll need someone to look after the women and the girls.'

'I could look after myself,' boasted Elizabeth, 'and, anyhow, my dad would go. He might be a bit old but he's tough. Driving piles is great exercise.'

'I reckon my dad will work out a way of coming home. My dad's a hero,' cried Toby. And he began a war dance, shouting it over and over again. '*My* dad's a hero! My dad's a hero! Your dad's just a builder, but my dad's a hero!'

Two days later, Elizabeth scrambled into the milk truck to find she was the only child in it. Toby was not there. The men in the front seats muttered to one another about the weather and jumped up and down, filling billies for the women who stood out by their front gates needing milk.

'Where's Toby?' she asked.

'Well, that a long story,' said Mr Lee. 'Toby's family – well, they've got a bit of trouble in their neck of the woods.' But then he swept on, talking to Mr Henderson about the fact that the Japanese seemed to be hovering around the top of Australia.

'Who'd have thought, eh? Who'd have thought!' said Mr Henderson. And he did not sound like a man playing an exciting game he was sure to win. He sounded almost terrified.

Elizabeth arrived at school. The bell had not rung and children were racing around in the playground, girls on one side of the front steps, boys on the other. Elizabeth looked for Toby but he wasn't there. The bell rang and they had to line up in their joggling lines with Miss Dalley walking up and down them, inspecting them, making sure they stood straight, making sure they looked respectful. Elizabeth looked for Toby again, but he just wasn't at school today.

'Where's Toby?' she whispered to Yvonne next to her, but Miss Dalley saw them and closed in on her, holding out her finger in a reproving way, then placing it over her lips. Shhhhh!

Mr Mowatt, the headmaster, put a record on the gramophone and they marched into school.

'Where's Toby?' Elizabeth asked Shirley.

'Dunno!' said Shirley. 'Hey! Is he your boyfriend?'

'No!' cried Elizabeth, 'I just wondered where he was.'

Miss Dalley tapped her desk with her pointer. 'Silence!' she said. 'Sit up straight!' And the class fell silent and shuffled themselves, sitting up straight. Miss Dalley's eyes wandered around the room. Her gaze stopped at Toby's empty desk.

'Toby isn't in class today,' she said. 'His family had bad news last night. His father has been killed – one of the brave men killed defending us in this terrible war. Toby'll probably be back with us tomorrow – or the day after – and we'll all have to be very kind . . . very understanding to him, because this is a very sad thing for his family.'

Elizabeth felt a sudden strange shift in the world around her. It was almost like an earthquake, except that the pens did not rattle and the desks did not slide. She wasn't sure if the change was in the world around her or somewhere deep in her own head. Perhaps it was partly the way voices and expressions in the outside world had altered. Perhaps her ideas about the world were struggling to fit themselves into a different pattern. Suddenly, the game seemed nothing but horrible. Suddenly she found she was deeply glad that her father was too old to go to war. Suddenly she understood why, when her mother was so excited and so sure of the good and bad of things, her father sat back, smiling his question-mark smile. And it wasn't just a secret joke, that question. There was something sad about it too.

At playtime only a few boys played the Spitfire game, and even they did not play it for long. Elizabeth thought that when Toby did come back to school that Spitfire game would be hard to play, even if, in the game at least, you were always shooting down the enemy.

She went home after school. The news of Toby's

father's death was like a scent in the air. She was breathing it in all the time, even in her own tin-hut home.

'He was a gallant man,' her mother said, not just once, but over and over again. 'He was a true warrior.'

'Warrior' was a heroic storybook word, but for some reason it was still hard to believe in that heroic story in quite the way she had believed in it yesterday.

When her mother went out of the hut and over to the caravan to look for some missing darning wool, Elizabeth turned to look seriously at her father.

'Dad,' she said. 'Dad, do you think Toby's father really was a gallant warrior?'

Her father looked sideways at her, then twisted in his chair to look at her directly, as if they were going to have a serious conversation.

'I think he probably was,' he replied, speaking in a quiet voice, 'but to tell you the truth, I think a lot of the German pilots are probably gallant too. And the ones that Toby's father shot down – they'll have mothers and children and friends being sad for them. I think war's a great mess.'

'But the Japs *are* baddies,' said Elizabeth. She wanted her father to help her feel certain about that.

'I know there are Japanese children who will be crying right now because their fathers have been killed,' her father replied. 'I'm much more mixed-up about things than your mum.'

'Toby played it as if it were a game – spitfires and Messerschmitts and . . .' Elizabeth hesitated and shrugged.

'I don't think it's a game,' said her father, 'not unless being alive's a game. Games and stories have shapes, and of course people put story-shapes on wars. But me . . . I think if you look at war really closely it loses its shape. I mean, for your mum, we are the goodies and they are the baddies – no doubt about it. But over in Germany – in Japan – there are thousands of people absolutely sure that *they* are the goodies and *we* are the baddies.

'Look, when I was away in my particular war, I lost friends. My best friend was shot down beside me. If the bullet had been a little bit to the left I would have been the one who was bowled over and he would have been the one running on towards the enemy. Anyhow, a few minutes later, there I was, firing my own gun and seeing this young man, round about my own age, stagger and fall. I don't know who he was, but he probably had a family who loved him. He would have been someone's best friend. Well, I'm not saying I'm sorry, even now. I was over there to shoot him and others like him. He was there to shoot me if he could. But by now it's gone all shapeless. And, like I said, games have a shape to them. These wars – they aren't games.'

'But you *do* want us to win,' Elizabeth said.

'Oh, you bet I do,' said her father. 'And, by the way, it sounds as if the Japs have come to a bit of a standstill, which I'm absolutely delighted to hear. So God bless the Yankees, even if they don't speak as nicely as the British.'

He and Elizabeth looked at each other. Her father smiled his crooked smile and, after a moment Elizabeth smiled back at him. And as she did this she felt that strange alteration inside her head coming out in her smile, so that her smile was a crooked one too – partly a smile and partly a question mark. The game had turned into a great question and, looking at her father, Elizabeth felt she might be asking that question over and over again for the rest of her life.

Joanna Davidson

wanted to write about a tragedy that is still unfolding, in Iraq, as I write this. The story centres on two brothers, Abbas and Hassen, whose lives are irrevocably changed by events far beyond their control. I also wanted to show the wider consequences of war.

After the Gulf War ended in 1991, Saddam Hussein ordered that the marshland – an area of some 7,700 square feet, to the south of Iraq – be drained. He wanted to punish the Marsh Arabs for rebelling against his forces and for giving sanctuary to those who fled into the marshes. Whole villages were torched to the ground and many people were killed. The Marsh Arabs – a civilization spanning five thousand years – bravely defied Saddam, only to be deserted by the Allies in their hour of need. They were effectively forgotten by the rest of the world.

As a consequence of this, they faced catastrophe. The marshes, home to thousands of different species of birds, were deliberately poisoned by pollution from the blazing oilfields. Their water was stopped by the damming of the Euphrates River. It took just a few years to wipe out the wetlands of Mesopotamia – an ecosystem that took millennia to be formed – a place many believe to be the setting for the Bible's Garden of Eden.

But there are now small seeds of hope. The Marsh Arabs really have begun to return, smashing down the gates of the dam that deprived the wetlands of water. But the marshes and the people can never be the same again; such is the enormity of the task of recultivating a land laid to waste by a war without end.

WHERE THERE IS WATER, THERE IS LIFE

The first shot cracked open the air, reverberating across the water, carried in a million ripples from the mighty Euphrates. Hassen plunged after his father into the reeds, wishing he, too, had a rifle instead of the ungainly spear he had been forced to carry.

He knew they were close now. High-pitched squeals rose from the yellowed sedge just ahead of them. Hassen pushed onwards, feet sinking into the clammy clay. The boy seemed oblivious to the trail of blood he left in his wake, where reeds, as sharp as razors, had slashed at his bare arms.

The wild pig was wounded, judging by the wild snapping of reeds as it floundered hopelessly in the mud. Then there was silence. Hassen knew this was when the danger was at its greatest. Many hunters had been gored at such a moment as this, falsely believing victory was already theirs.

Although now a fine hunter, Hassen still recoiled from the killing part. It was the thrill of the chase he loved. Unfit to eat, these brutes were considered vermin by the tribesmen of Zayad, demolishing the crops and attacking anyone who dared to disturb their endless feasting. In the flickering light of the campfires, villagers would tell tales of their close encounters, embellishing details (although no one ever seemed to mind), proudly raising their tunics to display livid scars, the result of an angry tusk.

Whereas Hassen found his life in the marshes a constant adventure, paddling to and fro between the islands in his little canoe, Abbas had felt trapped within a world that never changed.

It hadn't always been so. He had once risen, worked and slept to the ancient rhythm of his forefathers, happy in his ignorance. Until he had lingered, one day, chatting to the driver who came to collect the fish to transport to Baghdad. He described to Abbas his life in the city, where night and day no longer mattered, thanks to electricity, and clean water appeared at the twist of a tap. He displayed the gold watch strapped around a plump wrist.

'Your ways are dying, mark my words. Your family will depend on you in the future . . .' Abbas, lost in thought, missed the driver's oily smirk as he drove away.

'Why do you have to go?' Hassen pleaded with his brother.

'Haven't you ever wondered what lies beyond the reed beds?' Abbas asked, impatiently.

'Father says there is still fighting further north.'

'Pah!' responded Abbas. 'The war is almost over. I've heard that people live like kings in Baghdad,' he continued, looking suddenly dreamy. 'Men have Mercedes cars, not water buffalo.'

Hassen was unmoved. 'You will never come back. You will be killed – or forget all about us.'

He had never seen Abbas so angry as he was at that moment. 'Never speak that way again,' he warned him, his eyes black with fury. 'As God is my witness, I will come back.'

Abbas did not say goodbye. He left on a night when the moon chose to hide her face behind the clouds. Hassen was sad for months after his brother left them.

'I never want to hear his name spoken in our house again,' said their father. But the women wailed and tore at their clothes, as if for one already dead.

Hassen tried to compensate for Abbas's absence – to please his father, now lost in his private grief for a favourite son. How he longed to be like Abbas – impulsive and fearless, loved instantly by all those who encountered him. By comparison, Hassen felt as the moon to the sun. A pale imitation.

But now that Abbas had gone, it was Hassen who was left to fill the void. The days seemed longer now he was alone, herding the water buffalo out to pasture at dawn, returning them to the shallows in the violet dusk to give up their warm supply of milk. Nothing was wasted. Even the dung was moulded into small pats of fuel that filled the hut with acrid smoke.

Months passed, and there was no word from Abbas. It fell to Hassen, now he was thirteen, to accompany his father when he went hunting on the vast lake.

'You're my man now,' he told him, ruffling the boy's

dark head with a callused hand – the lines in his face etched deeper too since Abbas had gone.

Hassen watched his father halt just ahead of him, a small figure against the towering reeds. Wordlessly, he motioned for his son to stop as he pointed with the butt of his rifle towards a bank in the distance, shimmering in the wind.

Hassen was wading, waist-deep in golden water buttercups, when suddenly a roar so great, unlike any he had ever heard before, forced the reeds around him to bow down and touch the water.

He stood, transfixed, watching as his father raised his gun towards the sky and pointed it at the giant bird that loomed overhead. Silver and black, unlike any bird he had ever seen before, its vast wings caught them both in its shadow, blotting out the sun for an instant. And then it wheeled away as something fell, glinting against the blue sky, towards them.

He remembered afterwards how his father shouted, 'Down!', before everything went black. Hassen lay still, with nothing but the ringing inside his skull and the empty sky above him. Rolling slowly on to his side, he could see his father, floating on his back, a look of surprise on his face. Hassen knew then – he was dead.

Much later, as the light bled into the darkness, Hassen was found by passing fishermen, thrown like a rag doll, by the force of the explosion, against the forgiving mudflats.

The mourning lasted for many days after the funeral, with Hassen, now sole provider for his mother and two small sisters, Sadiya and Sabiha, forced to sit for hours on the tattered rug at the entrance to their hut, receiving all those who came to pay their respects, as was the custom.

During this time, Sheik Amara, the tribal head, came to pay his respects. This was looked upon as a great honour bestowed on only a few. Hassen's mother made sweet pancakes for the occasion, as the frail old man, accompanied by a small entourage, slowly lowered himself on to the frayed rug. The coffee was too bitter for Hassen and scalded the roof of his mouth. But he swallowed it all the same. He noticed the splendid dagger that hung from Sheik Amara's belt, the jewel-encrusted sheath flaming red and green as it caught the light. Hassen, in turn, proudly showed him his father's rifle.

Sheik Amara gazed from beneath his hooded eyes at the boy, pale olive against the white of his tunic. Seeing how heavily the burdens of grief and responsibility lay on those narrow shoulders, he reminded Hassen how, many centuries earlier, the king of Babylon had been forced to flee, like a bird to the marshes.

'But what have we done to deserve this war?' asked the boy.

'We chose to defy the tyrant Saddam,' the Sheik said with a sigh. 'We have risen up against him, giving sanctuary to those who flee his evil tyranny. So now we are like a thorn in his side. He punishes us because of the Marsh Arabs' refusal to give up their ways and their land and bow in abeyance, like a reed in the wind. We are a proud people and will not easily be crushed.'

Sheik Amara rose slowly to leave. Gazing out across the glittering waves caught by the morning breeze, he smiled. 'Where there is life, there is water,' he said. 'Until the Tigris and the Euphrates rivers run dry, there will be life in the marshes, and here we will stay.'

The boy took comfort from Sheik Amara's words. But he missed Abbas more than ever.

After his father's death, Hassen found he could not sleep. He would sit for hours into the night, fists clenched, as if made of stone, unable to close his eyes. When he did, he would see his father, pale and lifeless, floating away from him. The stars still shone hard and bright and the frogs still sang their midnight serenade and Hassen could only marvel at how the world continued, when his had stopped.

Hassen had started avoiding the evening fires where boys danced and sang until they dropped. Now the breadwinner, he had no time for such frivolity. He sensed his father's death was a bad omen for them all, since it had marked the beginning of many deaths in the marshes. There were to be many attacks on the Marsh Arabs after this – with stories of villages being torched, their inhabitants killed. The peace of centuries had been shattered forever.

A month after Sheik Amara's visit, Hassen was out tending the water buffalo with his friend Medhi. They had known each other since the cradle, born a few hours apart. Whilst Medhi was the joker, a skinny monkey of a boy who made everyone laugh, Hassen was tall and graceful, his seeming aloofness making him the reluctant object of every girl's attention.

Huge clouds bruised the horizon for days, and yet no storm came. No one could understand this freak of Nature. It was Medhi who provided the answer. While delivering fish to Basra, he had learned how many oil wells were now deliberately being set on fire.

'Saddam wants them to burn forever, like hell itself,' Medhi told Hassen, his monkey face looking suddenly wrinkled and old. 'If he can't flush us out, he will try to smoke us out.'

Birds, now airborne in their thousands, blotted out the light as they fled a storm that showed no signs of abating. Many dropped, like stones, their feathers congealed with oil.

For a while, the air was alive with the beating of wings – and then it was empty. And the world fell silent.

Hassen paused, spear in hand, and gazed beyond the waterline, black against the burnished sky. He had promised his dead father he would provide for his mother and two sisters. What if he failed? He felt truly afraid for the first time.

At first he thought he must be imagining it. The water level had begun to drop at the most alarming rate. No one had an explanation. Months passed, and the waters seeped away, revealing hideous lumps of slime, like the backbone of some monstrous beast, glistening beneath the sun.

The water buffalo, bewildered, stumbled further into the stagnant ponds. The powerful stench from the rotting reed beds grew as the arteries from the Euphrates and the Tigris rivers slowly ran dry.

Reeds cracked and turned to chaff beneath the baking sun as the marsh became jaundiced and withered in the heat. Fish gasped and grew bloated, rising to the filmy surface of pools which now resembled huge milky cataracts. A death rattle echoed through the dying bamboo.

There was panic among the villagers. Sheik Amara was forced to call another meeting.

'Our land has turned to desert – how can we live in a desert?' they clamoured.

Hassen noticed how he appeared to have shrunk inside his splendid robes. 'We have no choice,' he said, his voice little more than a whisper, chaff in the wind. 'We will have to move from the marshes. There is no life without water.'

When Hassen told his mother about the planned exodus, she cried pitifully. 'While there is breath in my body, I will not leave this place. Besides, how will Abbas ever find us now?' Weeping, she hugged Sadiya and Sabiha to her.

Hassen felt the anger rise up in him. Anger for the senseless death of his father, anger at Abbas for deserting them. Anger for having to be the strong one.

Hassen watched as many departed on foot, possessions piled high upon their heads. Medhi walked, looking straight ahead of him. He did not turn to say goodbye. Hassen understood. To look back would have made it impossible to leave.

'Five thousand years in a handful of dust!' Hassen thought to himself, watching the figures until they dissolved into the landscape. How were they going to live now? No fish, no birds, no water buffalo. No water.

In a matter of days, the little provision they had was running perilously low. The last of the water buffalo had died, knee-deep in the dried mud, now oblivious to the humming flies. Now there was no milk.

Sadiya, who was only ten, surveyed her brother with large brown eyes. 'My tummy hurts all the time now,' she told him. To distract her, Hassen fashioned a doll out of dried reeds.

Sabiha, who was twelve and very beautiful, had stopped combing her once glossy mane of dark hair. 'Too much comes out on the comb,' she wailed. Her teeth had begun to grow loose. Silently, Hassen cursed her for her vanity. At meal times, his mother now refused to eat her share, dividing it equally among her children. Hassen could not swallow a morsel.

As colour drained from the landscape, hope deserted Hassen too.

On the day Hassen finally decided they had no choice but to leave, he saw a cloud of dust in the distance. It was moving closer, and something gleamed as Hassen ran to fetch his father's rifle, sending the girls scurrying inside to their mother. He doubted such a visitation could be auspicious. Poised with the rifle cocked, he waited as the engine's hum grew louder.

Hands clammy with fear, his fingers slipped as he pulled the trigger and the first bullet bounced near the front left tyre, forcing the Mercedes to swerve to an abrupt halt.

When the dust cloud dispersed, a bearded figure emerged from the driver's side, both hands raised above his head, swaying slightly in the violet shadow of the door.

The man spoke in a voice which was all at once both strange and yet familiar. 'Please don't shoot my Mercedes,' he said.

Hassen loosened his grip on the trigger and watched as the figure stepped forward into the sunlight.

'And is this the way in which you greet your brother?' The voice was now indignant.

Hassen dropped the gun and started running towards him. 'Abbas!' he cried.

As Abbas shuffled towards him, Hassen couldn't help noticing how one arm hung, useless, the hand bent back like a lever.

'So you know me after all,' Abbas said with a laugh, embracing his brother with his good arm. 'Two years, and now you are taller than me!'

When they eventually stood back from each other, Hassen saw how much Abbas had altered. The eyes appeared to have retreated into their sockets and there was a grey tinge to his skin, as if he had been exhumed from the earth. But he had kept his promise. Nothing else mattered for the moment. Abbas was triumphant.

'I always said I'd come back. I told you I'd have a Mercedes. Just wait until they see.' Abbas nodded in the direction of their home, looking suddenly uncertain. 'I hope they can find it in their hearts to forgive me, too.'

Hassen remained by the car while Abbas went inside. He did not want to have to be the one to tell Abbas their father was dead.

When he eventually re-emerged, flanked by his mother and the girls, Abbas's face was set in stone. He knows, thought Hassen bleakly.

'We're going to the new settlement,' Abbas told him as he threw their few possessions into the vast boot. 'I have already made arrangements.' Hassen helped him, glad he did not have to make the decisions any more.

Abbas and Hassen surveyed the deserted village as it groaned in the dry wind. 'Do you think we will ever come back?' asked Hassen.

'I promise you we will,' replied Abbas. 'And you know I never break a promise.'

The girls clasped each other, slithering around on the leather seat, shrieking with laughter as the car lurched forwards with a purr from the engine. But next to them sat their mother, rigid with fear, her hands clapped over her eyes.

They drove towards the place where the sun fell off the edge of the world, because Abbas said they needed to get away from the marshes now.

Hassen sat next to Abbas in the front, his heart skipping a beat as the car accelerated away from the past. Much faster than a canoe – now he understood why Abbas had yearned for this thing called a Mercedes! He ran his hand over the cool walnut dashboard, but sprang back with fright when a voice came out at the turn of a knob. Abbas laughed, telling him it was only a radio. But Hassen wasn't convinced.

'There must be a man in the engine,' he declared, peering into the air vents.

Abbas switched to some music. 'So where have I hidden the orchestra,' he asked, eyes twinkling with mirth.

When Hassen saw his mother and sisters had fallen asleep in the back, he asked softly, 'What happened, Abbas?'

'You mean this?' said his brother, glancing down at the withered arm which hung, useless, on his left side.

'I was handed to the military police for a handful of

silver.' He spoke slowly, with great effort, as he described his betrayal by the driver when they reached Baghdad. 'They wanted information, but I had nothing to tell them – even when they broke my fingers and threw me into jail.' Abbas gave a hollow imitation of a laugh.

Soon afterwards, he had been seconded, along with many other prisoners, and transported to a place called Nasiriyah, a sprawling building site in the middle of nowhere. He was put to work on constructing a mighty concrete dam designed to block the mouth of the Euphrates.

'I knew I was doing a terrible thing,' Abbas continued, his good hand clenched over the steering wheel. 'How I wept inside as I helped cut off the lifeblood of the marshes. I felt like a murderer.'

He described how Saddam had exacted his ultimate punishment on the marsh people by building the Mother of Battles River to hoard the sapphire waters of the Euphrates, leaving the marshes to wither into desert.

'Many prisoners died, weakened by hunger and disease and from hauling huge stones on their backs,' he continued as they bumped across the shimmering landscape. 'It was a terrible place. Who could you trust? There was always fear in men's eyes. I learned to walk with my eyes to the ground.'

A boulder had fallen on him in the quarry, crushing his arm. So he was put on a truck with other sick and injured labourers. 'We were told we were being taken to hospital. But I did not trust them,' said Abbas. 'Too many had failed to return from such journeys.'

Abbas resolved to escape. On impulse, he had hauled himself off the back of the moving truck, falling with a thud, on to the bumpy road, before limping off, unseen, into the night.

'Did you find this car in the desert?' asked Hassen.

Abbas stared grimly ahead. 'Some questions are better left unanswered,' he said.

As the sun sank like a huge blood orange they arrived at the edge of a sprawling shanty town which stretched as far as the eye could see. Row after row of rectangular shacks, all built with the same type of bricks, all with the same rusted, corrugated-iron roofs. A dull chugging sound filled the air – the chug, chug of ancient generators pumping salt water down hundreds of small irrigation channels.

The family was allocated a small space in one of the huts. And so began their new life, squeezed among strangers, tending to the small plots of melons, onions, plump scarlet tomatoes and rich green cucumbers that thrived on the saline water.

It was hard to live among so many and fights often erupted over nothing. Abbas and Hassen kept their heads down, tending to their crops, hoping – as the days turned into months and the months grew into years – that one day they would go home. The Mercedes rusted and fell apart. Abbas reluctantly sold off the parts for scrap.

'So much for our dream!' he muttered, kicking a rusty hubcap.

'I never gave up after you left us, so you must keep faith now,' responded Hassen.

Abbas felt suddenly ashamed.

It was only by believing this state to be temporary, Hassen could make himself rise up each new morning.

*

117

The shanty town was far from safe. Saddam's henchmen came like flocks of crows in search of carrion. Sweeping in among the shacks, they beat and destroyed everything in their path, dragging off the young to fight their wars and build more dams. Abbas and Hassen grew used to hiding, lying face down in the shallow irrigation channels, concealed beneath the lush foliage.

American and British planes now came, dropping their loads of supplies randomly, leaving huge craters in which children played. Many became sick afterwards, but no one knew why.

Hassen tried to understand why it was that so many bad things happened in the name of peace. He had a radio now and followed the war as it unfolded. He yearned to return to Zayad and his dreams were full of star-filled pools where he swam, weightless and happy, with his father.

He was patient however. He waited as the years turned him from a youth into a man, and both Sadiya and Sabiha, dark and beautiful, married and moved to a new town. Tempted by the promise of a life that offered refrigerators and satellite TV, their mother went too.

But Hassen stayed. As he hoed the rows of vegetables, his mind wandered back through the reeds, along the silent waterways, until he reached Zayad, its huts drifting like a mirage above the mirrored surface of the lake.

Then news came that the war was over, and Saddam had finally been forced to flee his marble palaces. But there was little rejoicing. Years of uneasy silence had left Hassen, like many others, empty of words, dry of emotion.

But Abbas was jubilant. 'We are going home,' he told his brother.

Incredulous, Hassen thought he must have taken leave of his senses. 'But it is a dust bowl,' he reminded him.

Abbas just said, 'Come with me and I'll show you.'

They hitched a lift with one of the many American convoys rumbling along the main highway. Hassen feared they might be shot. But the soldiers were relaxed, even friendly. They offered them gum and cigarettes, pulling them up on to the tank with beefy arms.

The road was filled with people walking – many of them empty-handed – back towards the marshes. It was not until the convoy had rumbled through Garmat Bani Hassan, a small village close to Zayad, that Hassen saw it. A vast canal, that ran in a straight line until it merged with the horizon. Giant rusted gates threw their menacing shadow across the dusty plain beneath.

Hassen watched Abbas disappear into the crowd now gathering to peer over the concrete parapet into the abyss below. He waited, without knowing what, exactly, he was waiting for. And then it came. A high-pitched wail – filling the air as a mist engulfed him. Hassen thought, So this is how the world ends!

But as the mist turned to rain, he saw Abbas, standing beneath a huge rainbow, pointing triumphantly to the torrent of water gushing through the open gates of the dam, and down on to the parched earth beneath.

Soaked to the skin, Hassen and Abbas decided to walk the last few miles back home. Hassen sighed when he saw their village marooned in the sand, huts the colour of bone. There was no water. So Abbas had been wrong after all. Both men fell silent. They had travelled all this way for nothing.

It was late, so the brothers resolved to stay one last night and then leave Zayad for good. Lying side by side on the bare floor, they talked of the past.

Abbas reminded Hassen of the time before he could swim, when he had taken the boat without permission. A storm had blown in across the lagoon, and Abbas, returning with other fisherman, had found him clinging to the sinking hull, retching with fright. He had never told their father how the boat came to be taken, wanting to protect Hassen from a certain beating. Their father had been a good man, they both agreed, but quick to administer punishment.

Hassen recalled how they both used to sneak up to the Mudhif, the large reed guest house in the village. Sneaking under the raised building, they would slither on their bellies through the mud to a point where they could hear everything in the room above.

Their mouths watered at the memory of the hours spent with their father, gun at the ready, crouching in the small hide on the lagoon, waiting for a plump duck to take the grain they had strewn, returning triumphant to their mother's waiting fire.

Abbas, now just a shadow, laughed softly. 'I would give anything to have our time again, wouldn't you, little brother?'

But Hassen, exhausted, had already succumbed to sleep – a sleep in which his father came to him again. But this time he stood before him smiling. Hassen, suffused with happiness, stretched out a hand to touch him.

He awoke with a start and sat bolt upright. Through

the broken roof he could see the moon had risen some-where – and he could hear the calling of a bird. It was a marsh warbler and its sweet song stirred the empty air.

'I must still be dreaming!' he thought as he stumbled outside and stood gazing at the silvered river that now reached out towards him in the moonlight.

'Where there are birds, there is water,' murmured Hassen, rubbing his eyes with disbelief, as the stars began to dance to their reflection. 'Where there is water, there is life.'

In a short while he would wake Abbas. Then they would begin their life again. But, for the moment, he would watch the water return to greet him like a lost friend.

Tony Bradman

Several things have gone into the creation of this story. Anyone who was born like me in the 1950s grew up under the long shadow of the Second World War. Both my parents were in the services and they told me many stories about London during the war. I've read a lot about it too, and realized that by 1944 millions of young men from all over the world – many of them Americans, and quite a few little more than boys – were waiting to invade Nazi-occupied Europe. London just before D-Day (6 June 1944) was actually a pretty wild place, almost like a frontier town in the old American West.

I also thought that war often brings people together who would otherwise never have met, and that those encounters must have changed many lives forever – a host of small stories enclosed within a single huge one. British kids did love American films, and thought American soldiers were wonderful, and there was also a lot of crime and petty thieving – times were very hard for everyone. And on D-Day, the Eighth and Sixteenth

Infantry Regiments did land on beaches in Normandy, where a great many US soldiers were killed and wounded by the German defenders.

AMERICAN PATROL

Jimmy Wilson stood in a square of shadow cast by a wall a few yards from the corner of the main road. Most evenings the blackout meant the streets of Catford were in darkness, but tonight there was a full moon, a bomber's moon, its eerie light turning south London silver and grey.

Jimmy shivered, even though it wasn't cold. He was supposed to keep watch while Stan and Frank broke into one of the shops backing on to the alley behind him. They were after cartons of cigarettes for Stan to sell on the black market – Stan the Spiv, with his flashy suits and loads of cash, the man Jimmy had hated from the moment Mum had brought him home.

Jimmy had known Stan was trouble, even though he'd been nice at first, ruffling Jimmy's hair, telling him he was a good lad. One day Stan had got Jimmy on his own, said he had a little job for him, something he was bound to be good at, seeing as no one took any notice of kids – being a lookout while Stan and Frank 'liberated some stuff'. Jimmy had realized Stan was talking about nicking, and said no, but that had only made Stan cross. And the more Jimmy had resisted, the worse Stan's threats got.

Earlier that evening, Stan had come to the house and conned Jimmy's dozy gran into handing him over. Usually, Jimmy went to stay with Marge if Mum had to do the night shift at the big munitions factory in Woolwich. Marge lived up the street and had taken care of Jimmy back in the early part of the war. In fact, during the Blitz she'd almost been a second mum to him, and Jimmy knew she would never have fallen for Stan's old flannel. But Marge was busy, so Gran had been the one in charge.

'Thought I'd give the boy a treat, Gran,' Stan had said, smiling, showing his teeth. 'There's a Jimmy Cagney flick on at the Odeon, and you know how he loves Yank films. Oh, and don't wait up. We might be back late.'

Jimmy would have liked to see *Angels with Dirty Faces*, but as soon as they were outside, Stan had grabbed his ear and dragged him along the road. Frank had been waiting by the pub on the corner, the King's Arms. Jimmy hated the short, hatchet-faced Frank, too. Everyone said Frank was a deserter.

'Right, you're our lookout tonight,' Stan had hissed, his eyes narrowed to slits, his mouth tight and mean as he twisted Jimmy's ear harder. 'And don't even think about arguing. Not unless you want a taste of this.'

Stan had whipped his flick knife from his jacket pocket and clicked the blade out under Jimmy's nose. So Jimmy had done what he was told.

Suddenly Jimmy heard footsteps. Two policemen were walking along the main road. Jimmy retreated deeper into the darkness, rattling a pebble with his shoe as he did so. The coppers stopped, peered in his direction. Then Jimmy heard more footsteps – Stan and Frank coming back! Panic filled him. He knew if he moved or shouted, he'd give Stan and Frank away. But now the coppers were walking towards him. Towards the alley.

'Hey, who's there?' one of them called out. 'Show yourself!'

Jimmy turned and fled. There was nothing else he could do, even though he knew Stan wouldn't see it like that. As Jimmy ran into the darkness, his feet pounding the pavement, he couldn't stop thinking about Stan's knife. He could almost feel the sharp steel carving into his flesh . . .

Private First Class Scott Francis Riley was sitting in a small compartment on a train to Waterloo Station in London. He figured it was meant for eight people, but there were twelve servicemen squeezed into it now, and the narrow corridor beyond was packed with even more guys in uniform.

Scott was glad he'd managed to get a window seat. Looking out at the neat little English fields rolling past had kept him calm since the train left Portsmouth earlier that morning, had kept him from thinking of the terrible things that had been filling his mind over the last few weeks.

'Hey, buddy, got a light?' somebody said, and Scott realized it was the guy sitting beside him. He looked round, saw a soldier a couple of years older than him with a fresh Lucky Strike in his mouth, ready to be lit.

'Sorry, I don't smoke,' Scott said quietly. Sometimes

he thought he was the only guy in the US Army who didn't. He felt himself blush.

'Too young to have any vices,' said the guy, and laughed. A big sailor leaned forward and clicked a Zippo. 'Say, how old *are* you?' said the soldier. 'My kid brother looks older than you, and he's still in high school.'

'Old enough,' Scott murmured. 'I'm eighteen. I'll be nineteen in July.'

'Oh yeah?' The guy peered at Scott's shoulder flash. 'Sixteenth Infantry Regiment?'

Scott nodded.

'I'm in the Eighth,' said the guy, tapping his own insignia. 'I don't think either of us should be making plans for July.'

Scott stared at him for a second, then turned back to the window. He knew exactly what the guy was talking about. The Allies – the US Army, the British, the Canadians and all the rest – were almost certainly going to invade Nazi-occupied Europe soon, maybe in the next few weeks. And the scuttlebutt was that the men of the Sixteenth and Eighth Infantry Regiments would be among the first to storm the heavily defended French beaches.

Scott felt his stomach clench, his mouth fill with bile. That's why he had joined the army, he thought: to fight for freedom, to defeat an evil enemy. That's why he had left his mom and pop and his three younger brothers at home in Brooklyn. That's why he'd learned how to use a rifle and to get in and out of a landing craft with his platoon. But a buddy had told him the top brass expected at least eighty per cent of the men in the first assault wave to be killed or wounded and, since then, Scott's mind had been full of blood and death. He could almost feel the bullets ripping into the soft flesh beneath his uniform, the shrapnel shredding his muscles and bones, see it all happening to him as he ran from the landing craft.

It had gotten so bad he'd thought about talking to an officer, or maybe even a priest, but he just couldn't bring himself to do it. Then his platoon commander had offered the guys a two-day pass, the last they might get before . . . well, before the Big Day, he'd hinted. So Scott had grabbed the chance – hitched from the camp near Poole to Portsmouth, hopped on the first train to London. He was hoping he could clear his head, get a grip. Although there was this one, really crazy idea that wouldn't let him be.

A sudden burst of raucous laughter exploded in the corridor, but Scott didn't dare look round. He was too scared his face might show the others what was on his mind, the shameful thing he was sorely tempted to do.

He kept staring out of the window as the train rattled through the warm spring sunshine towards Waterloo.

Although now he saw nothing at all.

Jimmy spent his first night on the run hiding in a place he knew, the classroom where nice, tired old Mrs Percival had struggled to keep him and another forty kids under control until a few months back. But late one night a huge bomb had blasted half the school into rubble, and the rest was declared unsafe. Jimmy and his classmates had been parcelled out to other schools in the district, although most of them hadn't bothered to go.

It was strange sitting in the corner of a room that was both familiar and very different, the ceiling and walls badly cracked, the desks and floor covered with chunks of plaster and bits of broken glass, the ghostly moonlight shining through the shattered windows. Strange and scary.

Jimmy brooded on what to do. He couldn't go home. If those coppers hadn't caught Stan and Frank, he knew Stan would be after him with his flick-knife. Even if they had, Jimmy was sure Stan would get out of it and come looking for him. And Jimmy didn't feel he could talk to Mum. Everybody in the district knew Stan was dodgy, which meant Mum must have known as well. But she was totally wrapped up in Stan and didn't seem to care.

If only there was somebody else he could turn to, Jimmy thought. He wished his dad was alive, or that the school hadn't been bombed so he could have talked to Mrs Percival. He thought of Marge, and felt a surge of hope. Marge would help him, he was certain of it . . . then he realized Marge's house was too close to home, and his spirits sank again. Stan would probably catch him before he got anywhere near Marge's front door. No, he was completely on his own. Alone and utterly powerless.

Suddenly Jimmy heard a scuffling noise nearby. He froze, and peered into the shadows. A small, dark form was moving along the base of a wall. He breathed out, relaxed. It was only a rat searching for something to eat. Rats were so common on bomb sites, some of his mates even made them into pets. But Jimmy had never liked the look of their sharp, little teeth, or the way they scuttled, and he lobbed a chunk of brick in the creature's direction. It shot off through a hole in the skirting board.

Jimmy's stomach rumbled, and he realized it was hours since he'd eaten himself. Gran had made him bangers and mash, the sausages a present from Stan to Jimmy's mum the day before. Stan had given Mum some nylons too, and Jimmy had seen the smile on her face . . . He wiped the thought from his mind, concentrated on his most pressing needs.

He could get water from a drinking fountain. Food was going to be a problem, though, especially as he didn't have any money. Unless he went up west, Jimmy thought. There were plenty of places in the West End where he might be able to nick some food – shops, restaurants, cafes of all kinds. He knew stealing was wrong, but he didn't have much choice.

Jimmy dozed for a few hours, and woke stiff and shivering in a watery dawn light. He headed to a park where there was a drinking fountain, and by nine o'clock he was getting off a train at Charing Cross, hiding behind some office workers, slipping past a yawning ticket collector and immediately ducking through a side exit and out of the station. He walked up the steep hill of Villiers Street and turned into the Strand. There was a big cafe on a corner two hundred yards ahead of him.

Earlier that same morning Scott had left the American Red Cross club where he'd spent the night – a converted hotel off Park Lane – and gone for a walk in the park. It was Hyde Park, he thought, although he wasn't sure. Not that it mattered much. Wherever he went, the terrible images in his head went right along with him. And the terrible fear in his heart.

He wandered out of the park and into streets lined

with old buildings he didn't recognize. He'd spent the whole of the day before tramping the city, visiting places he'd only read about or seen in movie newsreels – Buckingham Palace, the Houses of Parliament, Westminster Abbey, St Paul's, still standing despite the Blitz. But all he'd seen was dead people.

They were there again today. The sidewalks were full of young guys in uniform, many just boys – Americans, British, Canadians, Australians, New Zealanders, Free French, Norwegians, Poles – young women too, any civilians seeming out of place. Scott couldn't help wondering how many were doomed to be slaughtered in the next few weeks and months.

Most seemed happy enough, Scott thought. Last night, the pubs and clubs and restaurants and dance halls he'd walked past had been packed with people laughing and drinking and having a good time. He had looked on, unable to join in, then had slunk back to the ARC club.

Scott slowed down, realizing he'd arrived at Trafalgar Square. He crossed the road, stood beneath one of the great stone lions and squinted at Lord Nelson high above him. The sun shone out of a clear blue sky, a crowd of pigeons strutted at his feet, buses and trucks roared by. Scott lowered his gaze. A few other people were dotted round the square. But heading straight towards him were a couple of US military policemen.

The boys back at camp called them Snowdrops because of the white helmets they wore. Nice name, thought Scott, but they were pretty tough guys, handy with the long wooden billy clubs they carried. Last night he'd seen a squad of them roust out a young GI from a pub and throw him in a jeep. The kid was AWOL, he'd heard a Snowdrop say, Absent Without Leave for a week. Not quite a deserter, but heading that way.

Scott hadn't said a word, just watched. Is that what would happen to him if he deserted? He knew that in World War One deserters had usually been shot, but he didn't think the US Army did that any more, or maybe only if you deserted in combat, facing the enemy. If he took off now and got caught, he'd definitely pull some stockade time back in the States. But at least he'd be alive, his body whole, the future ahead of him.

'Let's see your papers, soldier,' said one of the MPs. His cold blue eyes, just visible beneath the rim of his white helmet, were fixed on Scott's. The other MP stood to the side, tapping his billy club against his leg, lazily chewing gum, watching Scott fumble his ID and pass from his pocket. Scott felt himself blush, and again he feared his face might give away what he'd been thinking. But the MP only glanced at his papers and handed them back. 'OK, kid,' he said. 'Stay out of trouble, you hear?'

Scott watched them stroll across the square, the pigeons fleeing before them. Then he walked fast in the opposite direction, towards a long street he thought was called the Strand. His hands were shaking and his mouth was dry, and he was badly in need of something liquid, even if it was just a cup of that sweet, strange-tasting tea the English drank all the time.

He arrived at a certain cafe just as Jimmy was being thrown out of it.

It had all happened so fast. One minute Jimmy had been in the queue at the cafe – it was actually a large Lyons

Corner House – trying to sneak a Bath bun out of a glass case on the counter, and the next, somebody's fingers had a powerful grip on his ear. The same ear that Sid had twisted.

'Caught you red-handed!' shouted the person the fingers belonged to.

Jimmy could see now it was a woman; the manageress, he thought. She was middle-aged and scrawny and mean-faced. 'I'm sick of you street urchins coming in here to steal things,' she yelled, dragging him to the door. Jimmy glimpsed the people in the queue staring, heard them tutting. The manageress shoved him outside, and he fell, sprawling across the pavement. 'I've a good mind to call a policeman!' she hissed.

'Hey, what's going on?' said a voice from somewhere above him.

Jimmy looked up and saw a young GI with a puzzled frown on his face. The American was tall and thin and reminded Jimmy of James Stewart. He glanced down at Jimmy, then back at the manageress.

'None of your business, Yank,' she snapped. The GI stared hard at her. 'But if you must know,' she said, 'I caught the little scallywag stealing.'

'Stealing what?' said the GI. Jimmy stood up and rubbed his ear.

'A Bath bun,' the manageress replied haughtily, her chin raised.

'What's that – some kind of pastry?' said the GI, puzzled. 'Say, kid, you must be public enemy number one. Armed and extremely dangerous.' He glanced at Jimmy and smiled. Jimmy wanted to laugh, although he didn't dare. 'But seeing as it isn't the crime of the century, ma'am,' said the GI, turning to her once more, 'how about giving the kid a break?'

'Well, really,' spluttered the manageress, 'you Yanks come over here and think you can order us about . . . Oh, just go away, the pair of you!'

And with that she stormed back into the cafe, leaving Jimmy and the GI together outside. The GI took off his cap and gave a low whistle. 'Hey, nice lady,' he murmured. 'Makes a guy feel really welcome.'

'I hope the Germans drop a bomb on her,' said Jimmy. 'A big one.'

'It'd just bounce off,' said the GI. 'That dame is steel-plated, buddy.'

Jimmy did laugh now. The image of a huge black bomb covered in Swastikas bouncing off a steel-plated manageress was irresistibly comic. The GI laughed too, and put his cap back on. 'You OK, kid?' he said.

'Yeah, I think so,' said Jimmy, suddenly serious. 'And, er . . . thanks.'

'Don't mention it,' said the GI, smiling. 'That's what we're here for. I mean, to help you Limeys, although I didn't think I'd be protecting you from each other. Say, you look as if you could do with a square meal. You must be pretty hungry to try and steal one of those watchamacallits.'

'A Bath bun,' said Jimmy, his stomach rumbling, his mouth instantly filling with saliva at the thought of food. His whole being wanted this Yank to take him somewhere and feed him. But something else had struck Jimmy – what the GI had said about helping Limeys. Jimmy knew that's what the Yanks called the English.

He was a Limey and he needed help, didn't he? So maybe this American was the person to provide it . . .

'Well, I could use a cup of coffee and a bite to eat myself,' said the GI. 'How'd you like to tag along? I'm pretty sure Uncle Sam won't object.'

Jimmy grinned and nodded.

'OK, let's follow the yellow brick road,' said the GI and strode off down the street, Jimmy hurrying to keep up. 'I'm Scott Riley,' said the GI after a while. 'What do they call you, kid?'

'Jimmy Wilson.' They crossed to Trafalgar Square at the traffic lights. 'And what you just said, it's from *The Wizard of Oz*, ain't it? I seen that.'

'It sure is,' said Scott. 'You like the movies?'

Jimmy nodded again.

'Me too,' said Scott. 'So you're called Jimmy . . . just like Cagney himself. Say, maybe you *are* public enemy number one after all.' He smiled at Jimmy again. 'Just don't tell anyone when we get where we're going.'

'Where *are* we going?' said Jimmy. Pigeons scurried out of their way.

'To somewhere you'll like,' Scott murmured. 'To Rainbow Corner . . .'

Jimmy's painfully empty stomach couldn't wait for them to arrive.

Scott had eaten lunch at Rainbow Corner the day before. It was the name of another American Red Cross club, the huge place where everybody seemed to go, on Shaftesbury Avenue, just up from Piccadilly Circus.

Scott took Jimmy in through the main doors, under the big US flag on the outside of the building and straight into one of the dining rooms. The cooks were still serving breakfast and Scott got them both some ham and eggs, some pancakes with maple syrup, some waffles too, as well as a cup of good, strong American coffee for him and a glass of milk for the kid. Scott piled it on a tray and found a couple of empty seats at a table.

As he'd known, nobody minded the kid being there. In fact, the other guys round the table – a couple of Airborne troopers and a sailor – smiled and winked and said hi.

Jimmy didn't say a word. Scott could see he was shy, nervous, but excited to be there as well. And starving hungry.

'So what are you waiting for?' Scott said. 'Eat it while it's hot.'

Jimmy didn't need to be told twice. He grinned at Scott, then started wolfing down the food, barely pausing for breath between mouthfuls. Scott sipped his coffee, but hardly touched his own plate. He studied Jimmy instead, examining this British kid who had fallen into his path.

What he saw was a skinny boy, maybe ten or eleven years old, his hair cropped close to the sides of his head, a spiky tuft sticking up on top. He was wearing a shapeless blazer, a woollen sweater with holes in it over a rough grey shirt, those shorts the British kids all seemed to wear, knee-high grey socks and worn-out black shoes. Everything was grubby, including the kid's hands, his bitten fingernails half-moons of dirt.

None of that mattered. Scott had always hated seeing kids being pushed around, whoever they were, rich or poor. He could no more have stopped himself stepping

in to save Jimmy from that woman than fly. But there
was something about the kid that Scott had seen right
away – the British boy was a ringer for his youngest
brother, eleven-year-old Bobby. Clean Jimmy up, dress
him in a clean sweater and jeans and sneakers, and he'd
look like a regular American kid. Just like Bobby.

'So what part of London are you from, Jimmy?' said
Scott.

'Catford,' Jimmy mumbled, his mouth full. 'South of
the river.'

Scott had never heard of it. 'You live with your
parents?' he asked.

'Just my mum,' Jimmy said. 'My dad's dead.
Torpedoed.'

Scott didn't know what to say. Jimmy kept talking,
though, the words spilling out of him. He described
being evacuated at the beginning of the war, and living
in the country on a farm with strangers, which he'd
hated. There had been no bombing though, so his mum
had brought him back to Catford. Then the Blitz had
begun, and Catford had copped it bad, so he'd spent a
lot of nights in an Anderson shelter with Marge while
Mum was out at work, and then they'd heard about his
dad, who'd been a sailor. His ship had been sunk by a
German U-Boat in the North Atlantic.

'That's rough,' said the sailor at the table. He and the
Airborne guys had been listening too, spellbound.
'You've been having quite some war.'

Scott thought of Bobby going to school or playing
baseball while Jimmy was being bombed by the Nazis
and losing his father. He thought of the bad things he'd
seen in the newsreels: kids in Europe bombed out of

138

their homes, turned into refugees, made to suffer. He had a brief vision of the Nazis bombing Brooklyn, of Bobby being hurt . . . and realized he would do anything to stop that happening. And to help those other kids. Maybe even storm up a French beach with his platoon and get killed.

What else was he going to do, anyhow? Let down his buddies, the guys he'd trained with? Bring shame on his family? Spend the rest of his life knowing he was a coward? If this skinny British kid could take all of that, then he – Private Scott Riley of the US Army – could do the job he'd signed up for. He'd be damned if he wasn't going to give it a try, anyway.

'It ain't been *that* bad,' Jimmy murmured, his voice breaking into Scott's thoughts. The boy shrugged and wiped his plate clean with a piece of pancake. 'Not till my mum took up with that Stan the Spiv, anyway . . .'

Scott leaned forward. This was a story he definitely wanted to hear.

Whenever Jimmy thought of that day in the years to come, everything about it had a kind of rosy glow. How could it be otherwise? It was like suddenly being transported to paradise, or into a real, live movie. And he'd said and done all the right things too, just like a movie star would.

He'd been surrounded by Yanks giving him stuff – all the food he could eat, including ice cream and chocolate bars and packets of Wrigleys gum, as well as baseball cards and badges. He got a ride round the West End in a jeep with a couple of military policemen, too. Snowdrops, Scott called them, which was odd. He also said they were real tough guys, but they'd just been nice, cracking lots of jokes and doing a Jimmy Cagney routine because he'd told them he loved Cagney films, snapping 'You dirty rat' at each other and 'Take that, copper', and laughing a lot.

Then that afternoon Scott had taken him to the pictures, to one of the big cinemas in Leicester Square. It was a double feature, a cowboy flick with Errol Flynn which hadn't been very good, and *The Maltese Falcon*, with Humphrey Bogart, which had been great. He'd even enjoyed the Pathé news for once. The Russians were advancing, it looked like Rome was going to fall soon, and the Yanks were doing all right in the Pacific.

It had still been light when Jimmy and Scott had emerged from the cinema, a busy late afternoon, Leicester Square crowded with people.

'So what am I going to do with you, Jimmy?' Scott said softly. 'You have to go home some time, buddy. Maybe you should give your mom a chance and try talking to her, or ask that nice neighbour lady for help . . .'

'But even if I do, I still need somebody to protect me from Stan,' said Jimmy. He had been thinking about what to say all through the film. 'And I wondered . . . if you'd come home with me. I mean, you did say that's what you were here for, didn't you? To help us Limeys. And I just need some help to make it to Marge's house without Stan getting hold of me . . .' His voice trailed away. His heart was pounding in his chest as he stood watching the American's face. The young GI looked surprised and for a second Jimmy was sure he was going to say no. But then Scott laughed.

'I can do better than that,' he said. 'Let me talk to some of the guys . . .'

An hour later Jimmy was on the train back to Catford, but he wasn't alone. Sitting around him in a small compartment were Scott and the two Airborne guys and the sailor from earlier, as well as the two MPs. They were off duty now, but they were still wearing their white helmets and carrying their billy clubs. One of them was whistling a jaunty tune.

Jimmy recognized it instantly, a Glenn Miller song. He'd heard it often on the wireless at home, on the American Armed Forces network he and his mum liked to tune in to sometimes. They both loved that big band sound and Glenn Miller was the best. Even Gran thought he was good.

'Hey, that's "American Patrol", ain't it?' Jimmy said, and grinned.

'Got it in one, kid,' said the Snowdrop – and winked. 'That's us, amigo, the American Patrol, out to pacify the badlands south of the river . . .'

Marge was obviously glad to see him, if a bit surprised that he seemed to have acquired his own private American army since he'd disappeared. 'Blimey,' she said at the sight of all those Americans in uniform on her doorstep. 'I thought you lot were supposed to be invading France, not Catford.'

Jimmy was pleased to see plump, cuddly Marge too, happy to be hugged, eager to tell her what had happened the night before last.

'I always knew that Stan was a bad lot,' she said, 'and I told your mum; I said, "Doreen, you'll rue the day you took up with him." But it hasn't been easy for her since your dad died, Jimmy, you must understand that. She's been very lonely and frightened like the rest of us . . . but she won't have anything to do with Stan after this. Not if he's put you in harm's way. You matter a lot more to her than somebody like Stan ever could. She's been frantic, wondering where you were. She's even been to the police.'

'What about Stan, though, Marge?' said Jimmy. 'Did they catch him?'

'Course not,' Marge said with a snort. 'You mark my words, he'll be boozing in the King's Arms this minute, I expect, same as usual.'

'That's the pub on the corner, right, ma'am?' said Scott. Marge and Jimmy nodded. 'Wait here, kid. This won't take long. Come on, guys.'

Jimmy watched the band of Yanks march off up the street in the dirty pink light of a south London sunset – the Snowdrops swinging their billy clubs, all of them looking hard and determined. It seemed only seconds later that Frank shot out of the pub and ran up the street as fast as his legs would carry him, closely followed by an obviously terrified Stan – several very fit young Americans close behind them and gaining all the time.

No doubt about it, thought Jimmy. This was the best day of his life.

Four weeks later, on the morning of 6 June 1944, Scott was standing with the rest of his squad in a landing craft, one of the thousands of small boats heading towards the coast of Normandy, the sky above thunderous with the huge barrage from the battleships behind them. Cold sea spray blew in Scott's face as the boat's flat bottom hit each successive wave. He and his buddies were soaked already, most of them were seasick and all were afraid. Scott's stomach churned and he fought not to throw up.

'One hundred yards and closing!' yelled the bosun at the helm.

The cold air was rank with the smell of diesel fuel and vomit, and around him Scott could hear guys muttering prayers and the names of loved ones. He said another Hail Mary and thought of his mom and pop and his brothers. Suddenly he thought of Jimmy too, and how that day in London had changed things for them. He hoped the kid was doing OK . . .

'Fifty yards, and closing!' the bosun yelled. A fountain of water rose beside the landing craft as a shell exploded, drenching them even more.

The big fifty-calibre machine-gun mounted on the stern of the landing craft suddenly opened up over Scott's head, and he could hear enemy rounds pinging into the metal ramp at the front of the landing craft. He ducked, realizing the Germans in the pillboxes above the beach had got their range, and thought how strange it was that people he had never met were shooting at him. He gripped his rifle tighter, tried to swallow and couldn't, focused on the helmet of the guy standing in front of him.

'Hitting the beach, ramp going *DOWN!*' screamed the bosun. Thirty boys ran out of the landing craft, into the withering fire on Omaha Beach.

The rest, of course, is history.

Eleanor Updale

grew up in a time of peace, but close enough to the end of the Second World War to walk past bomb sites on the way to school. Like the children in this story, we spent every playtime re-enacting the battle against the Germans. At weekends we watched black-and-white war films on our tiny TV sets. Those playground games and films were all about the glamour of death, and it is the dead of the two world wars we count and commemorate every year. Even now, terrorist atrocities are measured by the number of corpses. A bomb that causes only damage and injury will not make it to the top of the news.

Yet far more people are affected, directly or indirectly, by the mental and physical wounds of conflict. This is the story of one family's experience and how the scars of war are still visible in the actions and attitudes of later generations. We should remember the survivors. Their agony lives on in unexpected ways.

I got the idea for this story from talking to my grandmother who, shortly before she died in her nineties, told me the truth about what had happened to my grandfather. After that, I understood all sorts of family quirks.

This is not her story, but it could be.

NOT A SCRATCH

It wasn't a bullet and it didn't kill him. At least not right then. Not with the instant force of a hand grenade, or the thrust and twist of a sharpened bayonet. It was a microbe, bred in a corpse and carried in a stream. He didn't even know it was there, lurking in the water bottle the men passed round as they cowered in their trench, relieved that the shell fire had stopped, thinking that they were the lucky ones.

Sidney took a swig and settled down with his tattered notebook to compose a letter to a young woman back in Derby. Not to his darling Maudie this time. He would write to her later, reassuring her that he was still alive. This letter was for Archie's wife – his widow now – to tell her of his brave death, hopelessly charging the enemy lines in the blistering August sun. It was only chance that had put Archie in the line of fire. A couple of inches to the left and Sidney would have taken the bullet. Archie would be writing to Maude now, struggling to find words of comfort and hope.

Sidney fumbled in his pocket for Maude's photograph, specially posed at a studio when she heard he was joining up. She had put on the serious look appropriate to the occasion, but he preferred to remember her laughing and happy, as she had been nearly two years ago, on the night he'd proposed. They'd been at a party, celebrating New Year's Eve as 1915 turned into 1916, the year they'd thought must surely see the end of the war. They had sworn to marry as soon as it was all over. It had been a long wait, and there on the battlefield he shut out the filth and the moans of the injured to imagine her as she would look on their wedding day: her jubilant face framed in delicate lace, with just a few soft auburn curls peeping out at the edges. When he was home they would go dancing together, spend Sundays riding their bikes out into the country, swimming in streams and watching romantic sunsets from grassy hills. He would hear her golden laugh again, and she would scream for him to stop as he tickled her when no one was looking. Until then, her grave photograph would bring him luck, as it had in battle after battle so far.

She had a picture of him, too: strong, healthy and cheekily grinning in his clean uniform; proud to be a soldier at last, setting off to an unknown destination. Maude carried that photo all the time. She had it with her at the station when the remains of his unit returned home, victorious. She thought it might come in handy in case she had to ask someone if they had seen him in the throng of men. It would have been no use. No one could have matched the emaciated body on the stretcher to the virile image on the card. But Sidney recognized Maude. For the first time in the flesh she resembled her picture, and he would get used to that serious look in years to come. But he was one of the lucky ones. Not a scratch, only a spot of dysentery that had scoured his bowels of food and water. He was so weak he couldn't stand, but he didn't count as a casualty. He'd survived, uninjured.

And at first it was a source of pure joy for Maude to see his face, and to watch him fattening up a little under his mother's care. Maude visited every day after work, and as the wedding approached Sidney's mother initiated her into some of the more intimate and unpleasant tasks associated with his 'problem'. It seemed the infection was still there, occasionally flaring up and sending him running to the toilet with painful bloody diarrhoea and vomiting, or 'd and v' as they preferred to call it. Sometimes, when things were really bad, the doctor visited. He could barely hide his distaste for Sid's symptoms, as he scrubbed his hands clean.

'I must be getting on. Just feed him up as best you can. Give him plenty of fluids, to replace what he's losing. There's nothing one can do about these bugs from the trenches. Bound to keep flaring up from time to time. Still, he should be grateful. I'm off to see to a man with only one eye – lost half his face at Passchendaele.'

He opened his bag and took out a bottle of orange liquid. 'Give him a spoonful of this three times a day. I'll send my bill round in the morning.'

'Yes, doctor,' said Maude, as politely as she could, closing the front door behind him. She knew the medicine would be ineffective, and that Sidney, lying weak in the bedroom, had heard the implied criticism – that his illness was less important than the injuries of the 'real' casualties. Maude despised the doctor. She resolved to keep out of his way, and to keep the doctor away from Sidney. She would nurse him alone, however unpleasant it might be.

Sidney's mother tried to encourage her as they mopped away the evidence of yet another futile dash to the lavatory.

'Don't worry, dear. It will wear off with time. Just thank the Lord that he's still here. It's nothing that a little disinfectant can't clear up.'

'Yes, of course,' said Maude bravely, plunging her mop into a bucket of pungent cleaning fluid. 'It's a blessing he's survived.'

And she meant it, as she prepared for her Boxing Day wedding. It was a quiet affair. She tried not to be disappointed. The girls she'd wanted as her bridesmaids had both lost their boyfriends in the war, and it would have been cruel to celebrate too wildly in front of them. Of course there couldn't be a honeymoon with Sid unable to travel. So they started married life under her mother-in-law's roof. No wonder there were no kiddies for five years.

And in those five years, how things changed. At first there was genuine sympathy from neighbours and old friends. Once Maude even overheard someone praising her devotion to her husband with his embarrassing complaint.

'I don't know how she does it. She must be a saint.'

But Maude's brief glow of pride subsided quickly as the woman continued: 'I couldn't live like that. I'd go round there to visit, but I just can't stand the stench. I can't bear to see Sid wasting away. He was such a lovely boy.'

Sid and Maude were together, but the old fun had gone from their lives. They sold the bikes. Sid couldn't sit in the music hall for long in case he had an 'attack'; and anyway the old gang, Archie and other friends, were gone. The war, a subject never off people's lips before 1920, gradually became unmentionable. New acquaintances didn't want to risk stirring up unknown troubles and a fresh generation of men, too young to have fought, took on the jobs vacated by their older brothers, lying cold in Europe and the east.

Sid grew stronger, but never strong enough to go back to his old work as a steeplejack, climbing high up church spires to repair their ancient stones, and maintaining factory chimneys across the county. His boss took pity on him and gave him clerical work back at the office, so he would never be far from a toilet and running water, but Sidney wasn't suited to it. He worked badly, and grew angry with himself and everyone else in the office. It didn't help that he arrived there every morning already exhausted after a night broken by stomach upsets or wild dreams about the horrors that had killed his mates. So it was no surprise that when the boss died, and his son took over the firm, Sidney was sacked.

He started on a round of casual work and disappointments. The pay was poor, and Sid had none of the prospects Maude had looked forward to when they'd met. Secretly, she envied Archie's wife with her widow's pension. Even more secretly, she coveted the status that came with having lost her man. At that first November remembrance service, a year after the end of the war, the widows were given seats round the temporary wooden memorial. They were still in the front row four years later, when its stone replacement was unveiled. Maude, who had been up half the night scrubbing sheets and was dizzy with pregnancy, still had to stand in the crowd with Sid. She looked at Archie's widow, elegant in black on her comfortable chair, dabbing her eyes with a lace handkerchief under the sympathetic gaze of the mayor.

'I bet he doesn't know she's seeing the butcher from Hatherley,' thought Maude unkindly, imagining their playful rendezvous by the canal. 'I wonder what Archie would have had to say to that.'

The congregation cheered a man with a crutch who hobbled on his one leg to lay a poppy on the cross. There were disdainful mutters when Sid had to leave suddenly before the prayers were over. If only they knew why. But Maude would never say. She had her pride.

The babies brought a brief interlude of joy. First Eric, then Margaret, rekindled some of the old closeness in the couple. Sidney and Maude laughed together as the children toddled around, rummaged in the dressing-up box, came out with unconsciously funny lines and asked silly questions. But there could be no country picnics, no trips to circuses or the zoo, at least not with Dad. It didn't matter to the children at first. They loved him as they knew him, and their tight little family was their model for how things should be. But everything changed when they went to school.

The adult world might have stopped talking about the war, but playground games were still steeped in it.

As soon as the children were let out at playtime, they sorted themselves into two groups – the English and the Germans – and set about chasing each other, firing invisible guns and throwing mock grenades (and real punches when the teacher wasn't looking). On wet days, shut in the classroom at lunchtime, pupils swapped titbits of family history. Eric and Margaret had nothing to offer. Eric tried to get information to share with his friends.

'Was Daddy in the war?' he asked innocently at tea time.

'Of course he was. That's why he's ill,' snapped Maude. 'That's where he picked up the germ that makes him sick. Now eat your food. We don't want to talk about things like that at the table.'

Having a dad with an infection didn't carry much weight in the schoolyard, where other children could boast of dead uncles, or fathers with glamorous wounds, exotic souvenirs taken from German corpses and stirring stories of bravery. Margaret tried to get more information.

'Didn't you fight at all, Dad?'

'Oh yes, I fought. I marched and charged. I slept in the mud and I watched my comrades fall dead all around me.' Sidney started to shake, as he remembered appalling sights he would never describe to her tender ears. He stared into the fire, his silence frightening both children. Their mother angrily bundled them from the room.

'Look what you've done, asking him all those questions. What do you want to go upsetting him like that for? Don't you ever let me hear you asking him about the war again.'

That night, and many nights afterwards, they were woken by the pitiful sound of Sidney squealing and bleating in his sleep. They heard their mother comforting him, or more often shouting at him, telling him not to let his mind stray among things that were in the past and could never be undone. They read the signs. They saw that their father's frailty made their mother angry, and they knew that she could never let herself admit it. She had to make a show of carrying on. Sid's illness dominated their lives, but they never spoke about it. They just knew it was embarrassing; that everything to do with the bathroom was secret and shameful, and that all bodies, not just their father's, were disgusting, disgraceful and bad.

When Sidney was very sick, the doctor had to come. When he did, Maude regarded the call as an admission of failure: her own personal disgrace. It was the same when Eric or Margaret were ill. They both reached their teens without seeing the inside of the doctor's surgery, and when Eric was taken to hospital by a teacher after breaking his leg in a football match, he felt more shame than pain. His mother's distaste for the place when she came to collect him couldn't be hidden behind her pinched and silent smile.

Eric stayed indoors with his leg in plaster, and no one came to visit. Maude never told the children why they were not allowed to have friends round to play. As they grew older, they didn't want to, anyway. They were embarrassed by the smells that would sometimes waft through the house when their father had 'one of his explosions'. At school, Eric and Margaret were thought to be stuck up and stand-offish. Their classmates' mothers said as much about Maude, loud enough for her children to hear.

'We're moving,' said Maude over breakfast one day, explaining weeks of tetchy, muttered conversations between the two adults. Sidney's mother had died and Eric had caught a reference to 'coming into a bit of money'. He'd allowed himself to fantasize about a life of luxury, so it was a disappointment when Maude finally broke the news officially.

'We're taking on the village shop at Currington. It's a post office and general store. It will be hard work, but it has to be done. That way, your dad can always be close to *facilities*.' She spoke as if she were making a huge sacrifice, demeaning herself by becoming a shopkeeper.

'Imagine, kids,' said Sid, trying to lighten the mood. 'You'll be able to have sweets and biscuits whenever you want.'

'They'll have no such thing!' snapped Maude. 'There'll be no eating the stock. We're going to need every penny we can make.'

Humiliated, Sid sank back into his now customary gloom, while Maude busied herself tidying the already spotless parlour.

The move was exciting for the children. There were trees to climb, strange country animals in fields, and a river. On the second day the children bounded into the shop with a couple of new friends. It was sunny, but their hair was wet. Maude greeted them, crossly.

'Where've you been?'

'Swimming,' Margaret said, laughing. 'I saw a fish, Mummy. A real fish in the river!'

Everyone was shocked by Maude's reaction. 'How dare you go there! Don't you know there are germs in that water? And who are these children? Dripping filth near food! Get out of my shop, and don't go interfering with my family again!'

The terrified visitors ran outside. Eric and Margaret tried to follow them, but Maude called them back.

'You two, stay here! I don't want you mixing with those country kids. We've got standards to keep up. Now, you keep yourselves to yourselves.'

Eric and Margaret wanted to defy their mother, and carry on playing with the local children, but it was too late. From then on they were frozen out, as alien new-comers from the city.

Maude's attitude to her customers didn't help. Her shame at Sid's 'affliction' stopped her asking anyone in to the flat above the shop. And, anyway, her work didn't leave time for friendships. Yet again she was seen as a snob and it was a role she slipped into little by little as she got to know more and more about the villagers. She developed grand airs: enjoying the power of granting them credit when they were in trouble, and refusing it when she chose. Behind the counter she took pride in cutting the cheese so precisely that it was only a sliver on the right side of short measure. Hating waste, she would scrape off mould and re-pot jam, rather than throw any-thing away. She was impatient with ditherers, or people who didn't have the right change, and she closed the door at five o'clock precisely every day (one o'clock on

Thursdays), even if she could see a customer running to buy something at the last minute.

Managing the shop was hard, and Sidney was less and less useful. His illness recurred, and his self-disgust at his failure to provide for his family made him too weak to fight it. Maude moved from martyrdom to bitterness. Sometimes she would lash out at Sid, and the children would pretend not hear, but most of the time her exasperation was expressed in sulky silence. The mood became so ingrained that she lost the knack of encouraging Eric and Margaret. No matter how hard they tried, they could never impress her.

Margaret skipped into the shop with some good news. 'I've won a book, Mum. You and Daddy are going to be invited to prize day at the end of term.'

'What do they want to go giving you a prize for?' said Maude. 'Do they think I've got all the time in the world to go traipsing up to a ceremony? Who'll look after the shop? I'll lose trade, and I'll have to shell out for a hat. And you know your dad can't go. He's taken to his bed again.'

Maude went off to shift boxes in the stock room, and Margaret slipped up to her parents' bedroom and stroked her father's thinning hair. He spoke softly.

'I heard what you said. About the prize. Well done. Don't take your mother to heart. She doesn't mean to be sour. Life's been hard on her.'

He was thinking of how, since the war, Maude's pretty face had sharpened and settled into a scowl that drew her lip up towards her pointed nose. Her hair was always scraped back into a tight bun for reasons of

157

hygiene, showing the bony outline of her skull. She was exhausted.

'We must make allowances,' said Sid. 'Try to understand her.'

But Margaret didn't understand. She was growing to hate her mother. At school the other girls called Maude 'the witch', and laughed about her funny ways. Worst of all, they thought Margaret was the same. No one would sit with her in the playground. When she walked into the classroom, intimate conversations stopped, and children held their noses and giggled. She had never told her father about that silent bullying, and was toying with the idea of telling him there, in the disinfected bedroom, when he interrupted her thoughts.

'Your mother was beautiful, you know, before the war,' he said, staring into his daughter's face. 'You're so like her.'

Margaret was horrified. The image of herself turning into a younger version of the harpy downstairs stayed with her from then on and she resolved to get away from Maude as soon as she could.

And now there was talk of another war. Day after day the newspapers and the radio spoke of the threat from Hitler's Germany. It made her father sicker. It made her mother worry about stock and suppliers, though, deep down, Maude felt a glimmer of excitement at the prospect of controlling the village's rations.

Eric came home from his job as an apprentice mechanic full of romantic talk about enlisting. 'I could join a local regiment, or the navy, or perhaps they might even take me in the RAF.'

'Imagine it,' said Margaret. 'You lucky thing. Flying planes – I wish they'd let girls do it.'

'Well, you're not going,' said Maude. 'I need you here.'

'How can you be so selfish when the whole country is threatened?' said Eric.

Sidney intervened. 'She's not just thinking about herself. She's thinking of what happened to me, and so many of our friends.' And, at last, Sidney found a voice for his despair about the waste of life in the last war.

'There's no glory in it. It's not fun. I've seen people blown to pieces, and I've killed men who were little more than children.'

But his son would not believe his accounts of mud, blood and pointless sacrifice. 'If it was so bad, why have you waited till now to talk about it?'

'That's *why* I didn't talk. I couldn't. I can't really do it now. It was so terrible.'

'You're just ashamed because you didn't really fight. Got out on a sick note!'

For the first time, it was out in the open. Sidney slumped back on to his pillows, too devastated to reply. Almost letting himself share his son's contempt. Wishing he had met a more glorious end.

Sidney and Maude were suddenly united in their passion to resist the jingoism of the newspapers. They both hoped for a diplomatic solution to German expansionism. They applauded Mr Chamberlain when he seemed to have achieved a last-minute deal with Hitler, but every night their children came home (Margaret from school, Eric from the garage) full of war talk and national pride. Sidney struggled to get out of bed once a day to eat with his family. But the meal, which for him was no more than some thin soup, always ended in slammed doors and shouting. He grew weaker, too weak to be moved to hospital, and early in 1939 he died, another victim of the Great War.

But the village didn't turn out for the funeral in the way it had for others twenty years before. They didn't rally round his family with stew, cakes and kind words. If he was spoken of at all it was as the henpecked husband with the stuck-up wife at the shop, who was rumoured to be keeping the best food behind the counter for herself.

Eric left to fight, but was reported missing in action. His loss made Maude even more unbearable to live with, and Margaret was gone within a year: away from school at the earliest opportunity, and helping out at an aero-drome, trying to live like an adult, though she was still really a child. She thought she had rebelled against her mother's attitudes, and yet Maude had left her mark and the cruel effect of the first conflict rattled down through the generations.

In 1946, Margaret chose an injured man for a hus-band, and found herself caring in her turn. She didn't mean to, but somehow she gave her own child, Susan, the message that bodies were shameful, that what went on in the bathroom should never be spoken of, and that doctors were to be avoided and distrusted. As time went on, and the medics discovered the dangers of smoking, Margaret said it was a plot to control the population by taking away harmless pleasures. She and her husband puffed on, and went to early graves. They didn't see

Susan reach adulthood in a time of prosperity and peace, or their grandchildren growing up in a new century, clouded once again by war and terror.

Those boys and girls barely knew Sidney's name, even though they had all inherited his deep brown eyes. Their mother, Susan, was everything Maude might have been: friendly and cheerful. But, without knowing it, she found herself replaying some of her grandmother's behaviour. The twenty-first century children wondered why lavatorial humour wasn't appreciated in their household, why toilet paper was smuggled back from the supermarket like some sort of contraband and why Susan tried every lunatic remedy at home before taking them to the doctor when they were ill.

Susan lay in bed night after night wondering if she should swallow her pride and face the shame of having the lump in her breast checked out. She could never explain, even to herself, why she feared doctors so. When she did go, it was too late, and soon Sidney and Maude's great-grandchildren were on their own.

It didn't say so on her death certificate in 2005, but Susan was another casualty of the First World War. That little microbe in the water bottle had set off a chain of events that had blighted lives and caused her death as surely as a bayonet or a shell. But nobody knew. After all, Sidney had been one of the lucky ones. It was a bit of an embarrassment, really. He hadn't had a story to tell. There was no family legend to pass down the generations. Lucky Sidney had come came back from the Great War uninjured. Not a scratch.

George Layton

Readers who are acquainted with my books *The Fib and Other Stories* and *The Swap and Other Stories* will know that they centre on a young boy growing up in a northern industrial town in the 1950s. Though works of fiction, the catalyst for each story is some distant memory tapped from my own childhood.

When Michael Morpurgo asked me to contribute to this anthology of war stories I went back to my earliest memories and they were all post-war: food rationing, cod liver oil, the radio comedy *ITMA* (*It's That Man Again*) and its star Tommy Handley, a time of austerity and hardship when a banana or an orange was a rare treat. More seriously: a time of diphtheria, rickets, infantile paralysis, doctors' bills and malnutrition.

This is a story of post-war Britain which tells how life and lives were affected immediately after the Second World War. As with all my stories, the conflict is in the boy's head. A self-proclaimed coward, he struggles with his demons as he grows up in a world he finds impossible to understand.

Some things never change.

THE PROMISE

'This is the BBC Light Programme.'

'Come on, Doreen, it's on!'

It's the same every Thursday night. We have to get our tea finished, clear the table, get the pots washed and put away so we can all sit round the wireless and enjoy *ITMA*.

'Doreen! She does it every time, goes out to the lavatory just as it's starting.'

Except I don't enjoy it. I can't understand it. I don't know what they're talking about.

'Tell her to hurry up, will you, love.'

I went out the back to call my Auntie Doreen but she was already coming up the path pulling on her black skirt. She'd come straight from work.

'He's not on yet, is he?'

He was. I could hear the audience on the wireless cheering and clapping the man who'd just shouted, '*It's that man again!*'

'Just startin', I think.'

She ran past me into the house.

'Freda, why didn't you call me?'

'I did.'

I can't understand what they get so excited about. They all come out with these stupid things like, '*I don't mind if I do,*' '*Can I do you now, sir?*' '*Tee tee eff enn.*' What's funny about that? Don't mean a thing to me.

'What's funny about that, Mum? "*Tee tee eff enn*"? It doesn't even mean owt.

'*Ta Ta For Now!*'

'*Ta Ta For Now!*'

They both sang it at me, laughing like anything.

'It's a catchphrase. Now shush!'

What's a catchphrase? Why's it funny? Who is Tommy Handley anyway?

'What's a catchphrase, Mum? Why's it funny?'

'I'll tell you when it's finished.'

They waved at me to be quiet.

'Turn it up, Doreen.'

My Auntie Doreen twiddled with the knob on the wireless. Oh, there he goes again: '*I don't mind if I do*', and they both laughed even louder this time and my mum started taking him off.

'*I don't mind if I do . . . !*'

My Auntie Doreen had to take out her hanky to wipe away the tears that were rolling down her cheeks.

'Oh, stop it, Freda, you're makin' me wet myself . . .'

What's he on about now, this Tommy Handley bloke? '*Colonel Chinstrap, you're an absolute nitwit!*' and my mum and my Auntie Doreen fell about laughing.

Nitwit. That's what Reverend Dutton called me and Norbert the other day when we ran into him in the corridor. 'You are a pair of clumsy nitwits, you two.'

Thank goodness his cup of tea wasn't too hot, it could have scalded him. If it'd been Melrose we'd run in to it would have been more than nitwits, more like the cane from the headmaster . . . Ooh no, the note! I'd forgotten all about it. I went out into the hall to get it from my coat pocket. We'd been given it at school for our parents. I was meant to give to my mum when I got home. I went back into the kitchen. They were sitting there giggling away at Tommy Handley.

'Eeh, he's a tonic isn't he, Doreen?'

The audience on the wireless were cheering and laughing.

'I've got nits.'

I handed my mum the note. She grabbed it. She wasn't giggling now.

'What do you mean, you've got nits? Who said?'

'Nit-nurse. She came to our school today.'

Next thing she was up on her feet and going through my hair.

'Oh my God, look at this, Doreen, he's riddled!'

'*Can I do you now, sir?*' the lady on the radio was asking Tommy Handley but my mum wasn't listening; she was halfway to the front door, putting on her coat.

'Get the kettle on, Doreen. I'm going down the chemist to get some stuff.'

'At this time of night? He'll be long closed.'

'Well, he'll have to open up then, won't he? It's an emergency. He can't go to bed with nits.'

She'd come back with two lots of 'stuff'. Special nit shampoo and special nit lotion.

'One and nine this lot cost! Come on, get that shirt off.'

She'd sat me at the kitchen sink while my Auntie Doreen had got the saucepans of hot water ready. Nit shampoo smells horrible, like carbolic soap only worse.

'Doreen, put another kettle on, will you. It says you have to do it twice.'

Another shampoo and then the special lotion. I'd had to sit there with it on for ages while my mum had kept going on about missing Tommy Handley.

'It's not his fault, Freda. He can't help getting nits.'

Then it had started to sting, the nit lotion.

'No, he's most likely caught them off that Norbert Lightowler. They're a grubby lot, that family.'

It had got worse, my head was burning.

'I don't like this, Mum. It's burning me.'

'Good, that means it's working . . .'

'Ow! Ooh! Mum, stop, please, you're hurting me . . .'

The nit lotion was bad but this was worse. She was pulling this little steel comb through my hair and it hurt like anything.

'Please, Mum, I don't like it . . . please . . .'

If I hadn't made her miss Tommy Handley I think she might have been a bit more gentle.

'You couldn't have given me that note as soon as you got back from school, could you? No, you had to wait till *ITMA* was on, didn't you?'

I don't know if it was the smelly nit shampoo or the stinging nit lotion or my mum dragging the metal comb through my hair, but I didn't feel very well.

'You know how much your Auntie Doreen and me look forward to it.'

I started to feel a bit dizzy.

'He's the bright spot in the week for me. I don't reckon we'd have got through this war without Tommy Handley, eh, Doreen? Him and Mr Churchill.'

'And Vera Lynn.'

'Oh yes, and Vera Lynn.'

It was getting worse. The room was going round now. Everything was spinning. What was happening? I don't feel well. I wish my mum would stop pulling that comb through my hair, she's hurting me. I feel funny. What are they doing now? They're singing. Why are they singing? Why are my mum and my Auntie Doreen singing?

'We'll meet again, don't know whe-ere, don't know whe-en . . .'
'We'll meet again, don't know whe-ere, don't know whe-en . . .'

Their voices seem miles away.

'But I kno-oo we'll meet agai-in . . .'
'But I kno-oo we'll meet agai-in . . .'

I'm fainting – that's what it is. I'm fainting. Now I know what it feels like. When Keith Hopwood had fainted in the playground I'd asked him what it had felt like and he'd said he couldn't remember much except that everything had been going round and round and everybody's voices seemed to be a long way away. That's what's happening to me. Mum! Auntie Doreen! I can see them and they're going round and round. I'm fainting! I can hear them, they're singing and they're miles away. I'm fainting!

'Some sunny . . .'
'Some sunny . . .'

I was lying on the sofa and and my mum was dabbing my face with a damp tea towel, muttering to herself.

'Come on, Doreen, where've you got to? Hurry up, hurry up.'

My hair was still wet with the nit lotion but she'd stopped combing it, thank goodness.

'What happened? What's going on?'

'You passed out, love, you scared the life out of me. Your Auntie Doreen's gone to fetch Dr Jowett.'

The one good thing about fainting is that everybody makes a fuss of you. After Keith had passed out the care-taker had carried him to the staffroom and while they'd waited for the doctor Mrs Jolliffe had given him a cup of sweet tea and some chocolate digestives. With me it was a mug of Ovaltine and a Blue Riband on the sofa while we waited for Dr Jowett.

'Have you any more Blue Ribands, Mum?'

'I haven't, love. And I won't be getting any more till I get my new ration book.'

Why does all the good stuff have to be on rationing? I bet nit shampoo and nit lotion's not on rationing.

'Will I be going to school tomorrer?'

That'd be great if I could get off school, worth faint-ing for. Double maths on a Friday, I hate maths. And scripture with Reverend Dutton. Borin'.

'Let's wait and see what Dr Jowett says.'

And Latin with Bleasdale. Then we have English with Melrose. Worst day of the week, Friday. English with

Melrose! Oh no! I haven't done his homework! I was going to do it after *ITMA*, wasn't I?

'I don't think I should, Mum. I might faint again. You never know.'

'We'll leave it to Dr Jowett, eh?'

'Breathe in. Out. In again.'

It wasn't Dr Jowett; it was a lady doctor who was standing in for him cos he was at a conference or something. I'd heard my Auntie Doreen tell me mum after she'd gone to get something from her car.

'Out. In. Cough.'

I breathed out and I breathed in and I coughed like she told me. The thing she was using to listen to my chest was freezing cold and it made me laugh.

'It's a relief to see him smiling, doctor. He looked as white as a sheet twenty minutes ago.'

The lady doctor wrote something on a brown card.

'Can I stay off school tomorrer?'

She carried on writing.

'I don't see why—'

Oh great. No maths, no Latin, no scripture, no Melrose . . .

'—you shouldn't go.'

What? No, no. 'I don't see why *not*.' That's what I thought you were going to say. That's what you're supposed to say.

'But I haven't done my English homework cos of all this.'

'I'll give your mother a note to give to your teacher.'

She smiled at me and gave me a friendly pat on my head. My hair was still sticky.

171

'I've got nits.'

My mum gave me one of her looks.

'Outbreak at school, doctor. You know what it's like.'

'Of course.'

'Maybe that's what made him faint. It's strong stuff, that lotion.'

She shone a light in my eyes.

'Unlikely.'

She looked down my throat and in my ears. After that she put a strap round my arm and pumped on this rubber thing. It didn't hurt, just felt a bit funny. She wrote on the brown card again.

'He's small for his age.'

'Always has been, doctor.'

'But he's particularly small. And he's anaemic. I'd say he's undernourished.'

I didn't know what she was talking about but my mum didn't like it. She sat up straight and folded her arms and the red blotch started coming up on her neck. She always gets it when she's upset.

'There's only so many coupons in a ration book, doctor. I do my best. It's weeks since this house has seen fresh fruit and vegetables. He gets his cod liver oil and his orange juice and his Virol. I do what I can. That nit stuff cost one and nine. It's not easy on your own, you know.'

The doctor wrote on the brown card again.

'Excuse me, I'm just going to get something from the car.'

My mum watched her go. The blotch on her neck was getting redder.

'Who's she? Where's Dr Jowett?'

172

'She's standing in for him while he's at a conference. She's very nice. Came straight away.'

'Very nice? I don't think it's very nice to be told I'm neglecting my own son. I'll give her undernourished!'

'Give over, Freda, she said nothing of the sort. Don't be so bloody soft, we've just had a war. We're all under-nourished with this bloody rationing!'

I don't know who was more shocked, me or my mum. You never hear my Auntie Doreen swear. You'd have thought it was my fault the way my mum turned on me.

'And why did you have to tell her you've got nits? Showing me up like that.'

My Auntie Doreen was just about to have another go when we heard the lady doctor coming back.

'I was going to write a prescription for a course of iron tablets but I remembered I'd got some in the car.'

She gave my mum a brown bottle.

'I don't mind paying, doctor.'

The doctor didn't say anything, just smiled.

'Now, I'll tell you what he really needs – a couple of weeks by the sea.'

My mum looked at her, then burst out laughing.

'A couple of weeks by the sea! Yes, that's what we all need, eh, Doreen?'

The lady doctor put everything back in her black bag.

'It can be arranged. And it won't cost a penny. I'll talk to Dr Jowett.'

I looked at my mum and my Auntie Doreen.

'He'll probably have to have to take time off school, but it would do him the world of good.'

A couple of weeks by the sea! Free! Time off school! Sounded good to me.

DEAR MUM,
I HATE IT HERE. WHY DID DOCTOR JOWETT
AND THAT LADY DOCTOR SEND ME TO THIS
HORRIBLE PLACE? I WANT TO COME HOME.
YOU PROMISED THAT IF I DID NOT LIKE IT
HERE YOU WOULD COME AND FETCH ME. I
DON'T LIKE IT SO FETCH ME WHEN YOU
GET THIS LETTER. MORCAMBE IS ONLY TWO
HOURS AWAY. YOU SAID SO YOURSELF . . .

Yeah, it sounded good cos I thought she'd meant all of us. Me, my mum and my Auntie Doreen. Nobody'd said I'd be going on my own. I wouldn't have gone, would I? My mum never told me. Dr Jowett never told me. He was in the kitchen talking to her when I got home from school on the Friday.

'Talk of the devil, here he is. Do you want to tell him the good news, Dr Jowett?'

He had a big smile on his face when he told me. I couldn't believe it. It turned out that because I'm small for me age and all that other stuff the lady doctor had talked to my mum about, we got to go to Morecambe for free. The council paid.

'And my mum doesn't have to pay anything?'

Dr Jowett pulled my bottom lids down and looked in my eyes, like the lady doctor did the night before.

'Not a penny. It's a special scheme paid for by the council to give young folk like yourself a bit of sea air. Build you up. You'll come back six inches taller. Now, do you want to go for two weeks or one?'

Why would I want to go for one week when we could go for two? I looked at my mum.

'It's up to you, love . . .'

If she'd have said, '*It's up to you, love, cos you're the one going not me, I'm not comin', neither's your Auntie Doreen, it's just you on your own,*' I'd never have said it.

'It's up to you, love – do you want to go for two weeks?'

It'd be stupid not to go for two weeks when it's free. So I said it. Just like the man on the wireless.

'I don't mind if I do!'

We all laughed.

DEAR MUM,
PLEASE COME FOR ME. I CAN'T STAY HERE.
I HATE IT. YOU PROMISED YOU WOULD
FETCH ME IF I DIDN'T LIKE IT . . .

After Dr Jowett had gone we sat at the kitchen table and looked at the leaflet he'd left for us. It looked lovely. I listened while my mum read it out.

'"*Craig House – a home from home. Overlooking Morecambe Bay, Craig House gives poor children the opportunity to get away from the grime of the city to the fresh air of the seaside . . .*" Sounds lovely, doesn't it?'

'Yeah. What does that bit mean?'

'What bit?'

'That bit about poor children. Do you have to be poor to go there?'

She looked at me.

'Well, it is for people what can't afford it, like us. That's why we're getting it for free.'

'Oh . . .'

We both looked at the leaflet again.

'There's nothing wrong with it, love. It's our right. Dr Jowett says. I mean, it'd be daft to give free holidays to them that can pay for it.'

Yeah, that was true.

'I suppose so.'

MUM, WHY HAVEN'T YOU COLLECTED ME FROM HERE? YOU PROMISED. YOU SAID IF I WAS UNHAPPY YOU WOULD TAKE ME HOME. PLEASE COME AS SOON AS YOU GET THIS. PLEASE . . .

It just never crossed my mind that I was going on my own. I had no idea. It wasn't till the Sunday night, when my mum was packing my suitcase, that I found out.

'Now, I've put you two swimming costumes in so when one's wet you can wear the other, and you've plenty of underpants and vests . . .'

Even then it didn't dawn on me. I'd felt good having my own suitcase, grown up. When we'd gone to Bridlington she packed all our things together but we'd only gone for two days. This time we were going for two weeks. I thought that's why she was giving me my own suitcase.

'. . . and I'm putting in a few sweets for you, some Nuttall's Mintoes, some fruit pastilles and a bar of chocolate. You can thank your Auntie Doreen for them, she saved up her coupons.'

I still didn't realize.

'Well, we can share them, can't we?'

'No, these are all for you.'

I thought she was just being nice, getting in the holiday mood.

'Now, this is important. I'm giving you these to take –' she held up some envelopes – 'they're all stamped and addressed so you can write to me every day if you like . . .'

You what? What are you talking about? What is she talking about?

'You don't have to write every day, I'm only joking, but I would like to get the occasional letter. They're here, under your pants.'

What was she talking about? When it all came out that I'd thought they were coming with me, she'd looked at me like I'd gone off my head.

'But why? What on earth made you think me and your Auntie Doreen were coming?'

'Cos you said.'

'I never. I never said we were all going.'

She was lying. She did.

'You did. When the lady doctor said I needed a holiday, you told her that's what we *all* needed, a couple of weeks by the sea. You ask Auntie Doreen.'

I'd cried and told her that I wasn't going to go and she said I had to, it'd all been arranged, I'd show her up in front of Dr Jowett if I didn't go. And it wouldn't be fair if I didn't go, it would be a wasted space that some other child could have used.

'It's not fair on me, cos if I'd known I wouldn't have said I'd go for two weeks. I wouldn't have gone for *one* week. I'm not goin', I don't want to go. Please don't make me go . . .'

I cried, I begged, I shut myself in my bedroom. I wasn't going to go, I wasn't.

'I'm not goin'. You can't force me.'

She couldn't force me.

'Listen, love, if you don't like it, if you're really unhappy, I'll get straight on the train and bring you home.'

'Promise?'

'It's less than two hours away.'

'Promise?'

'Course.'

'Promise!'

'I promise.'

My mum let me sleep in her bed that night cos I couldn't stop crying.

'Come on, love, go to sleep, we've got to be at Great Albert Street at eight o'clock for your coach.'

'You promise to fetch me if I don't like it?'

'But you will like it and it'll do you good.'

'You promise, don't you?'

'As soon as I get your letter.'

And I fell asleep.

> *Craig House holiday home*
> *far far away,*
> *Where us poor children go*
> *for a holiday.*
> *Oh, how we run like hell*
> *when we hear the dinner bell,*
> *far far away.*

OEAR MUM,
I HATE IT HERE. WHY OIO OOCTOR JOWETT
ANO THAT LAOY OOCTOR SENO ME TO THIS
HORRIBLE PLACE? I WANT TO COME HOME.
YOU PROMISEO THAT IF I OIO NOT LIKE IT
HERE YOU WOULO COME ANO FETCH ME. I
OON'T LIKE IT SO FETCH ME WHEN YOU
GET THIS LETTER. MORCAMBE IS ONLY TWO
HOURS AWAY. YOU SAIO SO YOURSELF . . .

That was the first letter.

OEAR MUM,
PLEASE COME FOR ME. I CAN'T STAY HERE.
I HATE IT. YOU PROMISEO YOU WOULO
FETCH ME IF I OIONT LIKE IT . . .

That was the second letter.

MUM, WHY HAVEN'T YOU COME . . .?

Why hadn't she come for me? She'd promised . . .

THIS IS THE THIRO TIME I'VE WRITTEN . . .

We'd been told we had to be outside the medical clinic
in Great Albert Street at eight o'clock for the coach. We
were going to be weighed before we went and they'd
weigh us when we got back to see how much we'd put
on. My Auntie Doreen came with us, and even on the
bus to town I made them both promise again. We turned

into Great Albert Street at five to and I could see lots of kids waiting on the pavement with their mums and dads and grandmas and grandads. There was no coach. Good, maybe it had broken down and I wouldn't have to go. My mum carried my suitcase and we walked up the road towards them. A big cheer went up as the coach came round the corner at the top end of the street.

When we got closer I saw that some of the kids looked funny. One lad had no hair, another was bandy. There was a girl with these iron things on her legs. My mum gave me a sharp tap cos I was staring at the bald lad.

'What's wrong with him, Mum?'

'Alopecia, most likely.'

'What's that?'

'It's when your hair drops out. Poor lad.'

'Do you get it from nits?'

'Don't be daft.'

My Auntie Doreen told me it can be caused by stress or shock.

'Do you remember that teacher we had at primary, Freda, Mrs Theobold? She lost all her hair when her husband got knocked down by a tram.'

My mum shook her head.

'Oh, you do. She had to wear a wig.'

'I don't.'

We stood outside the medical clinic next to a woman with a ginger-headed lad. His face looked ever so sore, all flaky and red. My mum gave me another sharp tap. The woman got a packet of Woodbines out of her handbag.

'Oh, don't worry, missus, he's used to young 'uns staring, aren't you, Eric?'

Eric nodded while she lit a cigarette.

'Eczema. Not infectious, love. Had it all his life, haven't you, Eric?'

He nodded again. My Auntie Doreen smiled at him.

'Two weeks in Morecambe'll be just what he needs, eh?'

The woman coughed as she blew the smoke out.

'Don't know about him but it'll do me a power of good. I need a break, I can tell you.'

Just then a man came out of the clinic and shouted that we all had to go inside to be weighed.

'Parents, foster parents and guardians – wait out here while the luggage is put on the charabanc. The children will return as soon as they've been weighed and measured.'

Eric's mum took another puff on her cigarette.

'I don't know why they bother. Last year he came back weighing less than when he went, didn't you, Eric?' Eric nodded again. 'And I swear he was half an inch shorter. Off you go then.'

I followed him into the clinic, where the man was telling everybody to go up the main stairs and turn left.

'Have you been before then, to Craig House?'

He'd been for the last two years.

'What's it like?'

'S'all right. Better than being at home.'

At the top of the stairs we followed the ones in front into a big room where we were told to take our clothes off. We had to strip down to our vests and pants and sit on a stool until we heard our name called out. There were four weighing scales, with a number above each one. I sat next to Eric. He didn't have a vest on and his pants had holes in them and whatever his mum had said he had, he had it all over, he looked horrible. I couldn't help staring. He didn't seem bothered, though. He just sat there, scratching, staring at the floor.

'Eric Braithwaite, weighing scale three! Eric Braithwaite, weighing scale three!'

He didn't say anything, just wandered off to be weighed and measured. I sat waiting for my name to be called out. The girl with iron things on her legs was on the other side of the room. Her mum and dad had been allowed to come in and were taking the iron things off and helping her get undressed.

'Margaret Donoghue, weighing scale one! Margaret Donoghue, weighing scale one!'

That was her. Her dad had to carry her, she couldn't walk without her iron things. Eric came back, put his clothes back on and wandered off. He didn't speak, didn't say a word. They were going in alphabetical order so I had to wait quite a long time before I heard my name. When I did I had to go to weighing scale number four. A lady in a white coat told me to get on.

'There's nothing of you, is there? A couple of weeks at Craig House'll do you no harm.'

She wrote my weight down in a book.

'Now, let's see how small you are.'

Couple of weeks? I wasn't going to be there a couple of weeks. Not if I didn't like it. And I *wasn't* going to like it, I knew that much.

'Right, get dressed and go back to your mum and dad.'

'I haven't got a dad.'

'Ellis Roper! Weighing scale number four! Ellis Roper, weighing scale number four! You what, dear?'

'I haven't got a dad.'

'Well, go back to whoever brought you. Ellis Roper please! Weighing scale number four!'

> *Craig House holiday home*
> *far far away,*
> *Where us poor children go*
> *for a holiday.*
> *Oh, how we run like hell*
> *when we hear the dinner bell,*
> *far far away.*

We were on our way to Morecambe and those that had been before were singing this stupid song. I was in an aisle seat next to the bald lad. He was singing, so I knew it wasn't his first time. I'd wanted to get by the window so I could wave goodbye to my mum and my Auntie Doreen but by the time I'd been weighed and measured I was too late. Eric was next to me on the other side of the aisle. He wasn't singing, just sitting there staring into space. Behind me a girl was crying. She hadn't wanted to go. The driver and the man from the clinic had had to drag her away from her mum and force her on to the coach. Her mum had run off up the street crying, with her dad following. They didn't even wave her off. My mum had had to get her hanky out cos she had tears in her eyes.

'Don't forget to write – your envelopes are in your suitcase under your pants.'

'Course I wouldn't forget. I had it all planned. I was

going to write as soon as I got there and post it straight away. My mum'd get the letter on the Tuesday morning, get on the train like she promised and I'd be home for tomorrow night. That's why I wasn't crying like the girl behind me. I was only going to be away for one day, wasn't I?

I was looking at the bald lad when he turned round. I made out I'd been looking out of the window but I reckon he knew I'd been staring at him.

'I've got alopecia.'

He smiled. He didn't have any eyebrows neither.

'Oh . . .' I didn't know what to say. 'How long have you had it?'

'A few years. I went to bed one night and when I woke up it was lyin' there on my pillow. My hair.'

I felt sick.

'It just fell out?'

'Yeah. It was after my gran got a telegram tellin' her that my dad had been killed at Dunkirk. I live with my gran. My mum died when I was two.'

I told him that I lived with my mum and that my auntie lived two streets away.

'Did *your* dad die in the war?'

'I don't know. Don't think so. I've never known him.'

He was all right, Paul, I quite liked him. He told me it wasn't too bad at Craig House. This was his third year running.

'It's not bad. They've got table tennis and football and they take you on the beach. And you get a cooked breakfast every mornin'. You get a stick of rock when you leave. It's all right.'

Maybe it wouldn't be as bad as I thought. Maybe I'd like it. Maybe I wouldn't want to go home.

DEAR MUM, YOU PROMISED. YOU SAID IF I WAS UNHAPPY YOU WOULD TAKE ME HOME. YOU HAVEN'T COME . . .

'Look – the sea!'

It was one of the big lads at the back who'd started the singing. Everybody leaned over to our side of the coach to get a look. Eric didn't; he just sat there, staring and scratching his face. For some of them, like the girl behind me, it was the first time they'd seen the sea. She was all right now, laughing and giggling and talking away to the girl next to her. The man from the clinic stood up at the front and told us all to sit down.

'We'll be arriving at Craig House in five minutes. Do not leave this coach until I give the word. When you hear your name you will alight the charabanc, retrieve your luggage, which will be on the pavement, and proceed to the home.'

The coach pulled round a corner and there it was. There was a big sign by the entrance:

CRAIG HOUSE

And underneath it said:

Poor Children's Holiday Home

We all stood in the entrance hall holding our suitcases while our names were called out and we were told which dormitory we were in. There was this smell and it was horrible. Like school dinners and hospitals mixed together. It made me feel sick. There were four dormitories, two for the girls and two for the boys. I was in General Montgomery dormitory and I followed my group. We were going up the stairs when I saw it. A post box. I'd been worried if they'd let me out to find a post box and there was one right here in the entrance hall. I could post my letter here in Craig House. It wasn't like a normal post box that you see in the street; it was made of cardboard and painted red and the hole where you put the letters was a smiling mouth.

I wasn't able to write it until late that afternoon.

When we'd been given our bed we were taken to the showers and scrubbed clean by these ladies and had our hair washed with nit shampoo. I tried to tell my lady that my mum had already done it but she didn't want to know.

'Best be safe than sorry, young man.'

Then we were given a Craig House uniform (they'd taken our clothes off to be washed). Shirt, short trousers, jumper. They even gave us pyjamas. And on everything was a ribbon that said 'Poor Children's Holiday Home'. You couldn't take it off, it was sewn on.

At last, after our tea, I'd been able to write my letter. I licked the envelope, made sure it was stuck down properly and ran down the main stairs.

'Walk, lad. Don't run. Nobody runs at Craig House.'

That was the warden. I walked across the entrance hall to the post box and put my letter into the smiling mouth. All I had to do now was wait for my mum to come and fetch me.

MUM, WHY HAVEN'T YOU COME? THIS IS THE
THIRD TIME I'VE WRITTEN. I HATE IT HERE.
THERE ARE TWO LADS THAT BULLY ME.
THEY HAVE TAKEN ALL MY SWEETS . . .

I hated it. I hated it. I couldn't see why Paul thought it was all right. Or Eric. Not that I saw much of them. They were in General Alanbrooke dormitory. I think I was the youngest in General Montgomery. I was the smallest anyway – they were all bigger than me. My bed was between the two who had started the singing at the back of the coach and at night after the matron had switched off the lights they said things to frighten me and they made these scary noises. I thought they might be nicer to me if I gave them each a Nuttall's Mintoe. When they saw all my other sweets in my suitcase they made me hand them all over. I hated them. I dreaded going to bed cos I was so scared. I was too scared to go to sleep. I was too scared to get up and go to the lavatory. Then in the morning I'd find I'd wet the bed and I'd get told off in front of everybody and have to stand out on the balcony as a punishment.

And I hated my mum. She'd broken her promise. You can never trust grown-ups.

DEAR MUM, YOU PROMISED. YOU SAID IF I
WAS UNHAPPY YOU WOULD TAKE ME HOME.
YOU HAVEN'T COME. I AM SO UNHAPPY.
PLEASE FETCH ME AS SOON AS YOU GET
THIS . . .

I licked the envelope and stuck it down like I'd done with all the others. I walked downstairs to the entrance hall and went over to the post box. I was just about to put it in the smiling mouth when I heard Eric.

'What you doing?'

'Sendin' a letter to my mum.'

Eric laughed. Well, it wasn't a laugh, more of a snort.

'It's not a proper post box. They don't post 'em.'

I looked at him.

'They say they post 'em but they don't. They don't want us pestering 'em at home.'

I still had the letter in my hand.

'I won't bother then.'

I tore it up and went back to the dormitory. The second week went quicker and I didn't wet the bed.

'You didn't send one letter, you little monkey.'

My mum wasn't really cross that I hadn't written.

'It shows he had a good time, doesn't it, Doreen? See, I told you you'd like it.'

She was annoyed at how much weight I'd lost.

Robert Westall

The late Robert Westall wrote this autobiographical piece about his time as a National Serviceman in the 1950s. Between taking a first-class degree in Fine Art at Durham University and becoming a postgraduate student at the Slade School, London University, he was called up to do National Service – a compulsory two-year period of conscription which operated from 1947 until 1963. He became a Lance Corporal in the Royal Corps of Signals.

Robert Westall had always been interested in writing; he wrote his first novel at the age of twelve to while away the long summer school holiday. However, it wasn't until 1962, when visiting an art exhibition, that he decided to write about it and sent the piece to a local newspaper. He was taken on as the art critic. He found he enjoyed journalism; it sharpened his style, and after a couple of years he started to write articles about Cheshire villages and buildings, complete with drawings.

Bob's son, Christopher, was born in 1960 and, when

he was twelve, became a member of a gang. Bob decided to write down, in the form of a novel, how life had been for him, also aged twelve, on Tyneside in the Second World War. He wrote in an exercise book, in his spare time from a demanding teaching job, and would read each chapter out loud. If Chris's attention wandered, Bob soon learned to edit his work. *The Machine-Gunners* was published in 1975, and Robert Westall's career as a writer had begun.

Lindy McKinnel

HARD SHIP TO EGYPT

As a writer, I shall always be grateful for my tiny war, because it led me into wickedness. If a writer doesn't understand wickedness from the inside, he's only half a writer, and all his villains will be cardboard cut-outs.

The war happened because the British Empire was still sitting on the Suez Canal, and Colonel Nasser wanted us out. So the Egyptians put in terrorist attacks. A bit like Northern Ireland only simpler, because all white faces were friends and all dark ones enemies, so you knew who to shoot at.

Aboard the troopship going out, we lived in a state of brittle, giggly nervousness that was good soil for wickedness to grow in. We were taught only one new military tactic: a judo-throw to use against an Egyptian coming at you with a knife, from behind. It did not increase our respect for Egyptians as human beings. There were rumours that if the Egyptians managed to knife you, they would cut off your private parts and sew them up in your mouth. Our private parts

191

rapidly assumed more importance than any Egyptian's life.

It didn't feel a tiny war when we docked at Port Said. Egyptian commandos had just blown up an enormous military warehouse, and the huge palls of black smoke hanging across the harbour made it feel as desperate as Dunkirk. There wasn't an Egyptian in sight ashore, but on every street corner were Brits playing with the triggers of their sub-machine guns, looking for an excuse to shoot somebody. It felt like a landscape of OK Corrals.

But the only signs of Egyptian attack in the harbour was a mass of frail rowing boats that nuzzled against our troopship like piglets to a sow, full of melons and oranges and men offering up brand-new Swiss watches at incredible bargain prices. There was an Egyptian policeman every ten yards along the ship's rail, clad in white with a red fez, and a rifle over his shoulder. Yet suddenly, incredibly, there was one of the bum-boat men among us, offering a genuine Swiss watch to my mate in exchange for his old English one. What happened next was too quick for the human eye. Suddenly, my mate's watch was on the bum-boat man's wrist and, equally suddenly, the bum-boat man had been felled to the deck by a blow of the Egyptian policeman's rifle. He lay there unconscious, blood trickling from his nose. The policeman took the watch off his wrist and gave it back to my mate, then stooped and picked him up and threw him overboard. We watched him sink; we watched him come up in a froth of bubbles and be hauled aboard a bumboat, still unconscious.

We landed under the swinging muzzles of other Brits'

Sten sub-machine guns. We'd been trained to use the Sten, a cheap weapon that looked as if a blacksmith had made it out of spare gas-pipe – famous for not firing when you wanted it to and suddenly firing when you didn't want it to. They'd missed out any safety catch, on the grounds of economy, and we felt as much in danger from trigger-happy Brits as from Egyptians, as we straggled up the quay with a heavy kitbag on each shoulder, unable to hear a thing and only able to see directly ahead, like animals being led to the slaughter. The sergeant in charge of us said the blown-up warehouse had contained only toilet rolls. He got that quick, brittle giggle.

It was better travelling down the canal by lorry, clinging to the back of the cab with the hot, dry desert wind streaming through our hair. Across the flat desert, wavering through the heat haze, appeared a long line of enormous brightly painted factories. Then we realized they were moving towards us – ships on the canal that didn't look half big enough to hold them, only a wretched little ditch, certainly not worth losing your private parts for.

The little mud-built towns were full of open-fronted cafes packed with Egyptian men sitting drinking. Until they saw us. Then every man was on his feet, screaming abuse, shaking fists, trying to spit as far as the lorries. A strange new unreal feeling – being hated not for what you'd done, not even for what you were, but for the uniform you'd been forced to wear.

But we were quite safe. From the lorry in front and the lorry behind, the Sten guns swung idly towards them, not even menacingly, but chidingly, like a teacher's finger. The Egyptians sat down, very suddenly. Only we, in the middle lorry, felt naked without guns.

Between towns, in a broken landscape of wadis and scrub, the tiny convoy stopped. The old hands in the other lorries jumped down quickly and began relieving themselves against the lorry wheels. We, in the middle truck, a little shocked, were a little slow to follow their example. So we were still peeing when the old hands jumped back into their trucks and roared away, shouting to our driver, 'Catch up!'

A deep silence descended, as our last trickle dried up; only the endless chirring of Egyptian insects. We scrambled back aboard quickly, glancing nervously round the empty landscape. Our driver pressed the self-starter. It whined out again and again, fruitlessly, into the deepening silence. We waited, gunless, remembering the burning warehouse and the hate of the towns. Then someone turned to the little bespectacled padre who had got down from the truck cab democratically, to pee with us. Pointed to his holstered revolver, the only gun we had.

'We'll stick close to you, sir, you'll see us right.'

The padre blinked and stammered, 'I don't know how to use it; I only wear it because they make me. I've never fired it in my life!'

'Better let me hold it, sir,' said the sergeant grimly.

'Actually, it's not loaded; I don't carry any ammunition. As a man of God it's against my conscience.'

We cursed his conscience and his God and huddled closer together, fingering our private parts inside our pockets, to reassure ourselves.

It seemed a long time before the other trucks came back for us.

Once we got Stens, we felt better. Carried them every-where, hung on our shoulders like a woman's handbag.

We lived in a camp, alone in the middle of a desert. A camp made of coils of barbed wire, full of tents without walls for coolness, that billowed with sharp cracks in the desert wind, like the sails of a whole sun-bleached fleet. No foxholes, no sandbags, no cover. A sandy billiard table. At night there were perimeter lights. But they didn't shine outwards into the darkness of the desert where anyone with a morsel of sense would've placed them. No, they shone directly down on the long path between two coils of barbed wire, where our sentries had to walk. You walked up and down, up and down, gift-wrapped in brilliant light for the first sniper who came crawling across the darkness of the desert. You had nowhere to run to, like a canary in a cage waiting for the cat to come. Two hours at a time, alone. With your eyes blinded, you learned to use your ears.

One night the world was filled with a stealthy rustling I couldn't place. I spun round and round like a dancing dervish, totally out of control, with my finger tightening and tightening on the trigger. Thank God I saw it in time: a tiny rag of desert-bleached Egyptian newspaper, snagged on the barbed wire. Another night the wire kept twanging softly, sporadically, and in the end I found two locusts mating on it, big as mice and green as the grass I'd left back home in England. Appalled, I listened to my own brittle giggle, glad there was no one to hear me within a hundred yards.

Every day was the same. We worked until noon, then lay naked on our beds while the sun flattened us. The walk to the tap was fifty yards and felt like climbing

195

Mount Everest – passing through a landscape of beds and naked, still, white bodies, while the nude pin-ups of girls that covered every locker leered and flapped at me in the furnace wind. Too hot to read, too hot to think.

One afternoon, I accidently crushed a huge scarab beetle with my foot, getting on my bed. Within seconds, a tiny file of ants emerged from a hole in the concrete floor. They entered the crushed armour of the beetle, as if it was a crashed car and carried out the wet, white contents, piece by piece, holding them above their heads. Then they dismantled its armour, piece by piece, bearing away legs bigger than themselves. Then, finally, five of them together carried off the crushed carapace. Waste not, want not. The ants rule here. They'd do the same to me, if I was dead.

As the sun got hotter, the tension in the regiment grew worse and worse. Worst of all was meal times. If the meal was one minute late, someone would start drumming on the table with his knife and fork. In a few seconds there'd be three or four hundred of us at it. You couldn't stop yourself.

People went mad. One bloke cut up his army boots for sandals and then wandered round the huge sand parade ground in the hottest part of the afternoon, challenging the sergeant major to come out and fight him. The officers gathered nervously at the edge and tried to reason with him as he walked round and round in circles, aimless as a rabid dog, a scarecrow figure in the shimmering heat haze. In the end, his mates had to go and catch him like a dog, and hold him down on the hot steel bed of a lorry, taking him to hospital. He whined and shivered like a frightened dog. We lay on top of him and wrapped our arms around him, stroking and talking to him as if he was a dog. It seemed to comfort him; I can feel his body trembling against mine to this day, and the fond animal sadness of my own body.

Anything to get out of the sun-drenched birdcage. Even the SDS run. The SDS was an open thirty-hundredweight truck that carried the mail. The Egyptian terrorists had a taste for them. So the truck carried front and rear gunners, with Stens. The front gunner, privileged, sat beside the driver. The rear gunner got thrown round the steel bed of the truck, trying to cushion his bones with the mail bags and praying his Sten wouldn't go off by accident.

At least it was a change of landscape. We saw many things and all steadily fed our contempt for the Egyptians. Their taxis, without headlights or windscreens, polished down to the bare silvery metal by sandstorms, with ten guys crushed inside, and ten more standing on the bumpers, the bonnet, the boot, bumping low and springless across the desert. The apartment blocks of the little towns, graceful concrete at ground level, but getting poorer and poorer in construction as they went higher, so the top floor was only a wretched agglomeration of sticks, corrugated iron and sacking. The refuse trucks that scavenged our camps, with figures sitting on top already sorting the rubbish while the truck was still in motion, figures so black and greasy that the rags that clad them seemed only black and greasy ridges on their skin.

It was very easy to believe we were the master race. We were really shocked to be offered fruit off a barrow covered with flies when we realized that in the middle of the fruit, equally covered with flies, lay a naked, writhing baby with sores round its eyes and mouth. Equally shocked when little boys of five and six ran alongside us in their blue-striped nightshirts, offering their sister: virgin schoolteacher, very clean. We pushed them off the side of the lorry with our feet and laughed like wolves when they went sprawling in the road.

Wolves with trucks and guns and that brittle giggle that made nothing in the world matter; everything was some kind of joke. Like when we stopped the huge, blue melon lorries by slewing our truck across the road in some narrow place. The filthy figures sitting on top of the melons would begin to wail and plead. We just pointed our Stens at them, cocking the cocking handles with loud expressive clicks. Then, still wailing and pleading, they would start to throw melons down on to the road, from the mountain of melons they were sitting on. When they'd thrown down enough, ten, twenty, we'd pull over and let them go sobbing past. We needed so many melons because some had burst upon hitting the road. But we'd pick up the ones that hadn't and go on our squishy rejoicing way, Stens in one hand and a half-melon in the other, until our faces and hands and triggers were thick and sticky with dried juice.

Whose melons? Whose melons did we squash deeper into the dust of the road on our return run? What the hell?

Then came the day we nearly massacred a whole village. I was rear gunner. Neither the driver nor I fancied the look of the front gunner, an Ulsterman, foul mouthed to the point of incoherence, with a bad case of Canal Zone twitch. He couldn't stop playing with his

Sten; it made your flesh creep. But he'd been put down for the duty, so off we went.

On the way home we drove into this village. We were always twitchy going through villages, with their narrow winding streets and close-clustered houses. Ambush territory.

At the crossroads of this one, we ran into a massive flock of sheep and goats that blocked every exit. We were marooned in a sea of goats. Two old men in night-shirts seemed to be in charge, helped by several small boys. When they saw us, they panicked, and panicked the flock until there were goats on the bonnet and sheep trying to get in the lorry with us.

It was a classic ambush ploy. Stuck there: a burst of fire, a hand grenade or even men with knives could have taken us without effort. I backed up against the cab, swinging the Sten wildly in all directions. Rooftops, dark windows, alleys, I couldn't cover them all at once. Wherever I pointed the gun I could still be shot in the back. I began that crazy dervish dance again, round and round, my boot-nails slipping and sliding on the steel bed of the lorry, the mailbags tangling round my feet, threatening to trip me up. Worse, I could hear the front gunner screaming, '*Imshi! Imshi!*' The only word of Egyptian he knew, probably. 'Quickly! Quickly! Hurry up! Hurry up!' Sheep, goats, old men and boys milled round wildly. A bleating sheep leaped over the tailgate and cannoned into me. Black-clad women began running from the houses screaming, trying to wade through the flock to reach their children. The mass of panic that enclosed us soared higher and higher. The front gunner's voice rose to a scream. '*IMSHI! IIIIMSHIIII!*'

Then I heard him cock his gun. I took a quick glance round. He was swinging it from side to side like the lead hose it was. Then he aimed at a woman and pulled the trigger.

Click! The good old Sten had run true to form. Jammed on a dud cartridge. Click again, and click again. He went on cocking and firing, as the dud bullets fell from the gun, scattering and tinkling in all directions. And all the time he was aiming and firing at real people. And he was screaming and crying, the dribble running down his face.

He went on until everyone had vanished from sight, until the sheep and goats had run away down side alleys, leaving us in total empty silence. Then the driver put the stalled truck into gear and we got out of there. We pulled up at the first empty quiet piece of desert. The front gunner was still raving on and on, about the way the army had sent him into danger with a dud gun. He went on until the driver hit him. It was a long time before the driver stopped hitting him. Then we threw him in the back of the truck and drove home, ignoring him.

It caused quite a stir back in camp, among the ordinary squaddies. Most of them agreed with the Ulsterman: he shouldn't have been sent out with a defective gun. What frightened me was that I'd seen him do it, and made no attempt to stop him. Watched him cock and fire at women and children, not once but many times.

I never went on SDS again. Soon after, the British government and Colonel Nasser signed a bit of paper, and the Egyptians suddenly loved us and only wanted to sell us brass camels and leather holdalls and their virgin sisters. We even had a trip round the pyramids, and soon after that we came home.

But Egypt made it possible for me to write about many things. Fear and heat; boredom and death; empire and the corruption that empire always brings; official stupidity and the fact that you have to train yourself to despise a people before you can kill them; madness and compassion. How can you begin to write about such things unless you've felt them in your bones? But if you have only a little of them, a spark, a true writer can fan a spark into a whole conflagration. In the heat and boredom, I did not go mad. I began to write: a story of what would have happened if the Egyptians had mounted one machine-gun just beyond our wire, out in the darkness of the desert, and massacred the lot of us. It was, believe me, a very vivid chapter of a book that never otherwise got written.

Jamila Gavin

Years ago, I picked up a book in an oriental bookshop called *Twenty Jataka Tales*, retold by Noor
Inayat Khan. The stories were of the lives of the Buddha
in his different animal reincarnations – nearly all about
sacrifice. The blurb informed me that Noor Inayat Khan
had been the war heroine, code-named 'Madeleine', who
had been a secret agent during the Second World War
and who was posthumously awarded the George Cross,
the MBE and the Croix de Guerre Gold Star.

Posthumously. That word always had a strange ring
to it: 'after death'. I vaguely wondered how she had
died. Twenty years later, when I was asked to write a
story about war, her name immediately leaped into my
head. As I researched, I wondered why – if she had been
such a heroine – was she so unknown, especially when
she was a princess too? There were hints that she had
been 'used' by powers in London to mislead the enemy,
and it seems certain that she was betrayed by a French
colleague. Now I found out why and how she died. She
was shot by the Nazis as a spy.

Some knew her just for her beauty and ephemeral qualities, but others were convinced that it was only because she was so imbued in the Sufi philosophy she had learned from her father that she was able to find the courage and strength to sacrifice herself.

I also wanted to pay tribute to the thousands of Indians and other Commonwealth fighters and agents who gave their lives for the battle against fascism in the Second World War.

THE PRINCESS SPY
Code Name: Madeleine

Others think they know me
But I am mine; what I am, I am.

In the darkness I see no light. But there is a light in my soul which shines out and illumines my prison cell.

What can the tiger catch in the dark corners of his own lair?

In the darkness I hear no sound, but in my head I hear music, of course! Music.

Only sweet-voiced birds are imprisoned.

In my mouth I would taste only bitterness if I didn't have the memory of sweet almonds and lover's kisses.

They keep me chained to the wall like a savage dog, but I am a swallow, soaring, circling high on the air currents. Whatever they do to me, I will not let myself down. I have not betrayed my country, I have not betrayed my masters. I am a princess. The blood of the great Rajah, Tipoo Sultan, runs in my veins. I am of the warrior class. They can interrogate me all they want and torture me too, but I will not betray myself.

*

205

Her name was Noor.

Her father was an Indian prince, Hazrat Inayat Khan, a Muslim, a musician and a Sufi mystic. His reputation spread far and wide for his wise counselling – even as far as Moscow. There, the strange, powerful Russian Orthodox mystic monk, Rasputin, asked him to come to the Kremlin palace and bring his Sufi philosophy of peace and love to comfort the Tsar of All Russias, Tsar Nicholas, in his time of trouble. Russia was in turmoil. Nicholas didn't understand why. How could he, closed away in his palaces, as far removed from his people as the sun is from the earth?

So, along with his young American wife, Nora, Hazrat arrived in Moscow. Their first child, Noor, was born in the Kremlin palace on 2 January 1914, when Europe was bristling with quarrels, intrigues and assassinations, leading up to the outbreak of the First World War that August. Russia, too, was seething with unrest and things were leading inexorably towards revolution.

The stone walls surround me, yet the chains fall from my limbs and I am an infant again, crawling up the long scarlet-carpeted staircase in the Russian palace. There is an outburst of girlish laughter, and a flurry of princesses surround me like swans, gathering me up, pinching my cheeks and passing me round like a parcel: Olga, Tatiana, Maria and Anastasia. 'Let me hold her! Let me!' Their voices tinkle like bells.

'Darling Alexis!' The princesses draw in their little brother – their precious boy who, one day, will be Tsar of All Russias. 'Here. Careful now, don't drop her!' and

I am passed into the arms of a boy who looks at me with sad, solemn eyes.

Their eyes gleam at me through the years of darkness. 'They came for us,' they seem to say. 'Now they have come for you.'

Look! There I am again, bundled up in furs, crammed in among the Russian princesses on the back of a sleigh, pulled by jingling horses, flying across the flat, white, rigid landscape, and plunging into birch forests, their branches drooping with snow. 'Baba Yaga, the witch, is after us,' they whispered in my ear, making me shriek with joyful terror.

They are all dead now. The tsar and his queen, my lovely swan princesses, all captured – not by Baba Yaga, but by the Bolshevik revolutionaries, who shot them all those years ago; Alexis too – my little tsaravitch.

My father's face bends over me so tenderly. His beard is like a cloud and his dark eyes are deep pools of mystery. 'Go to sleep, my little hare,' he murmurs.

A hare? Am I the hare? Lord Buddha came as a hare, and was willing to allow himself to be eaten to feed a hungry person.

'Tell me another story,' she whimpers in the dark.

How she loved stories and made them tell her more, more, and when there were no more to tell, Noor made up her own.

Princess Noor was born to enchant. She was beautiful and talented. A child of the Muses – full of poetry, stories, dance and music. A child of rhythm – but a rhythm of her own – shy, soaring, circling among the ideas and philosophies that her father taught her.

How could her stiff English masters understand that?

When she stood before them – this dark, gleaming young woman who looked more suited to the bohemian cafes of Paris than the tight-lipped, English-public school-discipline of the War Office – they must have asked themselves, 'What on earth has she to offer?'

'Like the hare, my little princess, you can offer yourself.' My father's voice counselled me in my head.

Oh, why did you have to die, dear father?

He is the only one I weep for. My torturers have made me scream and cry as they have tried in vain to make me talk, but those tears are different; they are because of my physical pain. The pain which makes me truly weep is deeper; it is the pain of betrayal and because I no longer know who is my friend and who my enemy. It is the pain of loss because you are dead and gone. Oh, Papa! We were all thrown into such agony when we heard of your death in India while we were so far away from you in Paris. Mama locked herself away in her room and would not come out. We couldn't bear to think that never again would we hear your music, never again hear your deep, silken voice and listen to your wise words. Yet now, in this empty silence, you speak to me. You are here after all, to give me courage.

'Death is just stepping into the light, dear daughter. Remember the hare? As he entered the fire to give his body so that others could eat, the fairy of light came and made the flames as cool as water.'

We are waves whose stillness is non-being.

It was 1940. The Nazis had overrun almost the whole of Europe and were now at the gates of Paris. 'We have to leave immediately,' Noor begged her mother, who had shunned the world for twelve years, leaving Noor to be the responsible one. 'We must get out now.' With great difficulty, she persuaded her mother to flee. They all joined a long train of refugees and headed for the coast, and managed to get on to the last boat leaving for England. There, Noor and her brother wanted to help the war effort. He joined the Royal Air Force and she the Women's Auxiliary Air Force – the WAAF – and was assigned to its transport section. She was keen and dedicated. But surely she could do more?

Pinstripe-suited men discussed her, sitting on one side of a long, polished table. 'She asks to do more? We need more people in Paris. We could use her, perhaps.'

They summoned her before them.

Here in the darkness, Paris gleams out in my mind. Beautiful Paris. The boulevards are scattered with sunlight. I walk gaily, composing tunes in my head on my way to school, sniffing the honey-roasted peanuts they sell in the Luxembourg Gardens, as I cut through to St-Germain-des-Prés. I wriggle my fingers, remembering the exercises I have been practising. Paris is my home; it's where my friends are. It's where I feel alive and truly myself.

'If you send me to France, you are sending me home,' I told them.

*

'Let's see,' said Pinstripe, looking at the notes and files in front of him. 'You have been living in Paris with your mother, brother and sisters for the last seventeen years. Music student, writer of stories –' he glanced down at his notes – 'for children? You've broadcast on Paris radio – so your French is fluent – and you know the city well.'

'It's my home,' she repeated. 'I want to help.'

'Yes, well . . .' They conferred while she waited outside. 'Perhaps she would be of use,' said one.

'It will be dangerous,' said another with some compassion. 'If they catch her, she'll be shot.'

'It's war. Sacrifices have to be made.'

To the men of the War Office she looked so unsuited to this work – too otherworldly, too innocent, too much of a butterfly. Not British. Most were sceptical. After all, they had never sent in a woman radio operative before. What's more, she was an Indian. India was already in conflict with the British – trying to kick them out of India. Could they be sure that she could be trusted?

'If she can't be trusted,' a cold, dark voice spoke, 'all the better for playing a game with, my dear.'

The game. What game? Everyone knew there was a game, but so few knew who the players were and what the rules of the game were.

'Send her into France as one of our operatives. Give her a radio. Ask her to send and receive messages. We'll send her information – false information. She's sure to be caught and sure to be interrogated. At first, she won't speak, but – I know these sorts of people – she'll crack. She'll spill the beans. But they'll be our beans, and they'll swallow them whole.'

So she received her instructions. 'We want you to

go to France. Meet up with the Resistance; be a radio operative. You will be given a transmitter and will learn the radio game,' they told her.

She was registered in her mother's name – Norah Baker – and her training began. For long weeks, she learned how to operate the radio, how to use the codes and ciphers they would give her. They told her about the Resistance cells all over France, full of people working to free France and the rest of Europe from the Nazis.

She would have to be flown in at night, landing in a field. She would have to connect with other agents and sympathizers, and be part of a group. She must learn how to collect information and radio it back to them, to live a double life. Her cover name was to be Jeanne-Marie Regnier, her code name, 'Madeleine'.

I am flying, flying! How beautiful. The darkness of my cell is illumined by the moon. I felt close to heaven, then, as we flew; and close to you, Papa, with the stars all around and the sea glistening below. How small I felt too. Infinitesimal. How could I make any difference?

Yes, daughter, you are but a drop of water in an illimitable sea, but each drop is there to make up the consciousness of the whole ocean.

The world looked marvellously tranquil in the cloudy moonshine that June night, when the Lysander took off from England. So peaceful. Impossible to think of the terrors and dangers that awaited her.

Suddenly, from far below, a shower of sparks from a fire sprayed upwards into the air like fireflies. 'That's them!' muttered the pilot, and the little plane circled and dropped lower and lower. It hadn't seemed real till then. Just one of her stories in which she was a character – a heroine: brave, unafraid, ready to die for the good of the world. Suddenly, she felt terror.

Here in my dark silent cell, my heart is thumping. I am afraid again. They will come for me soon.

The wheels struck the ground. There was a fierce bumping as the Lysander hurtled over the rough field. The dark shadows of trees whipped by like a smear from a paintbrush. Would they ever stop? They stopped, but the propellers kept spinning. The engine noise sounded dangerously loud.

'Out, out!' they yelled, pushing Noor through the door.

She was already dressed to look like a nursemaid. She was to pretend to be on her way to Paris to look after an old lady. So she was wearing a war-worn but well-tailored suit, a beret over her black short hair and black walking shoes. She would look as if she was on her way back from leave. They tossed her suitcase out to her; shabby and scratched, but hidden within its false lining, under her nurse's apron and cap, were her transmitter and her instructions.

'You will meet Garry,' they had told her. 'Your network is called Prospero. He will take you to them.'

No sooner had she leaped to the ground than the Lysander was already moving again and was sky-borne – before she'd even turned to meet the man standing in the shadows.

He grasped her hand in the darkness. '*Viens. Vite!*' He

snatched her suitcase with his other hand and began to run, tugging her along. They must get away from the field. Someone may have heard the plane. The Germans could be on their way. Already Noor had a stitch in her side; she was bent double, gasping – but kept running, allowing him to drag her along, pushing her through hedges and over stiles. At last they reached a small clearing. A car was waiting. Someone opened the door. 'Get in.' The case was thrown into the boot, then they were off – driving without lights – and hit the road to Paris.

'Garry!' My heart is thumping again. I call out his name. It has a hollow ring in this dark stone cell. 'Where are you now?'

Where are any of them? Gilbert, Antoine, Marguerite, Valentin. Some are dead. She had only been in Paris a week when the Nazis rounded up nearly all of the cell called Prospero. There was treachery everywhere, but the Gestapo didn't know her yet, so she slipped away and kept up radio contact with London.

She moved from one dreary apartment to another, hanging her aerial out of the windows to pick up signals from London, while trying to evade the direction-finding trucks which roamed the streets listening out for illegal transmissions.

I can still laugh – a croaking, gulping, last-gasp laugh – when I remember one fool of a Nazi coming in on me as I tried to fix up my aerial. He thought it was a washing line and helped me.

*

She lived like this for three months, the only British radio operative in Paris still free, still transmitting to London – staying on air a few minutes at a time, then moving on. A man called 'B' arrived from England to check out what was left of the Resistance.

'Come home with me,' he advised. 'You know you'll be shot if they catch you?'

She refused. 'They don't know me. I can still go on working for you. There's no one else left. You need me.' So 'B' returned without her.

But the Nazis were after her. Somehow they got to know her code name – Madeleine. Someone had betrayed her. She arrived back to her apartment one day to find a Gestapo officer in her room.

'She was like a wild cat,' he had reported later. She fought and bit and tried to get out. 'I had to pull a gun on her.' He phoned for help and other officers arrived. They ransacked her room and found her transmitter, notebooks, codes and ciphers. They took her to their headquarters at the Avenue Foch for interrogation.

'Just tell us all you know. Give us names, contacts. Tell us what the British are planning to do.'

'My name is Norah Baker. My number is 9901 – assistant section officer for the Women's Auxiliary Air Force Transport Service,' was all she would tell them.

'You're a fool.' They shook their heads with false pity. 'You'll soon speak. Take her away.'

She made another desperate attempt to escape by climbing through a window and slithering across the rooftops. But they caught her and dragged her back.

She was now classified as a 'dangerous prisoner'.

*

'They hurt me, Papa. They hurt me so much.

'We already know everything,' sneered the Gestapo. 'Your colleague broke. We know all about the plans. You might as well give in and save yourself more pain.'

'My name is Norah Baker, number 9901 . . .' She refused to give more than her name, rank and number.

Her masters thought she would break in the end. It was part of the plan. She would pass on false information; would tell them there was a plan to invade, that the Allies would land in Calais – not Normandy. But after five weeks of fierce interrogation, she stayed silent.

Love is action; action is knowledge; knowledge is truth; truth is love.

She was put on a train to Karlsruhe in Germany. There she stayed for ten months, in solitary confinement, shackled in chains. In September 1944 she was put on another train.

So this is where I am, Papa; Dachau. Not many people walk out alive from here. There are three other women from my section. We will meet for the first time in a few moments. I can hear the first birdsong of dawn. Yes – even in my cell, their song reaches me. I hear footsteps. They are coming.

'*Awake! For morning in the bowl of night has flung the stone that put the stars to flight.*'

Four women were taken out at dawn to a place all strewn with sand.

*

The sand is stained with blood.

I am a hare.

They were told to kneel. Four women – strangers to each other till then – held hands like sisters and knelt down together. An SS man came up behind them and, one by one, shot them dead.

Postscript: Princess Noor Inayat Khan was posthumously awarded the George Cross by the British and the Croix de Guerre by the French.

Joan Aiken

When the Second World War began in 1939, Joan Aiken had been sent away to a small boarding school in Oxford. At the time of the Blitz on London, two years later, her school had closed down and at seventeen she found herself a job at the BBC which had been evacuated out of London. Her 'war work' consisted of ruling lines on the backs of filing cards to save paper, which impressed her so strongly that all her life she saved paper by writing her new stories on the backs of old ones. Wanting to be more involved in the war effort she had, by the age of nineteen, found a job at the United Nations Information Office in a bomb-damaged building on the corner of Russell Square, near the British Museum. The Battle of Britain, the six-week battle in 1940, when the RAF defeated the German air force, was over, but the Germans were still sending hundreds of V1s, pilotless aircraft that fell and exploded, and V2s, which were huge twelve-ton rockets that made an incredible noise when they blew up. She even managed to joke about it: 'A V1 fell in Russell Square, blowing all the leaves off the trees, breaking the office windows, and messing up my filing system.'

But she stored the experience and it reappears in 'Albert's Cap', along with something she found much more frightening – the spirit of evil which causes humans to prey on the weakness of others. Joan Aiken went on to write over one hundred books. She died in 2004, aged seventy-nine – three days after sending off this story. She was a fighting spirit to the end, but her weapons against injustice were her words.

Lizza Aiken

ALBERT'S CAP

This story was told me by my gran. It happened to her in London. But not the London we know now.

It was in the war.

I had been sent away for a couple of years (said my gran) to escape the bombing. I stayed with cousins in Wales. It wasn't bad, but after a while I had a letter from my mum. (Your great-grandma.)

'Dear Gwenno,' she wrote, 'I've decided you can come back. I miss you such a lot. And Elsie Tarn says there's no more danger from raids here now. And if Dad got leave, he'd like to find you at home. So I'm sending the money for your ticket.'

Dad was in the navy, in submarines. I hadn't seen him for nearly three years.

Of course I was happy to go home. But it was a bit of a shock when I saw the district where we lived, around Well Street, Rumbury Town.

We'd always been in that part of London. Our flat, on the third floor of a block called Percy Mansions, was up six short flights of stairs. (Mind you – they didn't seem

219

so short when you were lugging a bike and a heavy duffel-bag up them). Inside our front door, on the right, there were three rooms overlooking the street; one of them was a kitchen. And on the left, a long passage. Halfway down the passage, a bathroom and toilet. At the far end, three more rooms. Or, at least, there *had* been, before. Now there was only one room. A family called Green had shared the flat with us, and lived in the back rooms. Now they were gone – Mum didn't say where – and Elsie Tarn lived in the one room that was left. The rest of the building had been sheered off, clean as you'd cut a chunk of cheese with one of those wires they used to have in grocers' shops. Two of the doors at the far end of the passage were boarded and bricked up – because outside of them was only space.

The first thing I noticed was that Mum had got very thin and pale and tired-looking. Her hair, that used to be bright red, was grey now. But she was really pleased to see me.

'I've been saving up flour, and my sugar and marge rations. And an egg!' she said. 'And some raisins. I made you Welshcakes for a treat.'

I hadn't the heart to tell her that, on the farm with Aunt Myfanwy, where no one took much notice of rationing – for there was plenty of milk, butter and eggs – we'd had Welshcakes almost every day.

Anyway, Mum's Welshcakes were extra good. But I did wish she hadn't invited Elsie Tarn to tea with us.

I couldn't remember Mrs Tarn – though *she* said she remembered *me*. She used to live, she told me, round the corner in Jugg Street. I didn't like her. She had thin no-coloured frizzy hair, she smiled a lot – all the time, just about – and she talked through her long nose. She sounded like the drone of a distant plane.

'No, *no*, there's *no* danger now, none at all,' she kept saying. 'Oh, Annie! Isn't it just grand to have young Gwenno back! I had such a job persuading your mum to send for you,' she said, giving me another of her long-play smiles, crinkling her eyes up till they looked like specks of grit in cracks. She smelled strange – sweetish, musky – like things that have been shut a long time in old cupboards.

'But what about the doodlebugs?' I asked.

They were the flying bombs, pilotless planes, that would buzz along rather slowly overhead, then suddenly cut out, and explode on the spot where they landed. I'd heard about them, of course, though they hadn't got as far as Wales.

'Oh, we just laugh at *them* – don't we, Annie?' said Mrs Tarn. 'All but old Tomkin – he goes under the bed.' She cast a look of scorn and dislike at our tabby cat. But I thought he showed good sense.

After tea I went out, to walk round the old neighbourhood. 'Don't go too far,' Mum warned. 'It'll be blackout time soon. And keep off the bombsites – specially the one round at the back. Some children did go on it and they just sank in – it's like a bog – they got stuck and they were only just rescued in time. The council say it's not safe to build there, it's unstable underneath. They'll have to put down hundreds of tons of concrete before building on top.'

Well, it was strange to see the old neighbourhood so changed. At the far end of Well Street, going south, you turn left into Pentecost Row. Then, left again into Jugg

Street. Then, left again, Ettrick Lane takes you back to Well Street. All that area – houses where my friends used to live, and lots of people I knew, as well as the laundry, the primary school, St Philip's Chapel, the Rumbury District Hospital, the bank – all of it was just flattened. Nothing but earth, rough and lumpy, inside a wire mesh fence, with some bits of brick and timber showing. And plants, bushes (beginning to grow), thistles, willowherb, buddleia with purple flowers. The back of our block of flats had been sliced off, sheer, like a cliff, and was now cemented over, with a couple of big wooden buttresses to support it.

'What *did* that?' I asked Mum when I got home.

'A landmine,' she said.

I didn't dare ask what happened to all the people who lived in those houses. Some of them must have been indoors at the time. Mum had been down in the air-raid shelter in the tube, she told me.

Our little street still stood, like a line of trees in the desert: Percy Mansions and the row of small shops and businesses beyond, butcher, cafe, cycle shop, baker, chemist and the pub, the Mousetrap.

'Funny sort of name for a pub, I'd say,' remarked Mrs Tarn, wrinkling up her long nose. 'That sign! It's common, if you ask me! Gives me the sick, it does.' The sign was a huge mouse, a lump of cheese and mug of beer.

Mum sighed. 'Jim and I used to go there, Saturday nights. It's not a bad pub. Now I haven't the heart. Wish we ever saw a bit of cheese like that *now*.'

The cheese ration was two ounces a week. Meat: one chop and a bit of gristle. Bacon: two rashers. (Mum used to swap her bacon for tea.) Sugar: a packet once a month. Soap: one bar. And a pot of either jam or marmalade. Real eggs you only saw one at a time, if you were lucky. What did we eat? Veg hotpot and baked beans.

London was very, very quiet in those days. No cars in the street. All dark at night, bar the searchlights, lancing about the sky.

And it was extra dark, extra quiet, in the space behind our block, I thought, in that wide, empty gap between Pentecost Row and Ettrick Lane.

Sometimes, of an evening, I'd tiptoe to the end of the passage and stand beside one of the two boarded-up doors, listening.

Mrs Tarn caught me doing that once. Quick and without the least noise – the way a mole suddenly comes out of the ground – there she was, beside me.

'Oh – Mrs Tarn – you made me jump!'

Her smell was very strong, there in the dark passage. 'Aunt Elsie – you must call me Aunt Elsie, dear!'

But I could never do that.

'What ever were you doing, Gwenno, love?'

'Just thinking how quiet it is – on the other side of that wall. Such a long way to the ground.'

'Do you know what I think?' said Mrs Tarn. 'Out there is empty ground. But it hasn't *been* empty like that, not for hundreds and hundreds of years. There's always been houses on top. Things must be stirring – and coming up – under that loose earth. Things that haven't been free to move – or seen the light of day – for *ever* such a long time—'

'How do you mean, Mrs . . . Aunt?' I said, not at all keen on the idea. 'Worms?'

223

'Oh – mercy – *I* don't know, ducky,' she said, laughing. 'When there are wars, they stir up all kinds of ancient things, left over from old ancient times – perhaps even from before there were people like us. Don't you think so? Just one of Auntie Elsie's funny fancies, you know.'

I suppose I looked puzzled and startled, for she said quickly, 'Never mind it! You've not been into *my* room yet – have you, Gwenno dear? Like to come and have a look-see?'

And she opened the third door, the door that was not bricked up, and drew me into her room.

Dark hadn't fully come yet, it wasn't quite blackout time, but Mrs Tarn quickly crossed the room and twitched down the heavy black cloth blinds over the window that looked over the bombsite. Then she switched on a light or two.

The room seemed to be full of clutter – bits of furniture crammed close together, boxes, bundles of cloth, jugs, basins, umbrella stands, all piled hugger-mugger. And there were rows of silver articles, not very big, sugar bowls, cream jugs, teaspoons, napkin rings, salt cellars, laid out on a dirty old newspaper, faintly gleaming in the dusky light.

'Polishing silver – that's *my* little hobby. While you and your mum are listening in to *Forces' Favourites*, I'm busy at my polishing. See, this is what I use . . .'

With her skinny, bony hand she picked up a thick, dusty circle of what looked like grey felt. An old beret perhaps.

'I *dip* this, you see, I dip it in a special mixture that I make myself – *nobody* else has the secret, only old

224

Auntie Elsie – and then I use it to polish up all my little treasures. Y'mum used to help me sometimes – but she's rather poorly these days, not so perky as she was, is she? Shame, she used to be such a live wire, such good company, your mum. You must brisk her up, Gwenno dear. That's why I made her get you back—'

'She misses Dad.'

'Ah, of course she does! And that would be the trouble, no doubt. Now, I'll tell you *another* use I have for this cloth—'

'It's an old beret, isn't it?' I said, trying to be polite, trying not to show how much I hated being in this cramped, fusty room.

'Clever girlie! I call it my Tarn-cap, you see. My little joke, that is! When I put it on my head – or would you like to try it? Maybe it's just a tiny bit on the big size for you? I must ask my brother – he has . . .'

The dusty cap smelled *foul* – a sick, stale, dusky smell. Like that of Aunt Elsie herself, but much stronger. I'd sooner have died than put it on.

I backed away, fast. 'Oh no – thank you very much—'

'Why, ducky, you aren't scared, are you?' she said, laughing. 'Now, your mum . . .'

But just then (thank goodness) I heard Mum herself calling, 'Gwenno? Gwenno! Where are you?' Quite frantic, she sounded. And I was able to nip hastily out of the door and along the passage.

'I'm stupid, I know,' said Mum. She was dead pale, a dew of sweat on her cheekbones. 'I heard you go down the passage and – sometimes – I get to think about those doors – opening on to thin air . . .'

'But they're all bricked up, Mum,' I said. 'Mrs Tarn was just showing me her things.'

Mum gave a sort of twitch, as if she'd heard the air-raid alert. But it hadn't sounded. The city was very, very quiet. Just, sometimes, the noise of a bit of stone or plaster falling. And the drip of rain. Not a car, not a bus. Tomkin curled up asleep in his basket. I thought of the earth on the bombsite, soft and wet and deep, going down goodness knows how far . . .

'Let's go to the pictures!' I urged Mum.

But she was too tired, she said.

That night I dreamed about the earth heaving and lifting up on the bombed site, as if there were mice, or worms, or moles, burrowing and churning and jostling just under the surface, with sometimes a claw showing, or an eye glittering among the dust.

I woke up with a yell, thankful to find old Tomkin sharing the bed with me, and to grab hold of his furry, solid shape for comfort.

Next morning Mum had one of her dreadful bad headaches. She used to get them before, but never as bad as this. There was nothing that could be done for her, only leave the curtains pulled and let her sleep it off. The whole day it took, sometimes.

'Could you – go and – tell Mr Schaefer I can't come?' she whispered faintly.

'Of course, Mum! Don't you worry. I'll tell him. Maybe he'd have me do the work instead. If I don't come back right away, that's where I'll be.'

I kissed her goodbye – I could tell she hardly understood what I'd said – left her with a cup of tea which she

226

probably wouldn't drink, and let myself out, quiet as a mouse, tiptoeing down the stairs so Mrs Tarn wouldn't hear me and come nosying. Most days, Mrs Tarn went out, and didn't come back till nightfall. Hunting about the ruins and bomb crates, Mum told me, looking for what she could pick up. I supposed that was how she'd come by her silver things.

Old Mr Schaefer lived in one of the houses in Ebernoe Square, east of Well Street. Mum had been housekeeping for him since before the war. He wrote poetry books. And these days he was something high up in a government office, analysing foreign news broadcasts.

Inside, his house was lovely. And – what I liked best – in front, on either side of the brick steps, were two stone lions. When I was small, sometimes Mum would take me with her when she went to work there. And I'd spend most of the day outside, with the lions, talking to them. Or, across the road, in the square, there was a big round garden. I was allowed to go and play in there. At that time it was railed off, locked up, private, but now those railings were gone. In the middle was a statue of a man in a top hat. Lord Palmerston, it said underneath.

I was very glad to see that the lions were still there. Made of black stone, they were, about as big as a sheep. The lion was looking sharp to his right, as if he was ready to pounce. The lioness looked straight ahead of her with big, round eyes. I didn't know which of them I loved best.

I gave each of them a pat, for old times' sake, before I rang the bell.

'Why – if it isn't young Gwenno,' said old Mr Schaefer, opening the door. 'How are you, my dear?

Bless me, how you've grown! The air of Wales must have been good for you. But I'm sure your mother was very happy to have you back. She's been talking of nothing else for weeks.'

I told him she was not well. Had one of her headaches. He shook his own head.

'To tell the truth, my dear, I've been worried about her. A good rest is what she needs. I'm glad you're back with her, Gwenno.'

'Can I do the shopping and cleaning for you today, Mr Schaefer?'

'Glad to have you, my dear. But you must run home at lunch time to take care of your mother.'

So I dusted and polished his house – it was very neat and bare; he explained he'd had all his best things, silver and china, sent away to the country for safety – and I did his shopping.

On the way back from the greengrocer I noticed a little hunched-up man, over the road, following and watching me. Then he crossed the street, mincing and skipping, came up to me and said, '*I* know who you are! Gwenno Everly – isn't it?'

I wasn't at all keen on this little creep making free with my name in the street. He was grubby, had a spiteful look, with his head tilted all on one side. His grin showed a lot of slanting yellow teeth. He came up only as far as my elbow. He wore dusty, drab, wrinkled clothes and a black beret. His face was all creased and dirty too.

'I'm Albert,' he said. 'Elsie's brother, Albert Neff. Elsie has told me all about you. And I daresay she's told you about me?'

'No,' I said, 'no, she hasn't,' hurrying along the pavement towards number three, Ebernoe Square.

'No?' He grinned even more. 'Well, I'm Elsie's loving brother. I know your mum. I'll be seeing you, at your place, one of these evenings.'

Not if I can help it, I thought, running up the brick steps and pulling out the key Mr Schaefer had given me. I don't care if I never see you again.

Albert gave the lions a glance full of dislike – in fact I thought I saw him aim a kick at one of them – then he turned back towards Well Street.

Just then Mr Schaefer himself came out of the house, in his bowler and carrying a briefcase.

'I'm off to Bush House,' he told me.

Right away, Albert began bobbing and bowing, up and down, up and down, like frantic puppet on the end of a string.

'Good to see you, lovely to see you, Mr Schaefer, sir!' he squeaked. 'I hope I find you well? Now, sir, can I clean your chimneys, can I come and do that? I'm sure they must be all choke-full of soot by now! They must need doing badly!'

'No they do *not*!' snapped Mr Schaefer. Very cold and brisk, he was. 'I haven't lit a fire since last January. No, thank you, I don't want them done. I told you, *no*!' And as the little man went on bobbing and pulling faces, he rapped out, 'Be off with you, man! Make yourself scarce, if you please. Go back where you belong!'

Albert scurried nervously away, kitty-cornerways, across the square, and Mr Schaefer said to me, 'Tiresome little wretch! He has taken to sleeping in the square, sometimes, on fine nights. The air-raid wardens don't like it at all. "The Fairy King", they call him. Let me know if he annoys you – or your mother – in any way. I'll tell the police. I've an idea they are keeping an eye on him.'

Mr Schaefer walked away towards the Underground station.

That night I woke with a start, all of a sudden, to hear the noise of a V1 bomber, or buzzbomb – which by now I'd got to recognize and distinguish from a proper plane – throbbing and throbbing over my head. A thick, bumpy noise, it was, like water slowly glugging down a half-blocked drain. *Zizz zizz zizz zizz.* Then – nothing. Complete silence. Tomkin whipped out from beside me and went under the bed. Then there was the most almighty crash. WHOOM! All our windows rattled and the house shook. A pane of glass clanked down in the passage and some plaster thumped on the floor.

'*Gwenno!*' came Mum's terrified voice. '*Are you all right?*'

'Yes, Mum!'

I jumped out of bed and went to hers and gave her a hug. 'Here I am, quite OK. How's your head?'

Last night it had still been dreadful.

'It's a bit better, thank you, love. That was a really close one!'

'Where do you think it fell?'

Fire engines were scudding past and slowing at the corner.

'Round in Ebernoe Square, perhaps.'

'Oh, I hope Mr Schaefer's all right.'

Mum said faintly, 'Oh, I'd just love a cup of tea!'

The gas was cut off, but Mum had a little spirit stove

which we used when that happened. I was surprised that Mrs Tarn didn't come to share our tea and gossip. But glad of her absence.

I didn't tell Mum that I'd met Elsie's brother Albert. We drank our tea and, shivering, went back to bed.

Next morning, when I shuffled, bleary-eyed, in dressing gown and slippers, to try the kitchen cooker, see if the gas was reconnected – there was a big grey rat, squatting behind the kettle on the stove top.

I let out a yell. 'Mum! Come quick! And bring Tomkin!'

Of course I'd seen plenty of rats on the farm, but none so big or so bold as this monster. It bared its teeth and squealed at me defiantly. Tomkin took one look and slunk away, back to our bedroom. *Mice* were his business, his ears and tail suggested, not a beast on this scale.

'Your cat's a coward,' said Mrs Tarn, slip-slopping along in her downtrodden feather mules and grubby candlewick negligee. 'Get out of here, you big brute!' And she shook the rolling pin at the rat, which, angrily squealing again, sprang off the stove, scurried across the lino and out on to the kitchen balcony. The door to it was open, unlatched when the bomb fell.

This balcony was never meant for sitting out on. It was for practical use: the dustbin stood there and, once a week, Fred the caretaker would lower the bin on a goods-hoist by a pulley and empty it out. (When I was smaller, boys in the flats sometimes used to go down on the garbage lift for a dare; but I never did. It was too grimy and nasty.)

Now the rat slipped easily over the edge of the balcony and ran down the iron support to the floor below.

'We'd better put out some poison,' said Mum, white as wax. I was sorry I'd called her.

'Oh – what's the use?' Mrs Tarn shrugged. 'There's hundreds more, you bet, down on the bombsite.'

She slapped the rolling pin back on the shelf, lit a fag and slip-slopped away.

'I think I'll have to go back to bed, dearie,' said Mum, who was swaying and looked sick.

I helped her lie down again and, when I'd eaten a bit of bread and marge, went up the street and round the corner to see where the bomb had fallen.

The middle of Ebernoe Square was all cordoned off and full of wreckage. Very luckily, it seemed, the doodlebug had landed right in the middle, among the flower beds and shrubs. No one was hurt, only the fronts of houses round the square had their plaster knocked off by the blast and windows broken; and the trees were shattered and had their leaves blown clean off.

But when I got to number three I had a sad shock: the front door was smashed in and the two lions I loved so much were just rubble and dust. Lumps of the statue of Lord Palmerston that had stood in the middle of the square were lying about. It was plain what must have happened: the blast from the buzzbomb had blown Lord Palmerston in his top hat right against Mr Schaefer's front door.

I stepped in through the open doorway and called. 'Mr Schaefer! Mr Schaefer!'

No answer.

'Step along there, move along now, none of your business,' said a warden, putting his head in.

'I've come to clean Mr Schaefer's house,' I said. 'Where is he?'

'Oh, well, that's different. He's in hospital. The Royal Free, Gray's Inn Road.'

'What happened to him?'

'Heart attack. He wasn't hurt. He'll be all right.'

When I'd tidied the house – it was a right mess, with dust and grit blown in – and seen that men were at work boarding up the broken windows and putting on a temporary door, I went home to make Mum some soup. She was a bit better. When I told her what happened to Mr Schaefer, she said I'd better go and see him.

'I'll take another nap,' she said. 'Don't let Elsie in – even if she asks – I don't feel up to talking.'

Just as I was wheeling my bike out the door there was a pit-pat up the stairs and – of all the bad luck – there came the grimy little man, Elsie's brother. He gave me his big, yellow, spiteful grin.

'Now, aren't I lucky? I'll just pop down the passage; see if Elsie's there.'

No indeed you won't, I thought. I'm not leaving you alone in the place unless Elsie's about.

But just then Elsie herself came out of the kitchen, carrying a bowl of wet washing.

She didn't seem a bit pleased to see her brother. 'I've *told* you not to come turning up here at all hours!' she hissed at him. 'Buzz off! Get away! I've enough to do – clearing up – after last night—'

He grinned at her some more, showing all his teeth. 'All right! All right!' he squeaked. 'Temper! Temper!

Don't get nasty now. I just thought . . . But I'll be seeing you later, then – usual place.'

And he slipped away, pit-pat, down the stairs, much quicker than I could manage with my bike. By the time I got to the street he was out of sight. And good riddance, too, I thought.

Mr Schaefer, in the high metal bed, under a neat white cover, looked grey and shrunk and old. But he seemed pleased to see me and to hear that there was not too much wrong with his house.

'I'll be back in a couple of days,' he said. 'Old age is all that's wrong with *me* – like the house. They can patch me up here and there with a bit of tar paper and a sheet of corrugated iron. And I reckon I'll last a while longer.'

'But, oh, Mr Schaefer – the lions! Your lions! It's so dreadful. They're just gone!'

'Well, Gwenno,' he said, 'maybe it was their time. Sometimes things come to their appointed end. We can't tell. Perhaps it was those lions that stopped Lord Palmerston from slamming right through my front door and pounding me to paste in my own front hall. In which case I'm certainly obliged to them. For I hope I still have my uses. And maybe the lions are glad to be free at last from those hard stone bodies. Who can tell?'

I was relieved to find him so cheerful, and gave him a little pot of bramble jelly that Aunt Myfanwy had sent with me from Wales.

'Look after your mother,' he said. 'Keep her away from those neighbours. They're not a good influence.'

When I got home I found Mum sitting in the old wooden fireside chair. Dusty yellow light came in the window. Mum looked as if she'd have been better off in bed, as she drooped against the worn dark-blue hessian cushions. All the bones showed under her skin, and that was pale as raw rice.

'Gwenno,' she said, 'I've been thinking. I didn't ought to have let you come back from Wales. It's not safe for you here. You better go back to Aunt Myfanwy.'

'Oh, come on, Mum,' I said. 'It's safe enough. The flybombs are getting fewer. Anyway, we're not likely to have another as close as last night's.'

And, I thought, you need me here.

'Maybe not,' she said, fairly crying now, tears trickling down, 'but there's other dangers. For one thing they say – it's said – that Hitler's going to send something worse, soon – much worse – another kind of flying bomb. Bigger. And that's not all—'

'*Who* says this?'

'Well – Elsie for one. And—'

'Mum,' I began, 'I don't much like Elsie. I wish you didn't see such a lot of her. I don't think—'

'Oh, that's it, that's a worse worry,' Mum gabbled on, in a soft, breathless voice, as if she were badly afraid of being overheard. Her eyes were fixed burningly, insistently, on mine. 'That's *another* thing, Gwenno. Elsie and her brother. It would be better – much better – if you didn't—'

'Hush!' I said.

We could hear voices outside, and footsteps. Elsie's high, breathy laugh and a man's voice that muttered something, quietly. I recognized it.

That nasty little viper again.

'Gwenno!' whispered Mum hastily. '*Whatever* you do, don't let—'

There was a tap on the door.

'Annie, dear? Are you better?' came Elsie's voice, dulcet and fluting. 'Can we peek in? Just for a quick looksee? Just to find if you're on the mend? Albert's brought—'

'*Don't* let him make you—' gasped Mum, and then the door opened wide and they came in.

Elsie was carrying a basket. 'Look!' she said proudly. 'Look, I found ever such a lovely teapot. In Chelsea, where they had two of them.'

'Two teapots?' I said.

'No, silly! Two flybombs. There's streets and streets of ruins. The wardens can't be everywhere.'

'And look what *I've* got,' said Albert the dwarf. He had sidled in after his sister, grinning like an alligator. 'Something for Gwenno. Just her size. She'll love it – won't she, Elsie? It'll make her look smart – and Frenchified!'

He displayed a crumpled bit of felt, a beret.

The front-door bell rang loudly. And Mum fainted dead away.

Outside the front door were police. Loud, official voices.

'Mr Albert Neff – we need to speak to him. We have reason to believe he's here.' I heard Albert's snarling whine. 'Why me? I've done nothing?'

'We'd like you to come round to the station for questioning.'

I didn't pay them much heed. I was rubbing Mum's forehead with vinegar, giving her sips of water.

I heard the bang of the door and the voices died away.

Where Elsie was, I didn't enquire. Maybe she had gone along too.

Presently Mum opened her eyes. 'Where is it?' she whispered. 'Where is what, Mum?'

'The cap. The cap that he brought. Don't touch it, Gwenno. *Don't put it on!*'

I'd forgotten all about it. But there it was, lying on the boards; a dusty, crumpled bit of black felt.

As I looked, I thought it gave a twitch. I could have sworn it moved.

'Don't touch it!' said Mum.

We had a pair of laundry tongs. I fetched them, picked up the dirty thing, wondered what to do with it.

I couldn't burn it, we had no fireplace, only gas fires. So – in the end – I carried it down the passage, intending to drop it out of Elsie's window on to the bombsite. But her door was locked. Maybe she was round at the police station, speaking in her brother's defence. I wondered what he was wanted for. Receiving stolen goods, perhaps.

I saw there was a gap in the bottom of one of the boarded-up doors – a gap the size of a grapefruit that had been *nibbled*. So I poked the black cap out through the hole, and pushed the tongs after it.

Then I went back to Mum.

She had a half-bottle of whisky she was saving in case Dad got leave; but it was on the table beside her, and a good two-thirds of it was gone.

'Gwenno,' she whispered. 'Don't ever, ever, put one of those caps on. I did once – just the once – and, do you know what? I thought – it suddenly seemed – as if I was all covered in grey fur . . .'

237

Her head dropped on the pillow, and she was asleep.

I put the bottle back in the cupboard.

Later in the night, I was woken by a sound and put my hand out of bed, feeling for the torch. My hand met *teeth*. Quicker than thought, I snatched it back.

Next door in the kitchen I could hear bumps and thuds and snarls. Pulling on my corduroy pants, I ran in and switched on the light.

Tomkin was at bay, facing two big grey rats who were snarling and squeaking and making running darts at him. They had him cornered.

I grabbed the kitchen chair, swung and bashed at the rats with it; managed to stun one of them and, with the leg of the chair, poked and shoved it though the balcony door and over the edge of the balcony.

The other rat had scurried off along the passage. Going after, I saw it nip nimbly through the hole in the boarded-up door.

So I went back to Mum, who was awake and trembling.

'Come on, Mum,' I said. 'You'll have to get up. We're not stopping here. It isn't safe. We'll go round to Mr Schaefer's house. I've got the key to his new door.'

That was what we did, carrying Tomkin in his basket. We slept on rolled-up carpets in his library. Not for too long, though. After maybe a couple of hours, we were woken by a bang.

And what a bang! It made the noise of the buzzbombs seem like the tap of a bone spoon on a soft-boiled egg. For five minutes after, our ears buzzed and we clung to each other in total terror.

'*What was that?*' whispered Mum.

And I said, 'It must have been that new thing you were telling about – the new thing that Hitler was going to send.'

Next day we found that I was right. It was the rocket they called the V2.

The V2s ploughed deep into the ground and did much, much more damage than the flying bombs. The things people think up! Though nothing to what they have now.

Luckily, not long after, the Allied armies fought their way to the launching pads where the V2s were sent off, and put a stop to them.

But the one we heard had landed harmlessly, in the area that was already clear, behind Percy Mansions. The authorities said that nobody had been killed.

Except some rats, perhaps.

Elsie Tarn was found next day, in the courtyard in the middle of Percy Mansions, where the dustbins were emptied. She had two broken legs and concussion. Nobody could understand how she got there. She was taken off to hospital in Stoke Newington and we lost touch with her. We heard the police had let Albert go, for lack of evidence, but after leaving the station he was never seen again.

I had my own ideas about what had happened to him.

A dirty old felt cap, found in the yard near Elsie, was thrown away.

When Mr Schaefer come home, I talked to him about it all. (I *never* talked to Mum. But she got better, after a while, and became almost her old self again. Specially after Dad came out of the forces.)

'Man thinks himself so much better than the other

animals,' said Mr Schaefer, 'in that he invented language, music and art. But in other ways he is worse, because he hoards. And he does things out of malice. Animals don't do that.'

He quoted a bit of a poem that he had made up.

'Lions, in pride and speed
Hunt and kill from need
Man, in shame and blame
Piles treasure out of greed.

'When we do something of which we have cause to be ashamed, Gwenno, we revert to animals. Do you understand?'

'I'm not sure,' I said. And then, 'Do you think Albert and Elsie turned into rats?'

'Perhaps they always had been rats. Perhaps they came out of that deep, buried place,' he said.

Anyway, that area has had tons of concrete poured in, and a high-rise block built on top. The new Rumbury Civic Centre.

London is a different town now.

But I reckon *people* are still much the same.

Eva Ibbotson

I was born in Vienna many years ago and when I was a small girl Hitler began rounding up all the people he didn't care for – Jews and gypsies and democrats – and sending them to camps where most of them died.

My own family and close friends all escaped and made happy new lives in Britain but I had a small cousin called Marianne, aged seven, who vanished with her family and was never heard of again.

She must, I suppose, have perished along with millions of others, but I have never quite stopped wondering about her, and sometimes I've imagined that somehow, somewhere, she was still alive. It seemed so terrible that I, who was the same age, should find safety in my new country and that she should disappear into darkness. And because I'm a writer I have thought of many ways in which her story could after all have turned out to have a different ending.

'A Place on the Piano' is one such story – the events I have described did happen – mothers did save their babies by throwing them out of trains . . . and perhaps, who knows, my little cousin Marianne was one such child, and lived.

A PLACE ON THE PIANO

I always thought the war would end suddenly but it didn't – it sort of dribbled away. Six months after I stood with the other boys in my class outside Buckingham Palace – yelling for the king and queen because we'd defeated Hitler – the barrage balloons still floated like great silver grandfathers over the roofs of London. The park railings were still missing, St Paul's cathedral stood in a sea of rubble and there was nothing to be bought in the shops.

My teacher had explained it to me. 'Wars are expensive, Michael,' he said. 'They have to be paid for.'

Rationing got tighter – you still had to have coupons for clothes and fuel. Worst of all was the food. You could hardly see the meat ration with the naked eye, and some very weird things were issued by the government for us to eat. Tinned snoek, for example. Snoek is a South African fish and when Cook opened the tin it turned out to be a bluish animal with terrifying spikes, swimming in a sea of gelatinous goo – and the smell was unspeakable.

'This time they've gone too far,' she said, and she tried to give it to the cat, who sneered and turned away.

I knew quite a lot about rationing because I was a sort of kitchen boy. Not that I worked in the kitchen exactly; I'd just won a scholarship to the grammar school, but I lived below stairs in the basement of a large house belonging to a family called Glossop, where my mother was the housekeeper. We'd lived there, in London, all through the war.

I remember the snoek particularly because we were just wondering what to do with it when the bell went and my mother was called upstairs.

When she came back she looked really happy and excited. 'Little Marianne Gerstenberger has been found. She's alive!'

It was incredible news. Marianne had been thrown out of a cattle train when she was a baby. It was her own mother who had done it. She'd been rounded up with some other Jews and she was on her way to a concentration camp when she found a weak place in one of the boards behind the latrine. She got the others to help her work on it to make a small hole. And then she bundled up the baby, and when the train stopped for a moment she managed to push her out on to the track.

We'd heard a lot about bravery during the last six years of war: soldiers in Burma stumbling on, dying of thirst; parachutists at Arnheim, and of course the Spitfire pilots who had saved us in the Blitz. But the story of Marianne caught us all.

'To do that,' said my mother, 'to push your own baby out on to the track because you knew you were going to your death . . .'

At first my mother had tried not to speak of what had happened when Hitler went mad and tried to exterminate the Jews. But my school was the kind where they told you things, and I'd seen the newsreels. I'd seen the bodies piled up when the Allies opened up the camps, and the skeletons which were supposed to be people. Marianne's parents had both perished, but now, as the news came through from the Red Cross in Switzerland, it seemed that the baby had survived. She had been found by a peasant family who had taken her in and was living in East Germany, close to the border with Poland.

'They're going to fetch her,' said my mother. 'They're going to take her in.' And there were tears in her eyes.

'They' were her employers – the Glossops – who lived in the house above us and who she served. The Glossops were not Jewish, but Marianne's mother had been married to the son of their Jewish business partners in Berlin. Glossop and Gerstenberger had been a well-known firm of exporters.

'They're going to adopt her,' my mother went on. She didn't often speak warmly about the Glossops, but I could hear the admiration in her voice.

'She'll live like a little princess,' said Cook. 'Imagine, after being brought up with peasants.'

Everyone agreed with this: the kids in my school, the people in the shops, the tradesmen who came to deliver goods to the basement. Because the Glossops, weren't just well off, they were properly rich. Their house was the largest in the square, double-fronted – and furnished as though the war had never been. To go up the service stairs and through the green baize door into the house was like stepping into a different world.

245

Mrs Glossop and her mother-in-law had spent the war in a hotel in the Lake District to get away from the bombs; and her daughter, Daphne, who was ten years old, had been away at boarding school, but the house had stayed open because Mr Glossop used it when he was in town on business, which meant that the servants had to keep it ready for him whenever he wanted.

So my mother and I went upstairs most days to check the blackout curtains and make sure the shutters were closed and none of the window panes had cracked in the raids – and I knew the house as well as I knew the dark rooms in the basement where we lived, along with the cook and old Tom, the chauffeur–handyman.

I knew the dining room with its heavy button-backed chairs and the carved sideboard where they kept the napkin rings and the cruets which Tom polished every week. I knew the drawing room with its thick Turkish carpet and massive sofas – and I knew old Mrs Glossop's boudoir on the first floor with the gilt mirrors and claw-footed tables – and the piano.

I knew the piano very well. I remember once when I was upstairs helping my mother I heard a V1 rocket cut out above me, which meant I had about half a minute before it came down and exploded – and without think-ing I dived under the piano.

It was an enormous piano – a Steinway Concert Grand – but I'd never heard anybody play it. It was a piano for keeping relations on. On the dark red chenille cover which protected it were rows of Glossops in silver frames: old Glossops and young ones, Glossops on their horses and Glossops in their university gowns. There were Glossop children in their school uniforms or holding cricket bats, and there were Glossop women in their presentation dresses ready to go to court. There was even a Glossop who had been knighted, and as I lay there, waiting for the bomb to fall, I wasn't in the least bit scared – I didn't feel anyone would dare to destroy a whole army of Glossops, and I was right. The rocket came down three streets away.

And now Marianne Gerstenberger, who was just seven years old, would have her own place on the piano, and be a Glossop too.

The preparations for Marianne began straight away, and we all threw ourselves into the work. It may sound silly, but I think it was then that we realized that the war was well and truly over, and that good things were happening in the world.

'We'll put her in the room next to Daphne's,' said Mrs Glossop – and she gave my mother a list of all the things that needed to be done. New curtains of pale blue satin to be sewn, and the bed canopied with the same material. A white fur rug on the floor, the walls repapered with a design of forget-me-nots and rosebuds, and a new dressing table to be lined with a matching pattern. Furniture was difficult to get – you had to have coupons for almost everything – but when you own three department stores the rules don't really apply. The Glossops had always had everything they wanted, and that included food. Parcels from America had come all through the war and they were coming still.

'She can have my dolls – I don't play with them any more,' said Daphne, but Mrs Glossop ordered a whole batch of new dolls and fluffy toys and games from the store.

'Of course she'll be a little savage,' said old Mrs Glossop. 'We must be patient with her.'

She sent my mother out to get one of the napkin rings engraved with Marianne's name and I imagined the little girl sitting in the big solemn dining room with all the Glossop ancestors looking down from the wall, carefully rolling up her damask napkin after every meal.

Actually, I knew exactly the sort of life Marianne was going to lead, because of Daphne.

Daphne didn't speak to me much; she was not the sort of girl who spoke to servants. A year earlier I'd pulled off an Alsatian who was holding her at bay as she played in the gardens of the square, and got quite badly bitten, and while my hands were bandaged she was positively friendly, but it didn't last.

Mostly Daphne was away at boarding school, but when she was at home she led a very busy life. On Saturday morning she put on her jodhpurs and Tom drove her to the park where she went riding – trotting down the sanded paths and greeting other children on well-groomed ponies. On Monday afternoon, she carried her dancing shoes in a velvet bag to Miss Bigelow's Academy and learned ballet, and on Thursdays she did elocution with a lady called Madame Farnari.

Marianne would do all this – but not for long, because as soon as she had her eighth birthday she would be taken to a school outfitter to buy a brown velour hat and a brown gymslip and a hockey stick and go off with Daphne to St Hilda's, where the school motto was 'Play straight and play the game'.

'When you think what that school costs, and the kind of children who go there – all those honourables and what have you – it'll be a wonderful thing for the little thing,' said old Tom, the chauffeur. 'Mind you, she'll have a lot to learn.'

As it turned out, we had several months to get ready for Marianne, because even the Glossops didn't find it easy to get the passports and permits and papers that were needed to bring Marianne to Britain. Things were made more difficult because the village where Marianne now lived was in the part of Germany that was occupied by the Russians and they were very strict about who could come into their zone and who could not.

But at last a permit came through, allowing two people to travel to Orthausen and pick up the little girl. The permit was for a particular week in July and now my mother was sent for again. What's more, she was asked to sit down, which was unusual.

'It's so awkward, such a nuisance,' said Mrs Glossop to my mother. 'But the permit covers the day of the royal garden party and I've been asked to attend. I simply couldn't miss that – and two days later it's Daphne's prize-giving at St Hilda's and of course I must go down for that.'

My mother waited, wondering why she had been summoned.

'My husband would go and fetch the little girl, but he has the annual meeting of the cricket club and then a very important Rotary dinner in Aberdeen at which he's been asked to speak.' She bent forward and fixed my mother with a stern eye. 'So I want you to fetch

Marianne. It's so convenient because you speak German.'

This was true. My mother had been studying modern languages at university when my father had married and deserted her, all in three months.

But my mother said she couldn't leave me. This was nonsense, of course, but she said it very firmly. I think she felt that the Glossops should go themselves to fetch their new daughter – or perhaps she was nervous. Since my father betrayed her, she had looked for a quiet life – a life where the two of us would be safe.

'Well, the permit is for two people. I don't see why Michael shouldn't go with you; we don't have to say that he's only twelve years old.'

So it was my mother and I who went to fetch Marianne Gerstenberger, but before we left we were given some very important instructions.

'Marianne has a birthmark on her arm,' said Mrs Glossop. 'Her mother wrote to us about it when she was born. It's on her right arm and it runs from her shoulder to her elbow – and you must make absolutely sure that she does have that mark and in the right place. It's one thing to adopt the daughter of one's husband's partner and another to take in any stray that wants a comfortable home.' And she told us that though Marianne's name had been pinned to her blanket, it was possible that in those frightful times the baby's things had been stolen and given to some other child.

'We will make sure,' promised my mother – and two weeks later we set off.

It was quite a journey. Ordinary people hadn't been allowed to travel all through the war and of course I was excited, crossing the Channel, getting a train to go through the Netherlands and Germany.

Or rather, five trains. Most of the rolling stock had been destroyed in Allied bombing raids. We stopped and started and were pushed out on to the platform and back in again. There was no food to be had on the train, or water, and I couldn't help wondering if it was because she knew how uncomfortable the journey was going to be that Mrs Glossop had decided to send my mother instead. We went through towns that were nothing but heaps of rubble and countryside with burnt and empty fields. It was odd to think that it was we who had caused all this destruction. I'd thought of bombing as something that the Germans did.

We spent the night in a cold and gloomy little hotel on the Belgian border, and the next day we travelled east through Germany.

I asked my mother if this was the route that Marianne's mother would have travelled on her last journey but she didn't know.

We were going through farmland now: fields and copses and little villages. The houses looked poor and small but there were a few animals: cows and sheep. The peasants were struggling to get back to a normal life.

We had to change twice more on to branch lines, travelling on trains so old that we didn't think they would manage to pull their loads. Then in the late afternoon we reached Orthausen.

The village that Marianne lived in was not directly on the railway. The woman who found her must have carried her bundle a long way to her house. My mother and I now walked that road, trudging along the white dust village street with our bags and turning off along a track which ran beside a stream.

Then, late in the afternoon, we crossed a small bridge and came to a wooden house standing by itself in a clearing.

Marianne was sitting on the steps of the porch. She was holding a tortoiseshell kitten on her lap and talking to it – not fussing over it, just telling it to behave. She spoke in German, but I knew exactly what she was saying.

She had thick, fawn, curly hair and brown eyes and she wore a dirndl, and over it a knitted jersey which covered her arms. When she saw us she put down the kitten and then she reached for the bag my mother carried and led us into the house.

The woman who had found Marianne on the railway track was called Mrs Wasilewski. She was very pale with a screwed-down bun of fair hair and a tight mouth. To me she looked like a death's head, so white and forbidding, and I was glad that we were going to take Marianne away from such a cold, stern woman. But Marianne went up to her trustingly and said, here were the visitors from England, and I realized that she did not yet know why we had come.

Mrs Wasilewski offered us some ersatz coffee and slices of dark bread spread with dripping. Her husband was away, working in a sawmill in the north of the country for the summer, to earn some extra money. When we had eaten, Marianne turned to me and took me by the hand, and said, '*Komm*,' and I got up and followed her.

When somebody takes you by the hand and says

252

'*Komm*', it is not difficult to guess what they are saying, but it still seems odd to me that from the first moment I understood Marianne so completely, and that she understood me.

The Wasilewskis had a smallholding, but the Germans had commandeered the horse at the beginning of the war and the Russians had taken the cow at the end of it. All the same, the animals that were left seemed to satisfy Marianne. She introduced me to the two goats – a white one, called Bella, and a bad-tempered brown one, called Sidonia, after a disagreeable lady who scowled at everybody in the church. She showed me the five hens and told me their names and the rabbits and the new piglet, honking in the straw.

Actually, it was more than showing – she sort of presented them to me, giving me the animals to hold as if hanging on to a squawking chicken or a lop-eared rabbit must make me the happiest person in the world.

It was far too late to try and make our way back that night – no one knew how the trains would run. Mrs Waslilewski – still unsmiling and gaunt – led us to a loft with two goose-down duvets on a slatted wooden board and we went to bed.

I was sure we'd leave the next morning, but we didn't. My mother helped Mrs Wasilewski with the housework and once again Marianne put out her hand and said, '*Komm*,' and once again I came.

She led me to a part of the stream where the water ran clear over a bed of pebbles. Both of us took off our shoes, but she kept on her jersey, and we walked along the river bed, dredging up bright and glittering stones.

'*Nicht Gold*,' she said, holding out a yellow-veined stone and shaking her head, but she was smiling. She didn't want gold, I could see that. She wanted brightness.

The stream was full of sticklebacks and newts and tiny frogs; all the creatures too small to have been stolen or pillaged in war.

After a while a boy and a girl appeared – a brother and sister – and Marianne introduced me, carefully pronouncing my name in the English way I'd taught her.

We came to a bridge where the current ran quite fast and we each chose a stick and raced it from one side to the other. I hadn't done that since I was at infant school, but you can't go wrong with Pooh sticks, and I found myself wondering if they played it at St Hilda's.

Mrs Wasilewski, still grim and silent, gave us lunch – pieces of salt bacon with beetroot and cabbage from her garden – and afterwards Marianne took me out and showed me the rows of vegetables, and picked a pea pod from the vine and opened it, dropping the shelled peas into my palm.

All that day Marianne stretched out her hand and said, '*Komm*.' She showed me a hedgehog asleep in the potting shed and a place where raspberries grew wild, and I made her a whistle out of a hazel twig. I'd brought my Swiss Army knife, and the whistle was a good one. They don't always work but this one did.

Even the next day my mother said nothing about leaving. We slept on the floor; the work she was helping with was far harder than any that she did in England and Mrs Wasilewski still went round like a zombie, but my mother didn't seem in any hurry to return.

That day Marianne showed me her special tree. It was an ancient oak standing on its own on a small hill and it was the kind of tree that is a whole world in itself. There were hollows in the trunk where squirrels had stored their nuts; beetles sheltered under the bark and a woodpecker tapped in the branches.

Marianne had not *built* a tree-house because the tree *was* her house. She explained this as we climbed up – and that it was in this house that she kept her treasures. They lived in a tin with a picture of cough lozenges on the lid, and she showed them to me, one by one. There was a tortoiseshell hair slide, a little bent; a bracelet made out of glass beads; a propelling pencil – and her most important possession: a small bear, carved roughly out of wood, which Mr Wasilweski had made on her last birthday. Then she took the whistle I had made for her out of her pocket and laid it carefully in the tin beside the other things, and closed the lid.

But the best thing about the tree was the view. Because it stood on a knoll you could see the surrounding countryside for miles. Marianne pointed to a small farm and told me that the man who had lived there had been killed on the Eastern Front. He'd been a German, of course – maybe a Nazi – but Marianne's face grew sad as she told me about him, which was strange because her mother's people had been so horribly persecuted by men like him.

If she was the child we thought she was . . .

But in the opposite direction was a low, red-roofed house and she told me that the man who owned it had a litter of sheepdog puppies and he was going to let her have one. There was enough food now to keep a dog, she said joyfully; it was no longer forbidden.

I didn't say anything. She would never be able to bring a dog into England; the quarantine regulations were far too strict, and the Glossops said it wasn't fair to keep animals in town. Even the cat we kept in the basement knew better than to make her way upstairs.

Then on the morning of the third day my mother called me into the kitchen. Mrs Wasilewski was there, more silent and morose than ever. There was a bundle on the table: the blanket Marianne had been wrapped in, I guessed, when she was found on the track, and a few baby clothes. Mrs Wasilweski called Marianne to her side and she came. For the first time, she looked puzzled and anxious.

'Wait,' said my mother. 'We must make sure we have the right child.' And very gently she said, 'Will you take your jersey off, Marianne, and your blouse?'

Marianne looked at Mrs Wasilewski, who nodded. Then she took off her jersey and undid the drawstring of her blouse.

Now she stood before us with both arms bare. From her shoulder to her elbow, her right arm was covered in a dark brown birthmark.

It was exactly what the Glossops had described to us. Without a doubt, the child who stood before us was the child who had been thrown from the train.

My mother and I looked at each other. Mrs Wasilewski stood like a ramrod, her mouth tight shut. Marianne, still puzzled, reached for her blouse and began to put it on.

The room was very still. Then my mother cleared her throat and looked at me again. She looked at me hard.

'What a pity,' she said clearly to Mrs Wasilewski. 'I'm so sorry. I'm afraid this is the wrong child. We can't take her back with us – her birthmark is on the wrong arm.' And then, softly: 'She will have to stay with you.'

The silence was broken suddenly by a gasp – followed by a kind of juddering sound. Then Mrs Wasilewski went mad. Her head dropped forward on to the table and she began to cry – but you can't call it crying. She erupted in tears, she became completely drenched in them, her hair came down and fell in damp strands across the table. I have never in all my life heard anybody cry like that.

When she lifted her head again she was a totally different woman; she was rosy, she laughed, she hugged my mother and me. And I understood what my mother had understood at once – that this woman who had made Marianne's world with such loving care had been almost destroyed at the thought of losing her.

In the train my mother said, 'I think we'll just say there was no birthmark. We don't want any further fuss about left or right.'

'Yes.' The train chugged on through what had once been enemy territory and was now just the great plain of central Europe. 'I'm going back,' I said. 'Later.' And then: 'Not much later.'

'Yes, I know,' said my mother. 'And I'm going on.'

(And she did too. She gave up her job with the Glossops and went back to finish her degree. We lived in two small rooms and were very happy.)

257

When we got back we were called up to the boudoir so that the old lady too could hear our story.

'Oh, well,' said Mrs Glossop, when we'd finished. 'It's a pity, when we had so much to offer a child. But it doesn't sound as though she would have fitted in.'

And my mother looked at the piano, with its two dozen important Glossops in silver frames, and said no, she wouldn't have fitted in. She wouldn't have fitted in at all.

Elizabeth Laird

I lived in the Middle East for a while, years ago, because my husband, David McDowall, was working there. We were in Iraq for a spell, and then in Lebanon. A civil war was raging at that time, and I watched at first hand as the city of Beirut sank into ruins. My skin would crawl with fright when the guns opened up and fighter bombers screamed overhead.

I've visited other parts of the Middle East several times since then, in particular the ravaged Occupied Territories of Palestine. Military occupation is an unbearable situation, terrible for the occupied and corrupting for the occupiers. This one has been going on for more than thirty years, and the pain increases day by day.

David knows Palestine well. He was there in 2004. He met many different people, and saw and heard many terrible things.

'Why?' I demanded, when he had told me about some of them. 'How can people deliberately kill other people?

What makes soldiers, who probably love their mums and feed the birds, turn their guns on the innocent?'

'Because they're angry and afraid,' said David, who had been a soldier once and knew what he was talking about. 'Or they're not used to power and it goes to their heads. Or they've suffered losses too, with friends killed and maimed, and they've *learned* to hate. They've stopped seeing their enemies as people like themselves.'

We thought about this for a while.

'I'll tell you a story,' he went on, 'that someone told me, last year, in Palestine. A story that actually happened. It's about a good man in a bad war . . .'

LEILA'S NIGHTMARE

The Israeli occupying forces were holding the cities of Palestine in a grip of steel. Tanks and armoured jeeps had been roaring through the streets, scattering everyone in their path. The Israeli soldiers, in their body armour and steel helmets, were jumpy and irritable. The Palestinians, angry, frightened and resentful, were trying to go on as normal, getting to work and to school, doing their shopping and visiting their friends.

Six-year-old Leila was sitting on a wall outside her grandmother's house in the city of Ramallah, kicking her heels against the sun-warmed stones. Behind her, in the house, the funeral of her mother's old cousin had been going on for hours. Aunties, uncles and family friends had been visiting all day, sighing and shaking their heads. Now the rooms inside were hot and stuffy, and Leila, who had been kissed and patted by too many people, was tired and bored. She had slipped outside and was wondering how to amuse herself.

She watched a cat leap daintily over a fallen lamp-post and called to it, but it didn't come to her. She looked round at the sound of some children shouting out of a window nearby, but they were out of sight.

The roar of an engine made her look the other way. An armoured jeep, full of soldiers, was approaching. Curiously, she watched it, then raised two fingers and gave the Palestinian victory sign, as she had so often seen the grown-ups do.

The jeep slewed to a halt. Hearing the sound of squealing brakes, Leila's Uncle Latif ran out of the house.

'No, *habibi*!' he shouted. 'Don't do that sign to *them*!'

Soldiers were already climbing down from the jeep.

'You! Terrorist!' one yelled at Uncle Latif, grabbing him in an armlock. 'Why are you teaching your children to insult us?'

Uncle Latif struggled to get away. The soldier cuffed him to the ground, and then the others joined in.

No one inside the house heard the sound of the soldiers' fists and boots thudding into Leila's uncle as they kicked and beat him. No one came.

Leila stood, still as a stone, watching, her face drained of blood.

At last, the soldiers stopped, piled back into their jeep and spurted off, down the road.

Uncle Latif lay still for a moment, then he slowly pulled himself to his feet. Blood dripped from his nose, one eye was half closed, and he clutched at a broken rib.

'Monsters!' he muttered over and over again, as he staggered back into the house. 'They're not human beings. They're monsters!'

'Monsters!' repeated Leila under her breath. She could feel a shudder run through her, a cold feeling that went deep inside. She hadn't realized that the Israeli soldiers were monsters. She hadn't known that they weren't actually human beings at all.

She crept into the house, squeezing between a group of large old aunts, and hid behind a sofa.

I'm probably safe here, she told herself, trying to think out what might happen if the monsters burst into the house. They probably wouldn't find me here.

Leila's nightmares started after that. Night after night, nameless, faceless beings kitted out in military clothing haunted her, chased her, imprisoned her. Carefully, she studied the small flat she had shared with her mother since her father had left to work abroad. She drew a map of the flat in her mind. There were safe places – under beds, in cupboards, behind chairs; and dangerous places – near windows, within sight of the front door, and on the balcony outside the kitchen. When she heard military vehicles outside, or the sound of soldiers shouting through loudspeakers, or gunfire in the distance, she would rush to whichever hiding place was nearest, and no amount of coaxing, no promises or threats, would lure her out until she was sure that the monsters had gone.

'Don't be so scared, *habibi*,' Samar, her mother, kept saying to her. 'You're safe here with me. I won't let anyone hurt you. You know that.'

Leila stared back at her mother, knowing it was useless to answer.

You don't understand, she was saying inside her head. You don't know what monsters can do. You don't know what I saw them do to Uncle Latif. What I see them doing, every night, in my dreams.

Samar was a schoolteacher, and thought she knew the minds of little girls, but she could only watch helplessly as Leila withdrew further and further into her own world. She did her best: holding Leila's hand tightly as she walked her to school; talking to her gently, trying to distract her as they went through an Israeli checkpoint; pretending she didn't notice the stiffness of Leila's body or her rapid, shallow breathing as they passed the helmeted soldiers.

And then one hot summer's night Israeli troops burst into the flat, on one of their routine searches. Leila, clutching her giant stuffed bear, which she always hugged tightly when she was in bed, had fallen into the first deep sleep of the night. She woke with a shuddering start when the banging came on the door. She lay trembling in fear as the door splintered with a crack and the soldiers rushed in. Then came raised voices from the sitting room next door. She heard Samar cry out, 'There's no one here, except me and my daughter. My husband's away. Please, I beg you, don't go in there. The child's terrified enough already. You don't know what you'll do to her!'

Leila covered her head with her sheet and made herself as small as possible, but the combined size of her small body and her fluffy bear made an impressive mound in the middle of the bed. The soldier ripped the covers off, and Leila stared up into the face of her nightmare. The man's helmet cast his face into shadow. All she could see were his eyes, looking down at her, the light glinting on the gun that dangled from his hand

and the pieces of strange equipment strapped to his flak jacket. She opened her mouth in a long, silent scream.

The soldier tossed the blanket over her again.

'Sweet dreams, baby,' he said carelessly, and went out of the room.

Now Leila knew that there was no safe haven, not even at home, where she could hide from the monsters. She redoubled her precautions. Every walk to school was a battle with terror. Every bedtime she had to fight away her panic. The picture of the soldier in her bedroom, the non-human of her imagination, was in her mind all the time. She could tell no one about it. People would only soothe her, lie to her, tell her not to worry.

The only way she could communicate her fear was with her crayons. Always good at drawing, she now spent hours bent over the pages of an old notebook, meticulously recording the terrors of her mind.

'I don't know what to do with the child,' Samar said, as she sipped coffee with her sister-in-law one autumn day, when the cool winds of winter were already sending dust-devils spinning down the city's cracked pavements. 'All our children have seen terrible things, God knows. Why is she so much more petrified than the others?'

'She's sensitive, poor little soul,' remarked her sister-in-law, popping a sugar lump into her mouth and sucking a mouthful of coffee through it. 'She's artistic, like you were at her age.'

'Artistic! I'll show you artistic!' snorted Samar. She reached down to the shelf below the coffee table and pulled out Leila's notebook. With a flourish, she opened it and laid it in front of her sister-in-law. 'Just look at that!'

Her sister-in-law leaned over and studied the page. The drawing was remarkably fine for a child of Leila's age. The soldier on the page radiated menace. Every detail of his clothing and equipment was perfectly drawn – the gun, the radio, the body armour, the helmet, the multitude of straps, the boots – it was an exact portrait down to the last button. But under the helmet, where the face should have been, there was a sinister space. No mouth, no cheeks, no chin: only two baleful eyes, boring out of the emptiness with terrible ferocity.

'It's good!' her sister-in-law exclaimed. 'She's captured it perfectly. Look at all the little details!'

'No, look again,' Samar insisted. 'Can't you see the terror? It's too much. It's . . . it's not normal. This isn't an Israeli soldier, it's something inhuman. What other child produces things like this? Look at your boys! Out all the time, up to all kinds of mischief – it would take an alien from outer space to scare them.'

Her sister-in-law smiled complacently. 'I know. They're little devils, I tell you.' She took another sip of coffee, and her smile faded as she replaced her cup on its saucer. 'But they worry me too, Samar. They're out of control half the time. How do I know what they get up to? Being cheeky with Israeli soldiers, throwing stones – making petrol bombs, for all I know – what they do is so dangerous! I tell you, I live in daily fear that one or the other of them will come home in a body bag. Since that time, last year – when Latif was beaten up so badly – they won't listen to either him or me. They've lost all respect. They even seem to think that getting a beating was their father's own fault! What'll I do if they get in with those hardliners and decide to go and blow themselves up?'

'They're much too sensible. Don't worry,' Samar said automatically, as she had done many times before. But her mind was elsewhere. 'You've made me realize something,' she went on. 'That day of Abu Hamid's funeral, when Latif was so badly hurt, it was that evening that Leila's first nightmare woke half the block of flats. Yes. It was then that all this trouble began.'

The next day was Friday, Palestine's one-day weekend.

Yesterday's autumn rain clouds had blown away, and the sun was shining over the broken city.

'Put on your sweater, my darling,' Samar said determinedly. 'We're going out.'

'Out? Where?' Leila looked fearful. 'No, Mama. There might be monsters.'

'Monsters? Don't be silly. You've been watching too many scary cartoons.' Samar made her voice enticing. 'We'll go to the ice-cream parlour. Your favourite place! We'll each have a huge ice cream. Mine's going to be a strawberry one. You can choose whatever you want.'

'Chocolate and vanilla,' Leila whispered.

'What, *habibi*? I didn't hear.'

'Nothing,' Leila said, but when her mother had turned away she picked up the sweater Samar had laid on the table and pulled it on.

The Israeli troops had withdrawn from the city for the time being, and the streets were filled with Friday shoppers. Stalls selling everything from socks to soap to scissors crowded the pavements. Leila clutched tightly at

Samar's hand, but slowly, reassured by the everyday normality of the bustling street, her grip began to loosen. Samar smiled.

Little by little, she told herself. I must draw her out little by little.

The ice-cream parlour was filled with families enjoying their Friday treat. Children, round-eyed with pleasure, sucked brightly coloured milkshakes through stripy straws. Mothers spooned sweet cold stuff into their babies' drooling mouths, and fathers wiped cream off their black moustaches.

Leila, scooping up the last precious dribble of her chocolate ice, licked her spoon slowly. Her mother was chatting to the family at the next table, admiring their toddler's bouncing curls.

Leila's glance fell on the window, and through it to the street outside. She froze. An Israeli jeep was cruising past. The soldier sitting by the driver was holding a bottle of water. Under Leila's scared, fascinated gaze, he lifted the bottle to his lips, tipped his head back and drank.

Leila tugged at Samar's arm. 'Mama! Israelis! Out there!'

Samar turned to look, but the jeep was already moving off.

'It's gone, darling,' she said quickly, looking nervously at her daughter. 'See? It's miles away now. Nothing to worry about.'

But Leila was looking more puzzled than scared. 'The soldier inside,' she said. 'It was drinking.'

'Why not? It's a hot day. He was probably thirsty.'

'They drink then? Like us?'

Samar laughed. 'Of course they do! Everyone has to drink.'

'And eat? They eat food?'

'Sweetheart, all human beings eat food! How can they live otherwise?'

'But they're not human,' Leila said positively. 'Uncle Latif said so. I heard him.'

Samar looked down at her, surprised.

'Of course they're human!' she said. 'What did you think they were?'

The waiter came over with the bill. Samar took out her purse and paid it. Leila took her mother's hand as they left the ice-cream parlour, but she clutched it less tightly than before, and when at last they reached home she settled down happily with her crayons to draw.

It was after dark that evening when the dreaded roar of heavy armoured vehicles echoed through the deserted streets of Ramallah once again. Samar, trying to distract Leila with a story, prayed for them to roll on past, but they stopped at the crossroads just outside the entrance to the flats. Voices shouted in Hebrew. The yellow light on the roof of a jeep flashed on and off: its lurid flicker reflecting into the flat, on to the walls, the mirror above the china cabinet and Leila's terrified face.

Samar went to the window and peered out cautiously from between the curtains. A prison van was pulling up now. Her heart sinking, Samar knew what to expect. The Israelis had come on a raid to take prisoners. That meant house-to-house searches. Already, several soldiers were running into the building next door. It would be their turn next, no doubt. The tramp of boots on the stairs, the shouts, the bang on the door would come any minute now.

'Don't worry, *habibi*,' she forced herself to say. 'They won't come here. It'll be fine. You'll see.'

Leila had buried her face in the sofa cushions.

The monsters are coming! The monsters are coming! she told herself over and over again.

Samar came back to the sofa and put her arms round her. 'It's all right, Leila. You're safe with me. There's nothing to fear, nothing at all.'

But the anxiety in her voice spoke louder than her words.

And then came the knocking on the door.

Samar hesitated for a moment, then a strange look – a determined, decisive look – came over her face. She scooped Leila up in her arms, went across to the door, and opened it.

'*Ahlan wa sahlan,*' she said courteously. 'You are welcome.'

Leila's head had been buried in Samar's neck, but her mother's calm politeness surprised her so much that she looked up. The two Israeli soldiers standing on the threshold were much closer than she had expected, and she would have ducked her head again if she hadn't seen the expression on the nearest soldier's face. He was looking as astonished as she was. He was hesitating, as if he wasn't sure what to do.

'Thank you,' he said at last, in heavily accented Arabic, and stepped into the flat.

'Anyone else in here?' the younger soldier said over his shoulder.

'No. Just me and my daughter,' Samar answered calmly.

'You deal with this lot then, Avi,' the second soldier said. 'I'll go on upstairs.'

'OK,' said the older soldier, his eyes still on Samar's face.

Samar shut the door behind him. 'Please,' she said, 'sit down.'

The soldier, encumbered as he was by his body armour, helmet and gun, followed her to the sofa and sat down gingerly on the edge of it. Samar, with Leila in her arms, made to sit down beside him.

'No, Mama, no!' whimpered Leila, shaking her head violently from side to side.

'It's all right, my darling. Stop that now.' Samar's voice was still calm. She turned and spoke to the soldier.

'Please,' she said, 'I want to ask something of you. I want you to let my daughter touch your hand. Just to feel it. Please.'

Leila's eyes, which had been tight shut, flew open, and she looked at her mother in horror.

'*Touch* him?' she whispered. 'I can't, Mama!'

'Look first if you like.' Samar was pointing at the soldier's palm, which was lying open on the sofa beside her. 'You see? He has five fingers. A ring, like Papa's. You can touch him. He'll let you. Put your hand in his.'

Slowly, daringly, Leila put her hand into the soldier's. His long slender fingers closed gently over hers. It was, without doubt, the hand of a man, warm and human.

'Look at his face, *habibi*,' Samar went on, in the same soft, insistent voice. 'See his nose? His mouth?'

Leila looked. The soldier was gazing back at her, but

271

in his face was only kindness and concern. Slowly, Leila withdrew her hand.

'Thank you,' Samar said at last, letting out a long breath.

'She has been so frightened?' The man almost sounded as if he was shocked.

'Yes. For a long time. She has seen things . . . heard things . . . She thought that . . .'

'For the children,' he said, his voice suddenly gruff, 'it is very bad.'

'You have children?' It was the question that Leila had wanted to ask.

'A daughter. A little younger than this one. Sometimes she gets scared too.'

Someone banged loudly on the door.

'Avi!' yelled a voice. 'Have you finished in there?'

Leila had shuddered at the sound and hidden her face again.

'Don't be scared,' the man said. 'It's only Ofer. He shouts all the time. It's just his way. You should hear him at the football match!'

He stood up. Samar did too.

'One day, *inshallah*, this will all be over,' she said, 'and we will be able to face each other, every day, as human beings. But now you had better get on and do what you have to do.'

'There's no need,' Avi the soldier said, opening the front door and stepping outside. 'You've shown me everything I need to see. Why should I look through your possessions when you've show me your hearts?'

ABOUT THE AUTHORS

Over the course of fifty years, **Joan Aiken** wrote over one hundred novels and story collections for children and adults, the most famous of which were the James III series, beginning with the modern classic *The Wolves of Willoughby Chase* and concluding with *The Witch of Clatteringshaws*, which features Joan Aiken's best-known heroine, Dido Twite. Joan Aiken worked as an advertising copywriter before becoming a full-time writer, and worked up until her death in January 2004.

Nina Bawden CBE is one of today's most distinguished and best-loved novelists for adults and children. She is perhaps best known for the semi-autobiographical *Carrie's War* (a novel about being evacuated during the Second World War, which has twice been filmed) and *The Peppermint Pig* (winner of the Guardian Children's Fiction Award). She divides her time between London and Greece, both of which have provided vivid settings for her work.

Tony Bradman has written a great number of books for children of all ages, and has also edited many anthologies both of poetry and short stories. His most recent books are *The Orchard Book of Swords, Sorcerers and Superheroes*, a collection of retellings of classic stories, and *Skin Deep*, an anthology of short stories about racism.

Joanna Davidson has been writing poetry and fiction since she was a small child. A graduate of English and Art History, she lives near Cambridge with her family and is writing a novel, *War Child*, about the consequences of war. She works as a freelance writer and charity consultant.

Jamila Gavin was born to an Indian mother and an English father, and her explorations of belonging to dual cultures has influenced much of her highly acclaimed work, including the three books in the Surya trilogy. Recently, she has published the Whitbread Award-winning *Coram Boy* and another highly-acclaimed historical novel, *The Blood Stone*.

Born in Vienna in Austria, **Eva Ibbotson** moved to England with her family when the Nazis came to power. After school she studied science and worked as a physiologist, but stopped to marry and raise a family. She began writing for magazines when her children were growing up and then switched to novels. Her award-winning books include *The Secret of Platform 13* and, most recently, *The Star of Kazan* (both of which were shortlisted for the Smarties Prize) as well as the now-classic adventure story *Journey to the River Sea* (which won the Smarties Gold Award, was runner-up for the Whitbread Children's book of the year and the Guardian Children's Fiction Award and was shortlisted for the Carnegie Medal).

Elizabeth Laird lives in Richmond but has been a traveller since the age of eighteen when she left her home in New Zealand to see the world. Along the way, she has witnessed first-hand the devastation caused by war and has written about it in novels such as *The Garbage King*, *A Little Piece of Ground* and *Kiss the Dust*. Her other books include adventure stories set in Africa and retellings of myths and legends from around the world – and comedies for younger readers, too.

George Layton is a highly successful actor and writer. He has created and written two award-winning television comedy series, *Don't Wait Up* and *Executive Stress*, and has written and starred in numerous others. His West End appearances include Fagin in the Cameron Mackintosh production of *Oliver!* at the London Palladium directed by Sam Mendes. His first book, *The Fib and Other Stories* has sold over a quarter of a million copies and is on the National Curriculum. This was followed up with *The Swap and Other Stories*, currently being made into a major feature film. He is now writing the third in the trilogy, which will include 'The Promise'.

Geraldine McCaughrean excels in retelling classic stories from the past and vividly re-creating the past in novels such as *A Little Lower Than the Angels* and *Gold Dust*, both of which won the Whitbread Children's Book

Award, *Stop the Train* and *The Kite Rider*. She used to write her stories while commuting to and from London while working in publishing, but she now writes full-time from her home in Berkshire.

Michelle Magorian worked in theatre, film and television before joining a novel-writing class where she took her first book, the Guardian Award-winning *Goodnight Mister Tom*, which is set during the Second World War and was made into a successful film. Her research for this book inspired her subsequent novels, which include *Back Home*, *A Little Love Song*, *Cuckoo in the Nest* and *A Spoonful of Jam*.

Margaret Mahy writes for all ages – picture books for young children through to complex teenage novels which have won many awards, including the Carnegie Medal twice (for *The Haunting* and *The Changeover*), as well as poems and short stories and television scripts. Her work is often characterized by its offbeat blend of fantasy and humour. She lives in Governors Bay in New Zealand in a house she partly built herself.

Michael Morpurgo combines writing award-winning children's books with running the charity Farms for City Children, with his wife Clare, from their home in Devon. Several of his books have wartime settings or are about the effects of war, including *War Horse, Waiting for Anya, Kensuke's Kingdom* and *Private Peaceful* (winner of the Red House Children's Book Award). In 2003 he was named the third Children's Laureate.

Celia Rees began writing thrillers and supernatural stories for teenagers while working as a teacher. Now she teaches creative writing and thrills readers with spine-tinging stories such as *Truth or Dare*. Recently, her historical novels have been highly successful – *Witch Child* was shortlisted for the Guardian Award while *Sorceress* was nominated for the Whitbread Award. Her most recent books is the best-selling *Pirates!*

Eleanor Updale is the author of the Montmorency books – a series of historical novels set in the late nineteenth century. These books have been translated into several languages, serialized on BBC radio and shortlisted for many awards; winning the Silver Smarties Prize and the Blue Peter 'Book I Couldn't Put Down Award'. When not writing fiction, Eleanor works as an academic historian. She has three teenage children.

More than a decade after his death, **Robert Westall** retains his reputation as one of the most powerful writers for children. He wrote many books, often reflecting his own childhood experiences of the Second World War on the home front in the north-east of England. These books include the Carnegie Medal-winning *The Machine-Gunners*, *Blitzcat*, *A Time of Fire* and *The Kingdom by the Sea* (which won the Guardian Award). He won his second Carnegie Medal for *The Scarecrows*. The introduction to 'Hard Ship to Egypt' was written by Lindy McKinnel, who knew Robert Westall for twenty-seven years and was his first reader and his partner for the last six years of his life.

OUT OF THE ASHES

Michael Morpurgo

This story is not a story at all. It all happened.

On New Year's Day Becky Morley begins to write her diary. By March her world has changed forever. Foot-and-mouth disease breaks out on a pig farm hundreds of miles from the Morleys' Devon home, but soon the nightmare is a few fields away. Local sheep are infected and every animal is destroyed. Will the Morleys' flock be next? Will their pedigree dairy herd, the sows with their piglets, and Little Josh, Becky's hand-reared lamb, survive? Or will they be slaughtered too?

The waiting and hoping is the most agonizing experience of Becky's life . . .

A powerful and moving fictional account of true events by one of the most acclaimed children's writers of our time.

The Wish House
CELIA REES

In the scorching summer of 1976, on holiday in Wales, Richard meets the inhabitants of the Wish House. Jethro Dalton is a famous artist. His sixteen-year-old daughter, Clio, the inspiration for his greatest paintings. The whole exuberant, talented Dalton clan amazes Richard when they smoke dope and sunbathe naked on the beach – and Clio entrances him utterly.

In a secret forest grotto she teaches Richard to play out her favourite stories. Clio is the powerful enchantress of ancient myths, he her heroic knight. Bewitched and in love, Richard ignores the dark truths of the Daltons' world. For within the Wish House the blazing force of Jethro's artistic genius is burning out of control. And the two innocent subjects of his final masterpieces may be irreparably damaged in the fire of his obsession . . .

THE WISH HOUSE is a brilliantly gripping and original coming-of-age novel from a superb writer.

A selected list of titles
available from Macmillan Children's Books

The prices shown below are correct at the time of going to press. However, Macmillan Publishers reserves the right to show new retail prices on covers which may differ from those previously advertised.

Joan Aiken
The Scream   0 330 39703 6   £3.99

Eva Ibbotson
Journey to the River Sea   0 330 39715 X   £5.99
The Star of Kazan   0 330 41802 5   £5.99

Elizabeth Laird
Jake's Tower   0 330 39803 2   £4.99
The Garbage King   0 330 14502 6   £4.99
Red Sky in the Morning   0 330 39867 9   £4.99
A Little Piece of Ground   0 330 43743 7   £4.99
Paradise End   0 330 98095 6   £9.99

George Layton
The Swap and Other Stories   0 330 39794 X   £4.99
The Fib and Other Stories   0 330 39795 8   £4.99

Michael Morpurgo
Out of the Ashes   0 330 40017 7   £4.99

Celia Rees
The Wish House   0 333 94739 8   £10.99
The Bailey Game   0 330 39830 X   £4.99
Truth or Dare   0 330 36875 3   £4.99

Robert Westall
The Machine Gunners   0 330 39785 0   £4.99
Blitzcat   0 330 39861 X   £5.99
The Watch House   0 330 39863 6   £4.99

All Pan Macmillan titles can be ordered from our website, www.panmacmillan.com, or from your local bookshop and are also available by post from:

Bookpost,
PO Box 29, Douglas, Isle of Man IM99 1BQ

Credit cards accepted. For details:
Telephone: 01624 677237
Fax: 01624 670923
Email: bookshop@enterprise.net
www.bookpost.co.uk

Free postage and packing in the United Kingdom